LIBER

Astrologia

SPHÆRÆ

Philosophia

*A Dialogue concerning
the Spheres*

AMOR · FACIT · MUNDUM · IRE · CIRCUM

COLIN A. LOW

Published by Digital Brilliance, www.digital-brilliance.com

Enquiries may be made to enquiries@digital-brilliance.com

First Edition 2022

ISBN: 978-0-9933034-2-5

DEDICATION

To my granddaughter Nina Rose.
To Carla and Owen.
You brought light into a dark time.

ACKNOWLEDGEMENTS

This book was conceived during the dark days of the 2020 Covid pandemic. I would like to thank all who were on my wavelength and kept me going through two years of isolation. In particular I would like to thank Duncan Fleming and Suzanne Cohen of the Rockwax Foundation; Sally Annett at *Atelier de Melusine*; Janine Marriott and the Bristol Bibliogoths; and my motorcycling chums.

I would like to thank Duncan Fleming and Don Karr for commenting on my early proofs, and Jane Bennett, Duncan Fleming, Geoff King, and Paul Welcomme for taking the time to winnow later proofs.

And Fabienne, who brought me countless cups of tea.

CONTENTS

DRAMATIS PERSONÆ

DUKE LORENZO FULCO, Duke of Rimona

DUCHESS YSABELLE GIROLAMI, Duchess of Rimona

SIGNORA EMELIA PASSARELLI, a companion of noble birth

FATHER GIOVANNI COLUCCI, a priest

PROLOGUE

DUCHESS YSABELLE: Emilia! What ails you? You are unwell? Is it grief that afflicts you?

SIGNORA EMILIA: Alas ... is my melancholy so apparent? It is mourning that afflicts me. I am not made for it. I was born for music and dancing and gaiety. In my seclusion I am learning Greek, and fretting over the loves of ancient poets. Necessity has made a scholar and a philosopher of me. And yes there is grief, but not the noble kind.

DUCHESS YSABELLE: How so?

SIGNORA EMILIA: If it was grief for my husband then the world would applaud and say I was a virtuous wife and a good mother. But it is not grief for my husband ... it is that most ignoble feeling, pity for myself.

What is to become of me, Ysabelle? I have two daughters but no son. My husband's brother is now lord over me, and I live in sufferance in a house that was mine and is now his. My husband

1

had some few qualities I admired, but his brother has none, and it taxes my patience to bear with his coarseness of speech. As for his wife, I am but a thorn in her shoe.

I would retrieve my dowry from the estate, but there are 'impediments'; my dowry is invested ... it may be recouped but with some loss ... it may be recouped but time and negotiations are required. Lawyers are arguing over linens and tableware and furniture. I fear they will cheat me and I must return to my father, who will find another husband for me. There is more ... will I continue or is this sufficient?

DUCHESS YSABELLE: It is sufficient, but you should continue.

SIGNORA EMILIA: My husband is but three months dead and already there is word of suitors. I have no stomach for another marriage or the bearing of more children. I fear it will be the death of me. How I resent the tedium of marriage suits—the ridiculous portraits, the parade of witless dolts, strutting peacocks, and blustering drunks. I should be like Penelope and weave a tapestry by day and unpick it by night. Alas, there is no brave Ulysses who will arrive and murder them all before I must complete my design.

See how sour I have become! I am vinegar where once I was honey!

DUCHESS YSABELLE: Let me sit with you, we will find some remedy.

SIGNORA EMILIA: Even if I am wed to the fairest, most eloquent and most noble man in Italy, a paragon of comeliness, he will still require a son of me. And if I refuse a marriage I will be hidden away in a convent.

DUCHESS YSABELLE: You desire to remain a widow?

SIGNORA EMILIA: I desire to remain a widow. Widows are the only free women in Italy.

DUCHESS YSABELLE: This is true.

SIGNORA EMILIA: I could retire to a convent, but I will not become as a child again, shut away, circumscribed by rules, denied books and argument, denied colour and music and dance. And what of my

daughters, whom I love dearly. Who will care for them if I am locked away? Who will approve of their husbands?

DUCHESS YSABELLE: Do not fret for your daughters—I am their godmother, and so long as I live they will be cared for. But I am loath to see you so unhappy, it tears at my heart.

SIGNORA EMILIA: Please Ysabelle, tell me the truth, how do you view the outcome?

DUCHESS YSABELLE: If you wish it, but the truth will not lift your spirits. You have two healthy daughters and you may yet bear sons, and so you will be pressed to marry.

SIGNORA EMILIA: You have spoken my thoughts.

DUCHESS YSABELLE: Perhaps an old man, too old to raise his flag?

SIGNORA EMILIA: Now you have made me laugh!

DUCHESS YSABELLE: And it is a pleasure to see you smile. Perhaps you are too much alone ... even in mourning there must be some laughter.

SIGNORA EMILIA: I have my daughters.

DUCHESS YSABELLE: And yet you are pale and melancholy—with good cause—but still, some other company to lift your spirits?

SIGNORA EMILIA: I could not bear to sit and sew with nought but gossip to entertain us. Whom should I marry? We must review all the possibilities. Would Marguerite restrain her tongue? ... no likelihood of that! I swear I will do her an injury with my sewing needles.

DUCHESS YSABELLE: You must not prick poor Marguerite. I have heard that in Urbino, ladies and gentlemen of the court meet together for learned discussions on matters of mutual interest. It is very select and modern.

SIGNORA EMILIA: How novel! Our sex is to be admitted to the higher discourse of men! Indeed, as if we were rational beings! And whom would we invite to such a conclave? The witless dolt, the strutting peacock and the blustering drunkard! Marguerite, with her simpering and blushes and tittle-tattle? And she has no Latin! She is eternally obsessed with *amore*, but not with *amo, amas* and *amat*!

DUCHESS YSABELLE: Emilia! I am shocked. I hope our court is not so bereft of learned company that we must invite fools and drunks. My confessor Father Giovanni is learned and wise.

SIGNORA EMILIA: Yes, of course, Father Giovanni. Forgive me, I am out of humour.

DUCHESS YSABELLE: My husband may oblige us. He studied at Padua before the war between Florence and Venice, and was reputed to be a sound scholar. Plus he is a man of worldly experience.

SIGNORA EMILIA: The Duke? That would be an honour!

DUCHESS YSABELLE: For us both I think ... he spends all his waking hours on public affairs. And I believe it would do no harm to your cause for the Duke to know you better than he does. What weighty matter should we discuss?

SIGNORA EMILIA: We must not be seen to shrink from matters of consequence. We are women of substance. The Cosmos ... we could begin with the Cosmos. No matter could be more substantial ... or less substantial, now I think upon it, being mostly of a celestial nature.

Indeed, it has become apparent to me that my soul is afflicted by black bile. My gaiety has fled. I must rise up to the Sphere of Saturn so that I may admonish him and tell him to leave me alone, demand that he find some other person to blight with his black humours.

I must also deliver some instruction to Venus concerning the prospect of future husbands. And perhaps Mercury will care to assist me with my Greek. Why, already I feel a lightness entering my soul.

DUCHESS YSABELLE: Excellent. A philosophical journey? Like Dante and Beatrice, we might ascend through the Spheres? Rising towards the divine!

Signora Emilia: A dialogue concerning all those powers that bear down upon our lives, that oppress us with their comings and goings upon the celestial sphere.

Duchess Ysabelle: I suppose that is another way of looking at it. I will seek out Father Giovanni and solicit his advice. And you must come and live with us in the palace while your affairs reach a satisfactory conclusion. There is an apartment of a good size and it is private. You may take your meals there when you desire solitude, as I know you often do.

SPHÆRA ELEMENTUM

DUKE LORENZO: That is a fine beard Father! Have you chosen to join the Eastern Church?

FATHER GIOVANNI: Very amusing, my Lord. Our Holy Father mourns for the people of Rome and has grown a beard to mark his grief.

DUKE LORENZO: My apologies Father, that was a thoughtless remark. And are all priests now bearded?

FATHER GIOVANNI: Those of us who share in the grief of our Holy Father.

DUKE LORENZO: Of course. I must say, I admire the beards of the Eastern clerics—they bring to mind the patriarchs and prophets of the *Bible*.

FATHER GIOVANNI: As they are meant to, my Lord, for I understand the Eastern Church shares with the Jews some notions concerning beards. These are set out in the books written by the holy Moses.

DUCHESS YSABELLE: Beards indeed! How fascinating! Father Giovanni, Husband ... my gratitude, we are well met! The Signora

Emilia and I are honoured that you have found time to meet and converse with us. Too often the ladies of our court are confined to needlework and *tarocchi* and other idle pursuits, and our opportunities for discourse are limited to gossip and scandal. Yes, we may find some pleasure in books, but books are solitary. How much we yearn for learned conversation!

FATHER GIOVANNI: Ladies, I am honoured. It is a rare pleasure to have some relief from pastoral duties.

DUKE LORENZO: Likewise, this invitation is timely. The duties of state are often tedious and filled with opposition and ill-feeling. I welcome some pleasure and refinement in conversation. I welcome the voices of women, for I am sure you have much to teach us.

SIGNORA EMILIA: Thank you, my Lord. You cannot imagine my gratitude.

DUKE LORENZO: The honour is mine, Signora. If I understand your proposal, it is that we should elevate our minds towards the stars so that we may ascend through the heavenly Spheres like Dante and Beatrice?

DUCHESS YSABELLE: It is but an idea ... the Signora Emilia and myself share a desire to know more concerning the realm beyond this world, those Spheres that encircle us. I surmise that we all know some small part of the matter. We thought that it would be a virtuous enterprise to share our understanding of the seen and the unseen ... how did you put it to me Father ...?

FATHER GIOVANNI: That we might better understand the power and sway of the heavenly bodies, how the celestial realm shapes the lives of all who walk upon this earth.

DUKE LORENZO: This is agreeable to me if the good Father feels able to speak freely on such contentious matters ... and will guide us if we stray too far.

FATHER GIOVANNI: My lord, I will greatly enjoy this discussion. Let me reassure you in this manner: it is impossible to be acquainted with theology without encountering opinions that are no longer considered sound ... and yet each novice must encounter these opinions anew, and feel the seductive power of careful arguments.

The blessed Augustine shows us the way here. He does not condemn the arguments of his predecessors. He examines them in detail, and if he refutes them, he does so with scholarship and reason. Be assured that I enjoy free debate, and you need not shrink from setting forth your views.

DUCHESS YSABELLE: Thank you both for your kindness. We will proceed with our plan. If we were students of a more serious bent we could muster a procession of black-capped scholars to fill our heads with ancient wisdom ... whom did you mention, Father?

FATHER GIOVANNI: Aristotle and Plato ... and Hermes and Solomon and Moses—these are but a few my Lady.

DUCHESS YSABELLE: Just so ... but there will be no procession of scholars. I hope our discourse will be much enlivened by what we share from our own learning and experience, however small ... and forgive me Father Giovanni, I mean no disrespect, for you are well-known as a scholar.

FATHER GIOVANNI: You relieve me of an unwelcome burden, for I have no wish to grow weary fanning such a small blaze as I can provide. We meet for the pleasure of company and exchange, and I will moderate my Aristotle and Aquinas in light of what you say, for I am eager to listen to such eloquent companions.

DUCHESS YSABELLE: And yet we need an introduction to harmonise our minds. Perhaps, good Father, you would be kind enough to open our dialogue with a broad view of where we are bound.

FATHER GIOVANNI: In that case, with the kind permission of this company, I can relate the outlines.

It is agreed by all that this earthly world we inhabit is at the centre of a great sphere composed of several parts. Above us are the Spheres of the Moon, Mercury, Venus, Sun, Mars, Jupiter, Saturn, and the *Stellatum*, or Sphere of the fixed stars.

There is more: to the roving eye of mystic or poet one might discern a Hell beneath us with sinners tormented according to sin;

and above the Sphere of the fixed stars there is a Heaven of angelic powers arrayed by spiritual potency and intimacy. Each Sphere has its inhabitants, and we may call them devils, daemons, spirits, or angels according to our inclination. These angels or daemons administer the power of a Sphere and manifest its nature according to degree and purity, just as a prince might appoint officers to administer his realm.

DUCHESS YSABELLE: An excellent summary! We shall journey through the Spheres like pilgrims. Today I propose that we will speak of the first realm, this earthly world as you termed it Father, the Sphere that lies beneath the Moon. Let us each propose an essential aspect of this realm. Husband, will you honour us by going first?

DUKE LORENZO: Then I will begin, but first I must ask a question. Father, how should we name this Sphere that we inhabit? I thought I might call it the Sphere of Nature.

FATHER GIOVANNI: Indeed, my Lord, those who look upon its outward aspect, where we find many forms of living creature, may call it the Sphere of Nature. Those who look beyond the surface to study flux and change, as do physicians and alchemists, might call it the Sphere of the Elements. Those who understand how God has chosen to regulate this Sphere with his decrees and laws and governance might call it the Sphere of Necessity.

DUKE LORENZO: Thank you Father, these are all very apt. I had not thought to view this Sphere both from without and within—I like the subtlety.

FATHER GIOVANNI: It is like standing by a lake, my Lord. On the surface we see the reflection of the world, but in the depths there are those mysterious things that alchemists show in their books— dragons, ravens, eagles, wolves, suns, moons, and the like.

DUKE LORENZO: Just as in the body there are humours, and physicians mutter about bile and blood and phlegm ... yes, very good. You spoke of Necessity and how God regulates this Sphere ... I am certain that there must be a minister or angel to whom He

Sphæra Lunae
Sphæra Mercurii
Sphæra Veneris
Sphæra Solis
Sphæra Martis
Sphæra Iovis
Sphæra Saturni

C. A. L. 2022

assigns so lowly a task ... I am reminded of a miller, who must regulate his ponds with gates and sluices so that his wheel is neither too fast or too slow.

FATHER GIOVANNI: The garden of Nature is watered and made fertile by divine blessings, my Lord.

SIGNORA EMILIA: Some speak of Nature as a mother, my Lord, and call her Mother Nature, for she is both bountiful and stern, and presides over the life and death of all livings things.

DUCHESS YSABELLE: But we are no longer pagans, Emilia ...

SIGNORA EMILIA: I think it is but a figure of speech, Ysabelle ... but I admit it recalls ancient times when every harvest was seen as a gift from the goddess whom the Greeks called Demeter and the Romans called Ceres. I digress, please, my Lord, you were speaking of how this world is ruled.

DUKE LORENZO: Indeed Signora, I was thinking of how we move from Necessity, which is the regulation of this world, to 'the necessary', which is the manner in which we must accommodate our lives to that rule. By this I mean those necessities the world imposes upon us.

We must obtain food and water. We must eat and drink and sleep. We must find shelter from wind and rain lest we sicken and die. So long as we live we must pay these dues.

To gain any comfort in this world we must learn to work its many parts according to the nature of each substance: of clay, the potter; of stone, the mason; of wood, the forester and carpenter; of iron, the miner and the smith; of clothing, the shepherd, spinster, weaver, and seamstress; of leather, the butcher and tanner. For food we must turn to the farmer, to the hunter, and to the fisherman.

DUCHESS YSABELLE: You have forgotten the cook, Husband, who labours so diligently in the kitchen.

DUKE LORENZO: And the cook, I must not neglect the cook, who has served us for so many years.

Where was I? So that each new generation retains some mastery of this world we have guilds to approve the masters of every craft.

They must learn each skill at great cost of time and trouble, only to lose all accomplishment as they age and die.

Necessity is the cause of unceasing labour. So much of a life's accomplishment is little more than obtaining some relief from her daily burdens. We cannot grow idle lest we suffer hunger or cold. We must be vigilant against those who would harm us, against those who would steal what we possess. Such comforts as we enjoy—our farms, our roads and bridges, our towns and cities— these are the legacy of our ancestors who toiled to leave the world a better place.

DUCHESS YSABELLE: Thank you Husband. You speak of Necessity as having the female sex?

DUKE LORENZO: Perhaps she is a cousin of Mother Nature ... it is but a figure of speech.

DUCHESS YSABELLE: Very well ... your point is clear: we must labour lest we suffer and die, and we win our comfort at great cost. Father, does the Bible say that God cursed the Earth, that we must labour to meet our needs, and that it would yield up thorns and thistles?

FATHER GIOVANNI: Exactly that, my Lady, just as you have said it: thorns and thistles.

DUCHESS YSABELLE: Then Nature is an accessory to God's judgement in this matter?

FATHER GIOVANNI: So it seems, my Lady.

DUCHESS YSABELLE: Thank you Father, let us continue. Emilia, I think it is your turn to speak.

SIGNORA EMILIA: Thank you Ysabelle. I do not wish to inspire melancholy, but I must make another complaint against Nature. My Lord, Father Giovanni, I had a mind to speak of the beauty of this world, of days when we walk in the sun and the air is filled with the perfume of flowers and the drone of bees. Days when the fields are golden with ripening wheat, and Ceres brings her bounty to us as she did to the Romans, so that we feel blessed by abundance. In my happy world I would have many such days.

And then I recall the truth of my days, and I cannot pretend this happiness, for there is much in life that is unpalatable. My eyes are opened to misery. Today I will be poor company, for I will speak of pain and the suffering it brings.

I desire to know: why is pain so painful? Why must it bring me to tears, and so often? Pain is our lot, men and women alike. Why must women suffer so at birth? Why must we die so often? Why do our children die so young? Have our children given offence to God that they must suffer and die? Would not a smaller quantity of pain in the world satisfy God? Are we to be chastened and made humble by torment?

FATHER GIOVANNI: I hear your complaint Signora. I had an aching tooth of late, and my thought, long sustained throughout the night, was the same as yours: why is pain so painful. Why must we suffer so? Yes, we were expelled from Eden and cursed to suffer pain, but a tenth as much pain would have been sufficient to send me running to the barber.

SIGNORA EMILIA: Father, do you think my suffering comes from God? As a consequence of Eve's sin? Or perhaps I am afflicted by a natural deficiency, a weakness of constitution, just as the axle on a coach will howl and squeal when it is dry and requires grease? We do not blame divine judgement when the coachman neglects his duties and a wheel falls off.

FATHER GIOVANNI: I do not think we would send for a physician if we truly believed our suffering came from God. The juice of the poppy brings some relief from pain, as does an infusion of willow bark. I doubt that God's will would be so easily thwarted.

DUKE LORENZO: You suffer from some pain, Signora?

SIGNORA EMILIA: It is merely the curse of womankind, my Lord, administered by the Moon, but tended and accomplished by malign spirits wielding pitchforks and harrows and pruning knives. I struggle to endure it.

DUKE LORENZO: You have my heartfelt sympathy, Signora.

SIGNORA EMILIA: I should not complain, my Lord, it is ignoble of me, and yet I cannot be truthful to the nature of this Sphere without some mention of pain: pain of the body, and suffering, which is pain of the soul. Sometimes I wonder what offence I have given to God, but then I recall the Medici of old were tormented by gout—father and son through generations. I have seen this in dogs, some bloodlines are strong, others are not so strong. My Mother, God rest her soul, was afflicted as I am.

DUCHESS YSABELLE: The Medici were, and still are, bankers and usurers. They give offence to God.

DUKE LORENZO: But what the Signora says is true, dear Wife; breeders know that if they select but one aspect in a breed, the line becomes weak. This is true in every kind, whether it is dogs or horses or cattle.

FATHER GIOVANNI: It is for this reason that the Church forbids consanguineous marriages. Families with great wealth might seek to retain that wealth by marrying across the family tree, but there is a price to be paid, for the blood is weakened.

DUCHESS YSABELLE: So a conclusion of this argument would be that we should not necessarily blame ourselves for weakness or sickness, that there is some humour that resides in the blood that disposes us to various maladies?

FATHER GIOVANNI: I believe this is so, my Lady, for it is easy to observe how often a child inherits not only the features of a parent, but also many of the same ills.

DUCHESS YSABELLE: I suppose there is some comfort in that, for I see God's will in every occurrence and I am often alarmed. Father, do you believe that God enacts judgements against us?

FATHER GIOVANNI: There are several prophets in the Bible who warned the people of Israel to mend their ways lest God enact dire judgements. The prophet Jeremiah warned the people of Judea that God would punish their idolatry, that the Temple would be destroyed, that they would be taken into captivity, and so it happened.

But we are not all prophets, and God does not speak through every man. There are those who preach in the streets and from the pulpit, that every drought, flood, storm or pestilence is a punishment from God for our evil ways. I have my doubts about such preachers. One can read about drought, famine and pestilence in the writings of the Roman Republic, long before the birth of our Lord, and the priests of that distant age condemned the people for offences given to Jupiter or Mars or Vesta. It seems to me that people at every time have had their share of poor weather and pestilence.

I also see vanity and arrogance in berating others for their sins. Why, one might argue, if a person suffers through God's will then we do not need to console them. What does our Lord say on the matter? That we should not judge others, motes and beams—you know the saying, my Lady.

DUCHESS YSABELLE: I have often thought that Father—that those finding fault with others and casting blame lack charity. Our Lord commands us not to cast the first stone.

FATHER GIOVANNI: Well said, my Lady.

SIGNORA EMILIA: There is consolation in your words Father. If the cause of pain lies within Nature then we might seek remedies within Nature, and pray that physicians might discover them.

FATHER GIOVANNI: I believe that Signora; that there is a world of knowledge within Nature as yet unexplored that might relieve us of many afflictions.

DUCHESS YSABELLE: It seems that Nature bears down hard upon us, but may yield healing just as she yields fruit and grain. There, I have called her 'she' and I am now become a pagan. Emilia, are you at an end?

SIGNORA EMILIA: Unless we discover some means to rectify Nature there will be no end to pain or suffering ... but my speech is ended and we can continue.

DUCHESS YSABELLE: Excellent. Father, perhaps you might share your thoughts on the nature of this Sphere?

FATHER GIOVANNI: Thank you, my Lady. I have a weakness for the philosophy of the Greeks, and so I would like to speak of the sense of order in the way the world changes. My lord, you spoke of Necessity; I observe a different kind of Necessity. It is so obvious and transparent I struggle to elaborate, so let me begin with a recollection from my childhood.

There is a game played by children with small rounded stones—not, I should add, for casting at sinners. Some use fired clay, some are made from the marble, the best are moulded glass. This game has many names, and doubtless you have played it.

DUKE LORENZO: To exhaustion and beyond.

FATHER GIOVANNI: As did I, my Lord; we played into the night until we could barely see our stones. If there is a place in Heaven for diligence in the casting of stones then I will be among the saints. And did you try to impress your will upon the stones?

DUKE LORENZO: I did. I would exert my will upon a stone until I thought blood would pour from my ears ... but the stone would go its own way. If there is a spirit governing stones then he is deaf to my entreaties.

FATHER GIOVANNI: I formed the conviction that stones were incorrigible—they went their own way. Whatever skill I possessed derived from my understanding of the nature of the stones. They did not adapt to me.

DUKE LORENZO: That is how it is Father. As a child one struggles against the incorrigibility of stones. As a youth I was required to learn the skills of archery, and it was the same. Arrows follow their own path, as you say, incorrigible. A good archer will tell you that the art is in the draw. Once the arrow has left the string it is too late to petition the saints that it should pierce the mark.

Please continue Father.

FATHER GIOVANNI: Thank you, my Lord. My point is this: some part of Nature is incorrigible. One cannot entreat or bargain with stones or arrows ... or dice it would seem, for there are no wealthy gamblers of my acquaintance.

So here is my point: when we try to work upon the world, it consults its accounting book, in the manner of a master mason or carpenter, and decides what the charge will be. Each manual skill struggles against the world; the world is harsh and abrasive, like a mill wheel or a cutler's grindstone. In every occupation something wears away: the carpenter's saw, the mason's chisel, the seamstresses' shears, the warrior's sword, the horse's shoes, the axle on the carter's wagon, the scribe's quill, all are quite worn down.

There is an obstinacy in the world. It travels its own path, as if it was obedient to a code, to a book of laws, the Book of Nature. We observe this most particularly with architecture and building, for stone has weight and bulk and rests in a particular place. When we desire to build walls, it takes us a great effort ... for stones are stones ... but we do not complain, for we like our houses to be fixed and enduring. This fixity of stones is a great convenience to us. We surround ourselves with permanence. Walls remain walls, chairs remain chairs, doors remain doors.

And so I will conclude by saying that the world forces a truth upon us. It exists upon its own terms and is quite incorrigible. We must learn its ways or perish. And its ways are stubborn and harsh, and men and women must wear themselves into the grave in the effort to win some shelter and sustenance and pleasure.

I do fear I have intruded upon your own points, my Lord.

DUKE LORENZO: But added much of value, Father. I like your point that the world keeps its accounts in ledgers and we must pay the bill.

DUCHESS YSABELLE: Thank you Father. It is with a sense of guilt I will admit that I am remote from the many trades you mention. Perhaps I will approach the masters of some guilds to find out what they do ... then perhaps I will be more in sympathy with the apprentice boys, who cause an uproar whenever they perceive an injustice.

FATHER GIOVANNI: I feel sure the guild masters would be delighted to engage your interest, my Lady. They will polish their woodwork until you are overcome with the smell of beeswax and turpentine. They will commission smart new livery for everyone.

DUCHESS YSABELLE: How jolly that would be! The rowdiness of apprentice boys leads me to my own topic, which is the spirit of contention and conflict among us that so often leads to violence. Why are we so murderously contentious, kin against kin, city against city, nation against nation? The prophet declares that a day will come when swords will become ploughshares and spears will become pruning hooks. When is that day?

DUKE LORENZO: For that day to come we must first placate the armourers ... but if I had to number the chief causes of conflict and violence I would begin with greed, and I would add vanity and honour.

SIGNORA EMILIA: There is also hatred, my Lord. Some are instructed in hatred from birth. We are taught to hate the heathen.

DUKE LORENZO: That is true Signora, and not only the heathen. Townsfolk north of the river insult those living on the southern banks. And what of the beasts? Father, is it Isaiah who declares that the wolf will live with the lamb and the goat with the leopard?

FATHER GIOVANNI: It is, my Lord.

DUKE LORENZO: And is there any sign of this? Or are foxes still stalking poultry, and do we still hunt them down? Do stags still clash in the autumn? Do stallions bite and kick? Do hounds fight to the death in the pits?

And birds ... birds have an evil disposition and exist to torment each other. In a day of idleness at Porto Pisano I watched gulls harass each other, pecking and flapping over every inch of rooftop. And fighting cocks! They leap and tear until one is dead. Geese ... if my men-at-arms had the temper of geese I would subdue Italy in a week.

I see a spirit of contention in the world, each kind fighting for sustenance and advantage in the world.

DUCHESS YSABELLE: Indeed husband! Well spoken, as you say, the spirit of contention is not only in our own kind. Emilia ... ?

SIGNORA EMILIA: Thank you Ysabelle ... I wished to agree with you, my Lord, in the matter of beasts and birds, and observe that a cause of contention is a general insufficiency.

    The Lord commanded that each kind multiply, and so they do, but a sow has fourteen teats to suckle as many piglets. If the boar was permitted to multiply its kind it would eat every acorn in Italy.

    In his wisdom the Lord made wolves to hunt the boar and check their numbers, so that there might be some acorns remaining to make oaks. In years of plenty the wolves gorge themselves on boar and grow their numbers until there are great packs of wolves in the forests, and they struggle to find prey. Then there is a harsh winter and this multitude of wolves begins to starve. The wolves come out of the mountains and bring terror to farms and villages, and so we unite to hunt them down.

    One might imagine that a benevolent God would allot to each being the necessities of life—sufficient food and drink so that some level of comfort would be possible without toil or violence. This is not so.

DUKE LORENZO: That is it Signora: insufficiency. The earth is bounteous but it can only give forth so much bounty for all the many kinds of creature that live upon it. And so much has been spoiled; the Romans took harvests from land that now is fit only for goats.

FATHER GIOVANNI: That is true, my Lord, we read that once there were forests in Spain, Libya, Sardinia, Sicily, and Attica and now the same land is stony ground.

DUCHESS YSABELLE: I accept this, that there is an insufficiency so that beasts prey upon beasts and men prey upon men. But is insufficiency all of the answer, or only a part? Forgive me Emilia, I feel I must pursue this, for I see more than insufficiency. The human heart is filled with violence even when there is sufficiency in all things. The nobles of Italy are famously given to murder. Father, your thoughts ...

FATHER GIOVANNI: My lady, I think it is evident why animals and birds must be fierce with each other. As you say Signora, they multiply and the earth does not. There is no more earth today than there was when Dido measured the boundaries of Carthage with an ox-hide.

Your question, my Lady: why is there still contention and violence in our hearts when we are blessed with sufficiency? Why do we divide ourselves by family, by parish, by city, and why do we war against each other?

Here is my thought. There is a belief among philosophers that the human soul has parts and is divided against itself. There is a portion of the soul that has the nature of an animal, so that we may liken it to a wolf or a goat. This soul is filled with lusts and natural violence, and although it may be appeased by sufficiency, it is not fulfilled. Like the stag, or the bull, or the cock, it inclines towards conflict.

The same philosophers also believe that we possess a part of the soul that is made in the image of God and enlightened with divine reason ... so that we may be moral and avoid sin. It is our moral duty to subdue and restrain the animal part, which, as we have observed, is filled with a natural violence.

DUCHESS YSABELLE: So the heart may be bestial and ignore the promptings of conscience, neglect God's laws, and fall into sin.

FATHER GIOVANNI: That is it, my Lady.

DUCHESS YSABELLE: And it is ordained that the wicked shall be damned and consigned to Hell where they will burn for their evil ways.

FATHER GIOVANNI: Unless they purchase an indulgence from an obliging bishop.

DUCHESS YSABELLE: You cannot condone this Father?

FATHER GIOVANNI: I do not, but neither do I wish that any soul should burn. I pray that reason should prevail over wickedness.

SIGNORA EMILIA: But are not scholars and churchmen, whom one might imagine to be enlightened by a sufficiency of reason, the most contentious men that ever were? There is no end to their disputation! They may be fed to sufficiency off the fat of the land

and still they quibble and split hairs. They publish furious letters filled with contempt for any who disagree on matters of essence and substance, the nature of the Trinity, whether angels require nutrition, whether faith is sufficient for salvation, or whether we require good works as well?

FATHER GIOVANNI: I see you are well-informed, Signora. Let us be charitable; they seek for truth in an imperfect world. And the only harm that comes from learned disputation is to vanity and error.

DUKE LORENZO: Unless a doctrine is so unpalatable that the Holy Inquisition takes notice.

FATHER GIOVANNI: The Church struggles against many errors of understanding, my Lord.

DUCHESS YSABELLE: And at this point let me intervene with a summary lest any vanity comes to harm. It seems to me that Father Giovanni's point goes to the heart of the matter: the world forces its truth upon us. My husband, you stressed that our daily necessities—food, shelter, clothing—have been won at great cost of effort, and there is no end to our labour.

Emilia, you have remarked upon pain and suffering. You have noted the pain visited upon women, and in a world imbued with divine reason it is difficult to understand this affliction without wondering its purpose, and what we have done to deserve it.

Father, you have noted the obstinacy of the world, its indifference to us, and how we wear away making anything out of it.

As for myself, I observe a spirit of violence between the creatures of this world. In Eden there was harmony between one creature and another, but we are fallen and the gates of Eden are barred to us.

DUKE LORENZO: I recall that Ovid describes a felicitous time? A Golden Age?

SIGNORA EMILIA: He does, my Lord. He tells us of a Golden Age untroubled by discord, when men ate fruits provided by nature and lived in harmony. But the poet says nothing of summer and winter, or of clothing and shelter, or what the foxes ate when they were in harmonious communion with rabbits. His verses do not venture far into the realm of common sense.

DUKE LORENZO: Ah yes ... what do wolves and leopards eat while they are living peaceably with lambs and goats? Poets and prophets are reticent about such details.

SIGNORA EMILIA: I struggle to understand how people might live in harmony. Must they all voice the same opinions, like a chorus singing in unison? No quarrels? No dissenting voices, never a moment of discord?

FATHER GIOVANNI: Consider this thought Signora: that our souls have fallen into a realm of darkness and error where truth is veiled. We can no longer discern truth, and false opinion seems equally plausible.

When this fallen world is restored to glory, truth will become apparent to all, and in a world where truth is apparent, there can be no basis for discord.

SIGNORA EMILIA: I look forward to the day when the glory of God is revealed ... but I am also discomfited. What will we speak of when there is but one view and all share it? God will set his immutable truth before us and win every argument. This truth shall strike us dumb. We shall be as Dante's angels, circling a glory that enlightens the dark within us and strips all dissension and variation from our souls. How shall I be Emilia if I am to be stripped of opinion?

DUCHESS YSABELLE: An interesting choice: to be one voice in the harmony of Heaven, or to be entirely oneself while lost in the darkness of error and strife.

SIGNORA EMILIA: And how would you choose, Ysabelle?

DUCHESS YSABELLE: I would recall all those of my acquaintance who thought most highly of their opinions. I am not learned; I cannot debate Aquinas or Augustine. If I am to defer to an opinion then I think I should defer to that of God. And if truth is apparent then we have less to quarrel over.

Signora Emilia: You are right Ysabelle, I would sooner submit to God than be subservient to some untutored opinion. But as we are speaking of conflict and harmony, I will observe that not all discord comes from opinion ... I recall how Satan was proud and would not defer even to God. He would not bow down to Adam. Discord can be rooted in temperament, and so we speak of animosity, a feeling of hostility that arises between people ... like two dogs who cannot abide each other and cannot be kennelled together.

Duke Lorenzo: So true, so true; sometimes every movement or gesture of another person is an affront to one's senses, and their opinions are to be abhorred on principle.

This transparency of truth troubles me for another reason. In the world-to-come, when our sullied vision clears, and God is revealed to all as an eternal truth, then surely games of chance are undone. A redeemed world will be sorely lacking in sport and entertainment.

Can we not then enjoy a game of *tarocchi* because there is no more concealment or bluffing? Will there be no more wagers on horsemen, or any other sport whose outcome is uncertain? And what of dice? Games of dice and knuckle-bones may plague the city magistrates as a cause of discord, but they are a great passion among the poor.

Father Giovanni: I cannot recall a scholar of theology who has given much thought to the matter of gambling in the redeemed world, my Lord. There is agreement that there will be music and joyful singing; I know nothing of sport and gambling. Dante does not mention it.

Duke Lorenzo: Very droll Father—perhaps I must content myself with singing. Perhaps my heavenly voice will be redeemed and I will sing in tune.

If I may, I would like to return to my topic of Necessity. You have said that the soul is divided ... a part that is moulded by the world of Nature and a part that is made in the divine image and imbued with reason.

The part that is in Nature you have likened to a wolf or a goat, because it shares with animals those needs of the body that we cannot neglect—we must conform to Nature and Necessity.

FATHER GIOVANNI: That is so ... we must conform to Nature by finding sustenance, shelter and rest.

DUKE LORENZO: But what of that other soul, made in the image of God? If it possesses reason then it is free to choose between good and evil. But what value is there in freedom if, at the End of Days, we are to be judged by God?

What I mean is this: we must conform to Nature lest we suffer in this life, and we must conform to God's law lest we suffer in the next life. The body tells us to rest, but not too much for that would be sloth. We are hungry and must eat, but not too much for that would be gluttony. We must multiply our kind, but not too much for that would be concupiscence. We must gather what we need, but not too much, for that would be avarice, or covetousness, or theft. We must guard what is ours, but not too much for thereby lies arrogance, violence and murder.

It seems to me that the seed of every sin is planted in the fertile soil of Necessity. We cannot avoid Necessity, and the hard choices it places upon us, but neither can we evade God's judgement. We are oppressed by Nature and judged by God.

FATHER GIOVANNI: You are correct, my Lord. God has given us his laws ... but they are not onerous. Permit me to explain ... the sins come from an excessive self-regard, a selfishness that requires more from this world than one needs. God requires only that we moderate our needs ... so that we do not resemble the fox that kills all of the hens in the hen-house. What does our Lord Jesus ask of us? Only that we love our neighbour as ourselves. And to love God.

DUCHESS YSABELLE: Bravo Father; what you say is true, charity and compassion are not so onerous.

DUKE LORENZO: They are onerous in Italy, where every man looks to seize what one possesses. In Italy the great are generous only when it magnifies their fame. The honest and charitable man looks like a simpleton.

DUCHESS YSABELLE: Husband, you are severe in your opinion.

DUKE LORENZO: Then let me arrive at the heart of the matter. It seems to me that between the demands of Nature, the demands of state and polity, and the judgement of God, my free will is but a notion. I am bound to a wheel like a donkey. Forgive me Signora, perhaps I speak too frankly.

SIGNORA EMILIA: You speak honestly, my Lord. None who are honest with themselves can be entirely at ease. Father Giovanni has said that the soul is sunk in darkness so that truth is obscured. How then can we choose wisely between the demands of Nature and the laws of God? We have reason to guide us in our choices, but often it seems that there are only poor choices and reason is bewildered.

DUKE LORENZO: Thank you Signora, that is it precisely—reason is bewildered. How can my reason guide me in God's way when each day I am confronted by unpalatable circumstances? And what is the value of my free will if it leads me to damnation?

Father is it true, as some Protestants assert, that the soul is too depraved by Nature to ever win salvation? What of the heretic Calvin, who preaches that nothing we can do in this world will win our salvation, that our fate has been known by God since the beginning of the world?

FATHER GIOVANNI: There are such doctrines, my Lord.

DUKE LORENZO: Then we would possess no more freedom than figures on a tapestry. If we are saved, then are we destined to become decorations for Heaven—your point I think Signora Emilia. And if we are to be damned, then it is God who has woven the pattern in which we are at fault.

FATHER GIOVANNI: These are ancient arguments. I have my own opinion, and some would quarrel with it.

DUKE LORENZO: Your opinions are safe with us, Father.

FATHER GIOVANNI: Thank you, my Lord. I believe that we are free, and the choices we make determine the future.

SIGNORA EMILIA: Then God must stand aside and watch us misbehave, for we are our own masters, and we can do as we please. We make our own future.

FATHER GIOVANNI: As did Adam and Eve, who chose of their own accord to eat the forbidden fruit. It was forbidden, but God gave them free will to choose.

My lord, you have questions about salvation and damnation. Our Lord Jesus explains this in the book of Matthew, with a parable of sheep and goats, where the shepherd (whom we take to be the Son of God) places the sheep on the right and the goats on the left. The sheep are the righteous, the goats are those who have sinned. Jesus asks: did you feed the hungry? Did you welcome the stranger? Did you care for the sick? Did you visit the prisoner? If you cannot answer that you have done these things then our Lord is harsh in his judgement. He tells us there is a fire prepared.

You might wonder how our Lord can preach compassion and yet be harsh in judgement, so I will put to you a question: how can there be a better world if the authors of evil and misery continue their works of destruction? How can a redeemed world contain those who are truly evil? Incorrigible? Unrepentant? Preachers of violence and authors of misery? It is better that they have their own place with their own kind.

DUCHESS YSABELLE: This is no more than we do to make our city safe. We do not permit thieves and murderers to roam the streets.

DUKE LORENZO: This is true ... and yet this world bears down upon people ... they suffer from evil circumstances, in the way that trees grow crooked where the wind is strong. We do not condemn a tree for growing crooked in a wind.

DUCHESS YSABELLE: If they behave like devils then they belong in Hell. And if they are not devils then they may repent, as Father Giovanni tells us.

DUKE LORENZO: I understand this ... if a man will not repent then he has an evil side. But I am still troubled ... that a man should be damned and consigned to the fires of Hell for all time because of inclement circumstances and youthful misdeeds. I met many such when I was soldiering, boys who had been cast out into the world, who learned to survive through any necessary deed, and who knew little of the Church. An ill-wind blew when they were born.

FATHER GIOVANNI: And yet I meet them in confession, my Lord, when they have grown old and are filled with remorse for the sins of their youth. They seek to turn their backs on evil, and find forgiveness. The Lord is merciful; he asks only that we repent of our sins.

DUCHESS YSABELLE: Evil circumstances may mould a youth, but boys become men and men know what is right and what is wrong. It is for this reason that the wicked prefer night and concealment, and speak lies so as to deceive their accusers. They fear discovery and they fear punishment, and by this they demonstrate their understanding of right and wrong.

DUKE LORENZO: I see that I am outnumbered and must retreat in good order, so here is my understanding. We may at any time choose good or evil. It is not our past that condemns us; it is the unrepentant present, the evil that clings to our soul, evil that we do not cast out. Our lives unfurl like a scroll and the record of our doings lies to the left, and to the right the scroll is blank. Even God cannot be sure what will be written.

FATHER GIOVANNI: I agree, my Lord, although this notion makes for uncomfortable theology.

DUKE LORENZO: I see that. We imagine that God must be potent in every manner and yet our freedom requires that He must wait upon my choices. He has no better knowledge of which rider will win the Palio at Sienna than I do.

SIGNORA EMILIA: Perhaps God is exceedingly good at guessing, my Lord.

DUKE LORENZO: I accept that, Signora. If He knows our hearts then perhaps He knows our choices. But a contest of many horses and riders filled with fierce competition? Perhaps God must place his bets just as we do?

DUCHESS YSABELLE: Husband! I am appalled! While gambling may not be proscribed, there is little to be said for it.

DUKE LORENZO: And yet God gambles that my soul will be righteous and not evil.

FATHER GIOVANNI: Very astute, my Lord.

DUCHESS YSABELLE: God does not gamble, Husband. There is no wager on your soul.

FATHER GIOVANNI: My lady, it is said that only one third of the angels fell and two thirds remained true to God. The odds of righteousness are good ... better than even.

DUCHESS YSABELLE: I think you are jesting with me Father, which means that we may have drawn as much water from this particular well as we can. Emilia, you wish to speak?

SIGNORA EMILIA: Thank you Ysabelle, I do, I have a question about the nature of this Sphere. Good Father, we have spoken of the obstinacy of the world, and yet there is change, as when wood burns to ash or water boils into steam. There is much talk of a first matter that precedes all definite form and may be transmuted to any substance, even gold. Can you instruct us?

DUKE LORENZO: Yes, please do, for I am pestered by mountebanks claiming that for a small investment in alchemical wonders I will be as rich as Croesus ... but I hear from my man in Prague that there is no end of purchases of furnaces and fuel and mysterious books. A great deal of gold seems to be transmuted into vapour. Many miracles are reported, but the market price of gold remains the same.

FATHER GIOVANNI: Yes, my Lord, you are wise to heed the market, for indeed, there is no new influx of mysterious gold ... barring that of the Spaniards from the New World. In answer to the question of the Signora, it is indeed said that there is a first substance that was present from the beginning of all things. Some call it chaos, because it is unformed, others *hyle* after the Greeks, but the sense is the same.

This *hyle*, either through divine *fiat* or some innate tendency, divides into four powers of a differing nature, and these are named fire, air, water and earth. According to Aristotle, fire is hot and dry, air is hot and wet, water is cold and wet, and earth is cold and dry. They order themselves by natural inclination so that fire moves upwards towards the Sun, air lies beneath and brings clouds and rain, water lies upon the earth, and the earth is below us, and through its generative nature it brings forth many wonderful metals and stones, so that miners dig down into the ground to seek them out.

It is this generative power of earth that the alchemists seek to harness; first to reduce earth to its primal form or *materia prima*, and then to let it reform and grow under propitious conditions into its most perfect form, which is gold.

SIGNORA EMILIA: That would be marvellous to behold. Duke Lorenzo, can we not have an alchemist with a furnace to bring clods of earth into a ferment of rubies, emeralds, and golden nuggets? It is but the art of the baker, and we much enjoy pastries and sweetmeats.

DUKE LORENZO: I will give a home to any wealthy alchemist ... and the more wealthy and ostentatious, the better I will respect him. I will leave the impoverished alchemists to practise their art at the expense of others.

DUCHESS YSABELLE: Well said husband; this court has no space for knaves and charlatans. But you are correct Emilia, an alchemical banquet of precious stones would be a marvellous sight. We would be as Sheba or Cleopatra, and poets would sing of our magnificence. Husband, if we do find an alchemist, be sure to find at least one poet as well.

DUKE LORENZO: I will seek out a poet in any case, and if he does not compare thee to Sheba, and to Zenobia, and to the Queen of all the Egypts, then I will not feed him until he does.

DUCHESS YSABELLE: I was hoping for alchemical wonders but I suppose flattery will be sufficient. What say you Emilia?

SIGNORA EMILIA: I would be content with flattery. Consider Cleopatra, long dead, her monuments broken, her jewels spread far and wide, her fair complexion withered in the tomb. We can read of her beauty, intelligence, and charm in Plutarch and the like. Eloquent flattery is proven to be ageless, baubles less so ... but ... on reflection ... I would not spurn baubles if were they sprouting like toadstools from an alchemical first matter.

But let me pause. Just now, as we were speaking of alchemy, I had a thought, and I desire not to lose it. Father Giovanni, I would question you again. You mentioned a Book of Nature. I assume this is a metaphor and not a new work from Amsterdam or Wittenberg?

FATHER GIOVANNI: Indeed, a metaphor, and one with a long provenance. I have suggested that the world forces its truths upon us. We grasp these truths imperfectly, like the parable of the blind men touching an elephant—one discovering a tree, another a serpent, and another a stout wall. If we could read these truths more clearly we might perceive the hand of the Creator and discover divine mysteries set there for the good of humankind, just as there are those who seek for hidden mysteries in the Scriptures. We spoke of this when we spoke of pain and its alleviation.

As is so often the case, there are two camps in disputation; one camp does not wish to dilute the authority of Scripture, while the other camp asserts that God gave Adam mastery of this world and if there are divine truths writ upon and within it, then we should learn to read the Book of Nature.

DUKE LORENZO: This metaphor is somewhat tenuous; what truths do you speak of Father?

FATHER GIOVANNI: If I may make an analogy, my Lord ... when a navigator encounters an unknown coast in the mist, he knows that the coastline—bays, estuaries, promontories, mudflats, reefs—is present whether he views it or not, and so he resolves to return under a clear sky with the instruments of a navigator's trade—

compass, cross-staff, sounding lead, hourglass and log. He will record his speed and deduce distances, and by taking bearings—angles to landmarks—he will, with dividers and protractor, mark these out in proportion upon a piece of paper and so make a chart. This chart he will esteem as highly as his ship. If he is Spanish then the Crown will take ownership of it as a state secret, guarded in the archives, never to be printed.

And now, to explain my analogy: this coast, concealed in mist, is akin to the truth that the world forces upon us. This coast of Nature is not revealed in a form we can easily comprehend, but it determines every part of our daily lives, and if we choose to live in ignorance of it, we will run aground. And so we must do as the navigator and devise such tools and instruments as will map a hidden truth, much as we map the outlines of a coast.

DUKE LORENZO: And this being but analogy, what form will this metaphorical coastline take when revealed to our minds?

FATHER GIOVANNI: Some say that the shape of the truth of the world will be revealed in the most sublime form of rational comprehension, that found in the work of Euclid and the like, and that beneath the exterior of the world we will discover the ideal forms of mathematics.

SIGNORA EMILIA: Geometry?

FATHER GIOVANNI: Indeed Signora.

DUKE LORENZO: And the metaphorical tools and instruments for navigating Nature?

FATHER GIOVANNI: The better perfection of what we possess, little more than the tools of the merchant and the mason, but employing the precision of the jeweller and less of the blacksmith. Already the timepiece is reduced from the bell-tower to the mantelpiece, and soon to the pocket. In like manner I would advance the measurement of weight, of length, of angle and bearing, of elevation. With accuracy of time and distance we can measure motion and discover its secrets.

Duchess Ysabelle: Your thoughts take you far from scripture, Father.

Father Giovanni: But not from reason, and if the world is imbued with divine reason, then my thoughts still incline towards the divine.

Duchess Ysabelle: Adroitly spoken! And what miracles of human devising might we expect in this brave new world? The arts of Vulcan and Daedalus revealed, metal servants to bring us food and guard the realm? Brass heads that speak of what is past, or passing, or to come?

Father Giovanni: Many would be satisfied with the lesser miracle of better steel and sharper blades, so that the praise and blessings of shearers, drapers, and butchers would ascend to Heaven. Every trade would make some demand for improvement: the seamstress would ask for an abundance of pins that she did not have to guard like a treasure. Likewise the carpenter for nails. The carter would ask for axles that did not squeal and howl and creak, the gunner for better powder with less smoke and filth. The tanner ... I feel for the tanner with his stinking vats of stale night-soil. There must be some better way to make leather as yet undiscovered. For the tanner, Eden would smell much sweeter.

We could proceed in the general direction of a new Eden by making innumerable small steps just as our forefathers have done, none miraculous, all within the province of human ingenuity.

Signora Emilia: I cannot help but notice that only the poor and downtrodden with useful trades are to benefit in this new Eden. What of us? A supply of pins and nails will do nothing for me. How will the leisure, abundance, and ease of gentlefolk be improved? Will gout be abolished, and likewise the pains of being a woman? Shall we live like Adam for a thousand years? Are there truly alchemical elixirs to cleanse mortal flesh of all infirmity?

Duchess Ysabelle: Yes, an excellent point, what of us? This brave new world must offer us more than happier butchers and carpenters. How will the man with thwarted ambition be relieved of melancholy, the loser in the joust be cured of resentment? The inadequate poet, the spurned lover, the singer whose voice does not quite reach the high note? Will the Book of Nature cure us of all imperfection?

FATHER GIOVANNI: Your point Lady Emilia, phrased with a blunt clarity, is that in this Eden of natural philosophy, the poor will labour just as much ... but with better tools. And that we, whom fortune has gifted with abundance, will be happy to leave them to their customary labours while taxing our physicians for elixirs and nostrums to make our lives of leisure yet more comfortable, so that we might be free of pain and immortal as gods. And your point Lady Ysabelle, that even in abundance we still fall short of contentment and fret at every unrealised ambition.

I have no answer. Every scheme for a golden age, or Eden restored, founders on the reef of human nature. The rectification of the human soul lies outside the Book of Nature I fear. As for elixirs and the like, I would find the tales more credible if physicians and alchemists lived longer than the rest of us. But yes, to be free of the pain of gout, or the pains of womanhood, or even rotten teeth, these are worthy aspirations.

DUKE LORENZO: If I may interject, we have voyaged far from the coastlines of Nature. When we talk of a reformation of the world we are entering the straits of Charybdis and Scylla, and we shall be sunk and drowned. As Duke, I am pressed day upon day with innumerable suits to reform this and improve that. My ears burn with pleas. Milder justice, stricter justice, lower taxes, harsher taxes, a smaller army, a larger army, more freedom to print, less freedom to print.

Those who talk idly of reform and change rarely understand how close we are to falling into civic uproar and administrative chaos. They fail to see how eagerly our enemies feed every sense of injustice. They seek out our weaknesses and ply with gold those who oppose our rule.

Much that seems fixed and immutable in our world is not; the Medici were exiled from Florence; the Visconti of Milan gave way to the Sforza; the Sforza were ousted by France. Great families have been ruined. Our lives are more precarious than they seem.

I devote my waking hours to affairs of state, and the longer I live, the less clarity I find. Those who wish to reform the world have not spent six hours listening to excellent—but contrary—advice in council, where each member brings a well-argued case that contradicts his neighbour. Each member represents some influential faction that seeks to gain at the expense of others. Some factions have deadly vendettas that were old with their grandsires, and routinely brawl in the streets and murder in the night.

In these councils I hold my course no better than a helmsman in a storm. This is my consistent experience of governance. As you say Father, the rectification of the human soul lies outside the Book of Nature and in a conjectured Eden of natural philosophy I would expect that knives would be greatly superior, but I would be stabbed in the back in same old way. Perhaps we should move on.

DUCHESS YSABELLE: And so we will husband, so we will. You are correct, it is easy for thought to dwell in the clouds and conjure fanciful realms that do not consider human nature. I will suggest a new theme: what personal qualities are best suited to match the nature of this Sphere. What say you? Emilia?

SIGNORA EMILIA: Personal qualities? Virtues? There are seven virtues … I will propose the virtue known as fortitude, or courage. As my Lord says, there is no safe path through life. Enemies seek to harm us. We are beset with pain and weakness. Fortune unravels many ambitions. We must accept that the Wheel of Fortune will ascend and descend, that the work of one year may be undone the next. If we are to accomplish any worthwhile thing we must persevere in the face of adversity, and not give in to melancholy and despair.

FATHER GIOVANNI: This is so Signora, and this year you have borne grave misfortune with an admirable fortitude.

SIGNORA EMILIA: Thank you Father. I owe my daughters nothing less.

FATHER GIOVANNI: And may they learn from your example. As for necessary virtues, I will add discipline and prudence. This world is unforgiving to those who are slothful and careless and who do not attend to details. It is for this reason that we try to teach the young the virtues of diligence and discipline. As for prudence, it is not in the nature of the young to be prudent ... too often they are contemptuous of the voices of experience and wisdom. Prudence is a virtue of age.

DUKE LORENZO: You have stolen my thoughts Father. Every petty lord fancies that his wayward and dissolute son deserves—at the very least—a bishopric or a senior appointment at court. Each day I must balance my need to build alliances against the burden of filling my court with fools, braggarts and incompetents. It is truly said that fools will inherit the earth.

DUCHESS YSABELLE: Shall we number the fools at court? Have I sufficient fingers? Toes? Shall we name them?

DUKE LORENZO: We shall not. It is enough to encounter folly once in a day and I have no desire to recollect it.

For my contribution to the theme of personal qualities I will suggest, not a virtue, but a vice. This Sphere promotes avarice. The poor are often charitable, but the wealthy never seem to achieve sufficiency. They grasp incessantly after more land, more wealth, more glory, and more titles, and they are the principal authors of misery in this land.

As for a virtue, I will suggest patience. There is an obstructive tendency in this world, so that if I am promised something in a week, I know it will take three. If I am promised a month, I assume the season will pass from spring to autumn before I see a result. If I am promised a year, then I must leave instructions to my grand-children. Wife, what have you to say about virtue.

DUCHESS YSABELLE: I agree with you husband, the poor are often charitable while the wealthy are not. And that avarice and greed are the authors of misery. I will counter avarice with charity, and I will strike at its heart with temperance. Temperance is a good

38

angel who inhabits the soul, counsels sufficiency, and restrains evil passion.

Duke Lorenzo: Temperance is the angel who mixes water with wine. I do not like to water my wine, unless it is high summer and some cool water or ice is refreshing.

Father Giovanni: I think dilution is a symbol, my Lord; the ancients intended that one should add reason to passion, and so exercise restraint over the desires of the body.

Duke Lorenzo: I see that Father, and yet I have wondered whether some passions should be enjoyed without restraint.

Signora Emilia: I can give myself to music and song without restraint. I am overwhelmed and sometimes I weep.

Duchess Ysabelle: I did say *evil* passion Husband. We may love God with all our hearts.

Father Giovanni: Bravo, my Lady, indeed we may love God with all our hearts. I have said that in this sphere of Nature truth is obscured. There is a veil before our eyes, so that truth seems folly and folly has the appearance of wisdom.

    The foolish believe that as we are in this world for a short span of time we should experience its pleasures to the full. However, Solomon observes that a fool gives full vent to his spirit; the wise man quietly holds it back. That is temperance.

Duke Lorenzo: So we should love God with all our hearts. We may indulge a passion for music, for music partakes of the air, which is far above the earth of this world and closer to God. So what are these evil passions? I hope you will not include horse racing, tourney, hunting, or undiluted wine in modest quantities?

Duchess Ysabelle: I had in mind those who are arrogantly proud and contemptuous of others; ill-tempered and violent; slothful and incompetent; jealous and suspicious; evil-tongued and slanderous; greedy and avaricious.

Duke Lorenzo: And how are we to reform fools who give full vent to their spirit? Can we decant reason into their heads. Are there sufficient angels in Heaven to perform this task?

Duchess Ysabelle: You must not mock me husband. Often you have said that those who do not know what they want will not obtain it. First I state what I want: that the evils of unrestrained passion should be diluted by reason, so that we may live passionately with no harm done. I leave it to future generations to elaborate the details.

Duke Lorenzo: That is sophistry my dear.

Duchess Ysabelle: It is, but there is also sufficient truth in it. As we cannot reform the world in this moment perhaps we should depart from this talk of folly which is dispiriting. What new topic shall we pursue?

Signora Emilia: I would discuss the living nature of this Sphere, something that is dear to my heart.

Duchess Ysabelle: Then you should begin.

Signora Emilia: Then I will begin by observing that in so many ancient authors the lives of gods and humans are intermingled, in easy commerce and to every degree, so that one can scarce tell whom is god and whom is human. Some are gods and immortal; some, like Heracles, are half-gods of mixed parentage, some are entirely human and yet might still be raised immortal to the stars.

There are no fixed boundaries: a man might become a stag, as did Actaeon, or a woman might become a tree, as did Daphne. We read that Poseidon's son Proteus could take any form, and would reveal the future to any who held him to one shape. The gods of Olympus changed their shape to work many kinds of mischief, such as Zeus, who took the form of a bull to carry off Europa. There is Ovid's book that speaks at great length of the flux and motion between forms, so that one must doubt the primacy of outward shape and look past appearance at the soul that moves it.

And so the ancients saw living spirits in trees and groves and spring and rivers, calling them by names according to their outward forms: *Dryads* in oaks, *Daphnaie* in laurel, *Meliae* in ash, *Naiads* in springs and lakes and rivers, *Nereids* and *Tritons* in the sea. They named the four winds, and the mountains, and the shapes made by stars, and built temples and shrines to the hidden life in every part of nature.

Even now Italy is filled with sacred springs and groves and shrines that the peasant folk name after local saints, and elaborate their miracles and martyrdom with fanciful tales, but in truth these are the same springs and groves and shrines that were there before the time of Rome. And one can still find household gods in cottage nooks, and small shrines set apart from the road, and boundary stones as revered now as they were in the first days of Rome and dedicated to the god Terminus.

What are your thoughts Father?

FATHER GIOVANNI: That the Bible commands us not to worship false idols and for this reason we have saints where once there were spirits, or *genii* as the Romans called them. Whether our saints have overcome the Roman spirits I cannot say.

Some say the spirits are devils from Satan's legions, and the temples of Rome and Greece were habitations of devils grown corpulent on burned offerings. That is why men took crowbars to the old temples and mined them for stone, burning the fine marble of statues in kilns to make lime.

The Protestants say our blessed saints are just as much false idols as the ancient deities of the country folk and seek to tear down their shrines in turn. They would cleanse the world of its hidden life and leave it clean and clear as polished marble with not the smallest speck of idolatry.

There is another view, which I incline to: that the world and all its creatures are holy and would not exist for a heartbeat without the power of God that sustains all things. No matter what we worship, or what shape we give to it, it is still God. But then the perverse of mind dream up strange notions and ask if we should find God in scorpions, and serpents, and ordure, and what seems like a beautiful idea becomes as ornate and tangled as the politics of the Holy City.

DUKE LORENZO: And do you believe there may be spirits in springs and groves and rivers, and those places where the heart is filled with awe and reverence? In my days of soldiering in the war against the Venetians we crossed the mountains using old roads made by the Romans, much fallen into decay, and there were wild places far from habitation where our skin crawled and hair stood on end and the men crossed themselves and muttered prayers. Perhaps we would find an old Roman altar to the *genius loci*, and the men would leave offerings of food and drink for safe passage and sound sleep. I have done so myself many times and never thought there was ought of the devil in those places.

FATHER GIOVANNI: In my time I have walked many ancient paths in wild places and felt just as you have, my Lord. There is an aspect of reverence, as you say, and an aspect of fear, as if one had entered into the province of a powerful ruler, and so one resolves to pay all duties and bribes for a safe and easy passage. And as you say, one sleeps the better for it.

SIGNORA EMILIA: I would love more than anything to walk those ancient roads and leave offerings on altars used by Romans ... and you may denounce me for idolatry if you will. Alas, I would be obliged to travel in a coach drawn by a team of four horses, and accompanied by two maids, a steward, a cook, some scullery maids, assorted pavilions, wagons, grooms, muleteers, men-at-arms, their companions of questionable virtue, dogs, cats and a troubadour. Any *genius loci* would sense our coming from a distance of five leagues and retreat as far as Greece or Persia.

FATHER GIOVANNI: I have no wish to encourage idolatry, but there is a friar of unquestionable virtue who is much afoot in these parts, taking the word of the Lord out to remote hamlets. Perhaps he could be persuaded to take a smaller entourage to places within a day's horseback ride, places known to be especially pleasing to the saints on account of their sanctity, being ancient springs or groves that still retain some memory of that golden age of Saturn as recalled by Ovid.

SIGNORA EMILIA: Yes! Yes! What a splendid notion Father.

DUKE LORENZO: Excellent Father! In addition I will instruct the steward to arrange a visit to the villa at San Gennaro. The huntsman there knows many remote places of great beauty. I would enjoy some relief from affairs of state. What say you, Wife?

DUCHESS YSABELLE: I would like to exercise the falcons. I hope they remember me. Emilia, Father Giovanni, you must come, we can remove these conversations to another locale and see what new perspectives we find. Nay, do not answer now, think on it, and find if it suits your convenience.

Husband, I will be mildly discourteous and guide the discussion back to a previous point that intrigues me. Father, you said that God sustains all things, or God is in all things, or all things are entirely God. A stone cannot move of its own volition, and yet God is omnipotent, so how can a stone be God?

FATHER GIOVANNI: A pertinent question, and perhaps I can explain it by analogy. When I play chess, I choose—for a short time—to confine my attention to the surface of a chessboard. The rules are understood and each player agrees to play by the rules (for if there were no rules there would be no play as we understand it, merely two people ignoring each other, and each would tell his own story about what was taking place).

But we agree to play by the rules and so each player has common ground, and there is a shared meaning about the positions of the pieces that comes from long experience. A player can look at a board and decide who has the advantage.

Because I have agreed to the rules, then when I play as a pawn, my pawn will move as a pawn is supposed to move. When I play as a knight, I will move differently. When I play as a queen I can move in any direction. In myself I am unchanged, but my power and value when playing as a pawn is much less than my power and value as a queen. It is my choice to be a pawn and my choice to be a queen, and it is by limiting myself in this way that a game of great interest and complexity is created.

Perhaps we can say that God chooses to play as a stone, and a tree, and an ox, and a human being. The world is like a game of chess, where God chooses to be the board and all of the pieces.

43

DUCHESS YSABELLE: I sense an unorthodox doctrine here ... have you been delving in the Greeks again?

FATHER GIOVANNI: Not the Greeks, my Lady! When I journeyed to Ferrara in the spring I took the opportunity to meet with some scholars of the Jewish community. They have little inclination to communicate their thoughts, as most of their fathers and grand-fathers suffered grievously for their beliefs, but the physician Mordechai in this city—whom I am sure you have encountered—has a cousin by marriage in Ferrara who is a rabbi there, and he kindly wrote me an introduction.

They spoke to me of the outer mysteries of the Cabala, which is their secret understanding of the *Bible*. Although there is much active debate among them, I can say that the central understanding of evil is greatly different from ours. We read in John that the whole world lies in the power of the Evil One, and we read in Paul that Satan and his devils are in league with all the unbelievers and heretics, and Satan will remain prince of this world until Christ comes again to crush him under foot. The Hebrews have none of this. There are some among the scholars of Ferrara whose belief is just as I have said it: that all things are God, that there is only God, there is no thing apart or separate from God.

DUCHESS YSABELLE: So they give no credence to the Devil and his minions?

FATHER GIOVANNI: They do not, for they reject all doctrine that undermines the unity and primacy of God.

DUCHESS YSABELLE: But the Devil is permitted to work his malice only for a time, and then he will be vanquished forever.

FATHER GIOVANNI: That is so, my Lady, but nevertheless these Jews prefer the doctrine that the realm of evil is brought to life by human sin and has no foundation separate from God.

And as you have mentioned the Greeks, I will observe, to your consternation perhaps, that the aerial spirits of the upper regions between Earth and Moon that the Greeks called daemons were not, in the distant past, considered to be of an evil purpose. The

Greeks (and by this I mean Plato and his many successors) believed that any two dissimilar principles in communion did so through some third thing. If Heaven is immutable and eternal, and Earth is mutable and ephemeral, then between them must necessarily be some intermediate medium, which they called air. As all things that exist share some measure of divine life, this medium must be filled with living beings of an extremely fine and scarcely discernible nature. These they called daemons.

SIGNORA EMILIA: And are these daemons akin to the spirits that inhabit trees and groves and springs? Or are they perhaps of another kind?

FATHER GIOVANNI: Of another kind I think. This race of daemons would seem to be most apparent to those of a philosophical temperament, and philosophical spirits are lean and spare, like racing dogs bred for gambling. They are so lean and agile they may dance on the heads of pins, dozens at a time.

The spirits that inhabit trees and groves and springs are given shape by popular imagination, and embellished by poets so that we may easily mistake them for ourselves ... these earthy and watery spirits are driven by curious and inexplicable passions that entangle human actors in unlikely fates.

DUKE LORENZO: The French are masters at this kind of popular tale— Arthur and his knights, Roland, quests, enchanted forests, prohibitions, fairy women—I have a volume that was given to me as a gift. *Lancelot* I think, something of the sort. Signora Emilia, it is in French but I expect you will have no difficulty. You may have it if it is to your taste.

SIGNORA EMILIA: I would be delighted!

DUKE LORENZO: Excellent. Wife, how are we progressing through this Sphere? Are there more topics that come to mind?

DUCHESS YSABELLE: There is the matter of how the planets work their influence upon this world. Father?

FATHER GIOVANNI: Yes, there is much to say on the matter of sympathy, which is to say, how the nature of one thing resembles the nature of another, so that the greater may act through the lesser. In this manner we can say that a certain herb or stone contains the virtue of the Moon, and another plant or stone the virtue of the Sun, and there is much discussion about how these sympathies yield a practical benefit in the arts of the physician.

One can also talk about the sympathy between the several organs of the body and their ruling lights in the sky. This is important in understanding the causes of sickness and health. Ficino, whom you may have read, would summon the rays of Jupiter and Venus to overcome the melancholy that Saturn inflicted upon his soul.

In this matter of sympathies there is a tedious profusion of lists; Agrippa has many such, purloined from the *Book of Secrets*, and from Pliny, and from countless other sources. This soil is not barren, but there are many weeds. We will doubtless uncover matters of relevance when we deal with other Spheres, and I fear we would choke on the matter if we attempted a recitation. Indeed, I am convinced, we should leave this matter for our discussion of the next Sphere, which is that of the Moon.

DUCHESS YSABELLE: In that case, let it be so. I retract my question, and will save it for another day. Will we conclude, and begin again when Moon is full?

SIGNORA EMILIA: An enchanting thought!

DUKE LORENZO: In the orangery perhaps?

FATHER GIOVANNI: These are excellent proposals, and I thank you for your company and courtesy.

Sphæra Lunæ

Duke Lorenzo: I had a dream of my old dog Tesoro last night. It was him in every detail. I swear I could smell him and hear his panting. I woke with such a feeling of loss. I see him even now in my mind's eye.

Duchess Ysabelle: Perhaps his shade is unquiet. He seeks you now in your dreams as he did in life?

Duke Lorenzo: I recall most his affection, his easy company, his love of simple pleasures—any small communion between us brought him joy.

Duchess Ysabelle: He lives on in your soul. Bella, of most fond memory, lives in mine. When I am downcast I recall her.

Duke Lorenzo: But Wife, you are never downcast!

Duchess Ysabelle: Not so, not so ... I am often downcast, but I conceal my melancholy. I keep my melancholy close, lest she builds a nest in *your* soul and hatches her chicks there.

DUKE LORENZO: Your melancholy has the shape of a bird? And builds nests? And has chicks?

DUCHESS YSABELLE: She flies away in summer and returns in winter when I must sit by a fire with my ladies for many weeks and months. We gripe about every manner of thing. We gossip. We are oft affronted and appalled, concluding that we live at the End of Days, and that the Antichrist is even now returning to complete the ruin of the world. The air fumes with outrage until we are all quite downcast. Oh, the black bird of melancholy hatches many fledglings.

DUKE LORENZO: The Antichrist returning? The prelates talk of little else, of how we must direct our thoughts towards sackcloth and penance. But this glorious eve ... the Moon is full, the white jasmine yields up her perfume to the night air, and the nightingale murmurs in the branches. There is yet joy.

DUCHESS YSABELLE: Indeed there is. Father, do you hear us, do you find delight in the cool of a summer's eve? Father ... ?

FATHER GIOVANNI: I hear you, my Lady. Yes, most delightful. I was thinking on your words, the memory of things long departed, images still alive in our souls. In my mind's eye I recall Milan as it was when I was a child. I was quite lost in memories.

It is said—and you may know this—that the soul is an image of the world, a *microcosmos*. We recall the smell of lavender, the touch of marble, the acid bite of lemon; we recall the images of countless things we have encountered, all somehow living within us. Even the streets of Milan as they once were. Scholars name this faculty the *Mundus Imaginabilis*, which means nothing more than what I have just said, a world within that reflects the world without.

DUKE LORENZO: And my Tesoro, as real as in the flesh. Well, I say real, but there is a fleeting quality to dreams, they do not hold fast.

DUCHESS YSABELLE: Which is a mercy, for not all of our dreams are good.

DUKE LORENZO: In that case the soul does not contain a true image of the world, for the world has a substantial quality, a fixed and enduring stubbornness. This fountain here has endured since the time of my grandfather. Our dreams and imaginings are mutable and fleeting.

SIGNORA EMILIA: Perhaps the soul is an image or reflection after another sense, like a storeroom filled with paintings of everything we have witnessed. In our dreams and imaginings we can recall these scenes ... as we do when we walk around the Stations of the Cross in the cathedral and witness the passion of Christ?

FATHER GIOVANNI: Yes, in our mind's eye we can view and review our own daily passions, minor though they may be, as if in a gallery of images. And you are not the first to note the similarity of the mind's eye to a treasure house or storeroom of images.

SIGNORA EMILIA: Ah, pray tell us more, good Father!

FATHER GIOVANNI: There is a practice among rhetoricians of various stripes—lawyers and demagogues and other garrulous types— where they imagine a gallery or theatre filled with images, and they fasten a part of their speech or argument to each image so that by strolling around this imagined gallery they may recall their case without the irritation of requiring notes. The practice is, as the Signora Emilia has already noted, similar to recalling the events in the passion of Christ by meditating at the Stations.

DUKE LORENZO: I made some use of these tricks while a student at Padua, where I would take part in public debates, or deliver an oration on a set topic. I would imagine a route through the chambers of this palace, which I have known since a young child.

SIGNORA EMILIA: I would be most obliged if you were to conduct us along your route.

DUKE LORENZO: It would give me pleasure, and I can recite arguments from long-dormant orations as we proceed. What did we debate? Whether Day or Night is more excellent? Does learning make men happier than does ignorance? Ah, I see your warning eye my dear, you wish to guide me away from the memories of my student days and back towards the topic of tonight's discussion.

DUCHESS YSABELLE: Thank you, I did not wish to seem discourteous, but just as a ship needs a helmsman to hold a course, so our port is best reached through small touches to the rudder. Good Father, would you kindly introduce this topic.

FATHER GIOVANNI: With the greatest ease, for we are already bound to port!

DUCHESS YSABELLE: Excellent! How so?

FATHER GIOVANNI: Our topic for this evening is the Sphere of the Moon. By tradition the Moon governs the lower parts of the soul, those parts that most closely mirror this world.

DUCHESS YSABELLE: The soul has parts? So it would not be a digression to continue our discussion by asking in what manner the soul is divided?

FATHER GIOVANNI: It will not be a digression so long as I am brief. I adhere to a view—contentious, but it is my considered view nevertheless—that identifies the soul with the activity of a living thing. When the thing—a person, a dog, a tree—possesses a power of action, we say it is living, and when it loses that power of action and begins to decay we say it is dead. That is plain I believe?

DUCHESS YSABELLE: Indeed.

FATHER GIOVANNI: Many have followed Aristotle in observing that each kind of living thing—whether a person, or a dog, or a bird— lives in a unique manner and has a unique activity. We easily recognise the differences in how a cat moves, how a dog moves, how a horse moves, how a bird moves, how each kind of creature differs in its habits, its choice of food, its need for companionship. If we are to assert that it is the soul that invests each living body with its activity, then the soul must be particular to the body it animates.

DUCHESS YSABELLE: There are no two dogs alike. Nor horses. And certainly not people. All share in their creaturely necessities such as sleep and food, but differ in their preferences and temperament.

C.A.L.2022

LIBER SPHÆRÆ

FATHER GIOVANNI: Yes, indeed, in every variety of living thing we find commonality and variance. We know an oak by its bark, by its leaves and its acorns, but each oak differs in its branches. So with every plant or creature; we recognise it by how it resembles others of its kind, but in every case we find some difference. So it is with the soul: in its similarities it partakes of the nature of its kind, and in its differences it is unique. It is of the commonalities of souls that I wish to speak.

The notion that the soul has parts comes from the differences between stones, plants, animals, humans, and angels. Stones have no movement of their own. Plants are fixed to one place and their movement is limited to growth. Their growth comes from the soil, from the sun, and from water, as every farmer knows. Because they are fixed to a place, they have no need for organs of sense, although most are vigorous in growing towards sunlight.

Animals are not fixed to one place. They must seek out their sustenance, which may be plants or other animals. They have a means of movement, and organs of sense as we do—sight, sound, smell, taste, touch—so that they can find what they need to survive and avoid becoming prey. However, even the best of animals, animals raised in our ways such as dogs and horses, must be trained to perform simple tasks. We are amazed if they comprehend our purposes, or understand our needs. Their powers of comprehension, of recall, and of communication, are small by comparison with a young child.

Humans resemble animals in our limbs, senses, and bodily functions, but in addition we possess language and reason, and many ingenious and complex skills which are acquired by instruction. We speak our thoughts that others may comprehend our actions. We also possess arts to preserve whatever is considered great and noble and memorable, so that even after untold centuries we still recall the quarrel of Achilles and Agamemnon, and the death of noble Hector. In a similar manner we recite the exploits of Roland, and those of Arthur and his knights.

Lastly, there are angels, nourished by divine effulgence and superior to us in comprehension of the divine. What we comprehend through the power of reason, they perceive directly through a superior intellectual power. It is said that to each of us is appointed a guardian angel to guide us and protect us, and that this angel is a part of the soul concealed from us until a time when it may be revealed in fullness ... for we are as inferior in our comprehension of God's purposes as animals are in comprehension of our own.

And now I will conclude my digression by stating a notion shared by many philosophers, that our soul has parts: a vegetative or nutritive soul akin to plants; a sensitive soul akin to animals; a rational soul that is unique among our kind; and an intellectual soul akin to that of an angel.

SIGNORA EMILIA: And the lower soul, the part ruled by the Moon, comprises the vegetative and sensitive souls? I see the sense in that; the Moon has sway over the ancient wildness in us, that part of our being that is at home in dark forests and desires to live free of society. I see that clearly, for Diana was ever the wildest of the gods, content to run and hunt and live without attachment.

FATHER GIOVANNI: Indeed.

DUKE LORENZO: So the Moon governs the lower part of the soul, the part that is closest to this world, and with it she governs all the creaturely needs and impulses that have sway over our higher aspirations. And the higher soul is presumably ruled by the Sun?

FATHER GIOVANNI: You are correct, my Lord.

DUKE LORENZO: I have felt the wildness of which you speak, Signora Emilia ... mostly when hunting, sometimes when soldiering, when I am reduced to eyes and ears and a fierce slyness. All noble and worthy thoughts depart like swallows in the autumn, and I am a creature of the woods in all but clothing and title.

Hunting is not a vocation for philosophers. There cannot be many who enjoy the hunt who have not imagined living wild in the forest, a simple life far from the society of civilised men.

SIGNORA EMILIA: And far from the society of civilised women too, my Lord, for the wilds call to us equally. There are women who would rather live on the fruits of nature and hunt with a bow than spin and weave and sew.

    The wild witches of Thessaly were famed for their knowledge of herbs and healing, and it is said they had power over the light of the Moon and could draw it down to Earth. There is an idyll in Theocritus—it is the second idyll I think—where a woman is spurned by a lover and makes a spell, and sings to Diana and Hecate that she might have redress.

FATHER GIOVANNI: Theocritus, eh? It seems your Greek has progressed ... the tutor I appointed has been useful?

SIGNORA EMILIA: Father Alonzo has spent many hours on verbs, but he blushed and stammered when I mentioned that I had procured a volume of Theocritus from a printer in Venice. He said its discussions of love were not suited to one in his vocation. And so I have made my own study.

FATHER GIOVANNI: He is young, and Theocritus was Greek and liberal in matters of physical affection. As it happens, I know the idyll you mean: the woman who falls in love with a wrestler. His feelings are transitory while hers are not; and so she suffers the agony of rejection and calls upon Luna and Hecate to work a spell that is an equal mixture of love and spite.

    Diana has ever been a goddess for women. She lived in the wilds with her nymphs and despised the company of men. It is said that there are wise women in Italy to this day who minister to women in childbirth and seek the aid of Diana instead of the Mother of God.

DUCHESS YSABELLE: From the time I became a woman I knew the Moon ruled my body, just as she rules the sea and the tides. The only relief from her dominion came when I had children, and for a time I was no longer subject to her monthly cycle. Is this not so Emilia? Women use the Moon as a timepiece? Ask any woman and she will tell you at what phase of the Moon she bleeds. We

increase and decrease according to the changing light of the Moon
... forgive me Father, this is womens' talk.

FATHER GIOVANNI: I listen to the confessions of many women, my
Lady, and the dignity of the Church is not disturbed. This matter
of increase and decrease ... ?

DUCHESS YSABELLE: There is a monthly tide ... you tell him Emilia!

SIGNORA EMILIA: The Moon draws water into our bodies until the
time of blood and then it is released again. Unless we are with child
... then there is no blood and the fullness increases until after birth
and we are subject once again to the rhythm of the Moon. This is
truly womens' talk Father ...

FATHER GIOVANNI: You are saying that the water in your body
moves with the Moon, flowing and ebbing as the Moon changes?

SIGNORA EMILIA: I will speak plainly. In the days before my bleeding
I feel like a bladder that has been held too long under the pump.
And there is pain too, sufficient to bring me to tears. Forgive me
Father, forgive me my Lord, it is not decorous to speak of these
things.

DUCHESS YSABELLE: But you speak truly Emilia, the Moon has this
power over us.

DUKE LORENZO: Signora Emilia, you have my gratitude for your
candour. When my good wife first suggested we attempt these
discourses, the Spheres seemed distant, a matter for the poet or the
philosopher, and an opportunity to revisit the *Cantos* of Dante
Alighieri. Your talk of tides within the body has reminded me that
these are matters of immediate consequence and personal signific-
ance.

SIGNORA EMILIA: This is true, my Lord. There is a monthly tide that
brings with it great discomfort and pain. Is it not true also with
the sea, that there are monthly tides as well as daily tides?

DUKE LORENZO: Indeed. As the Moon becomes new or full, the tides
increase in their rise and fall. When the Moon shows but half her
face the tides are at their smallest flood. It is ill-luck to ground a
craft on a sandbar at the full Moon, for it will be stuck fast as the

tides drop away and they will not return to the same point for two weeks.

FATHER GIOVANNI: With this talk of tides I will relate that sailors have seen the creatures of the deep sea rise to the surface for the purpose of procreation at the time of the full Moon. It is thought among scholars and philosophers that the Moon has dominion over all the mysteries of generation.

DUKE LORENZO: By generation you mean ...?

FATHER GIOVANNI: Procreation, the means by which male and female multiply their kind. both the organs and the act. The union of two bodies to make a third that has some part of both, and the embodiment of the soul so that the offspring has its own life.

DUCHESS YSABELLE: I have felt life quicken in my womb. Such a miracle! Now my sons study Latin and fret at their tutor, and fret at Horace and Cicero, and despise any task that interferes with running headlong around this garden with our wards and pages.

SIGNORA EMILIA: We do not possess them for long, Ysabelle. My daughters also have an errant and reckless wildness in them. Father, those scholars and philosophers of whom you speak are in agreement with a line of women reaching back to the time of Eve, or Pyrrha as the Greeks called her.

They knew that the mysteries of generation are under the dominion of the Moon, because their bodies told them so. They gave offerings to Diana for protection in childbirth. When they saw the increase of the Moon they saw the promise of new life, and in the decrease they saw old age and death. Diana shepherded the soul as it entered this world, and when the body was weary and the soul departed, Hecate would conduct it to the underworld.

I am intrigued to hear that grey-beards have arrived at this understanding; perhaps a woman should address a conclave of scholars on these matters ...

FATHER GIOVANNI: I expect a grey-beard must have spoken to a woman at some point in history ...

Liber Sphæræ

DUKE LORENZO: Very droll Father ... this talk of generation recalls to mind something I heard at Padua, where many studied Galen and Hippocrates. Forgive me ladies, once again we must breach the bounds of good manners in the interests of our investigation. It is said that to make a child, the mother gives the blood of the Moon, and all that is white comes from the semen of the man.

FATHER GIOVANNI: I am familiar with these opinions. I think some Greeks believed that semen is the froth of the blood; that it is separated in the white matter of the brain and flows down a channel in the spine into a man's organ of generation, where it is kept in readiness.

The white matter in the body of a child—bones, sinew, brain—comes from the father. It is written that the whiteness of semen is a sign that its nature is lunar.

I have have also read that pearls are the transformed semen of Leviathan.

DUCHESS YSABELLE: Pearls? These? Semen!

SIGNORA EMILIA: I think he jests Ysabelle ...

DUCHESS YSABELLE: So he does, there is whimsy in his eyes.

FATHER GIOVANNI: Whimsy, or perhaps a caution that we should test the value of opinion. There is an excellent new work from Basel by one Vesalius—he studied at Padua, like yourself, my Lord—that does not find the supposed channel from the base of the spine to the male organ for the transport of semen descending from the brain. We must amend the marvellous traditions of Greek thought in light of this new passion for investigation.

DUKE LORENZO: I have seen a great deal of anatomy on the battlefield, in the surgeon's tent, and in the aftermath of the hunt. I will seek out this book if you recommend it. I would enjoy some study at leisure.

FATHER GIOVANNI: I have no copy of my own. Cardinal Vespucci of Bologna has a copy and he was eager to display it to me. It was graven in Venice but printed in Basel, a masterpiece of printing, profusely illustrated, and dedicated to the Emperor Charles.

DUKE LORENZO: Then I will seek it out.

DUCHESS YSABELLE: Yes, you most certainly should—I would see it too. You must write to your agent in Venice in the morning. So Father, the woman provides the red matter and the man provides the white. What about the soul? How is the soul conducted into the child? Is there a guard of angels to conduct it from Heaven?

FATHER GIOVANNI: With celestial trumpets and hosannas and a carpet of palm leaves ... you have chosen one of the most contentious topics in all of theology. If I can make an observation about scholars it is this: the fewer facts we possess, the more heated and enduring the debate. Hundred of authors and opinions are referenced to throw light on the same few sentences in scripture. You ask about the body and the soul ... may I curtail my reply?

DUCHESS YSABELLE: Perhaps some brevity ...

FATHER GIOVANNI: In that case I will reduce much argument into three strands of opinion. The first strand is that the soul is immortal. It exists prior the body and continues to exist after death. The soul possesses autonomy and may be regarded as the administrator of the body. These beliefs were held by many of the ancients, and come to us by way of Hermes, Orpheus, Pythagoras, Plato, Plotinus and many others. They held that the soul descends through the celestial Spheres into this world, is embodied in flesh, and ascends again at death. The soul can leave the body and encounter spirits and devils and angels and such like. It can travel from place to place in visions and dreams, and witness events both in the present and in the future. It can ascend into Heaven, as Paul describes in *Corinthians*. It may have been created at the same time as the angels, an opinion held by some of the Church Fathers. I am told that the Hindoos of India believe that after death the soul may inhabit a new body, and then another.

The second strand of opinion is that the soul is immortal and that it is newly created along with the body. This is the belief of the Church: that the soul is newly created by God and embodied at a time when the body of the child is developed to receive it. I know nothing about an honour-guard of angels. Whether this new soul is pure or marred by original sin is a subject of controversy and I will not inflict the tedium upon you. Whether it will be saved or damned is likewise a subject akin to the Gordian knot—and unlike Alexander I have no blade of sufficient quality to remove it.

The third strand of opinion is that the soul is an intimate part of the body, like the liver or stomach or heart, but diffused throughout so that it can direct the activity of every part and harmonise each activity with its purposes. One might imagine it to be like the general of an army, invisible among all the companies, and using messengers to direct and coordinate each part of the host. In a similar manner the soul can direct the body to run from danger, or jump a stream, or make great and wonderful works like those of Michelangelo or Raphael. Some believe that the soul shares the substance of the body and so is mortal, while others are reluctant to discard their belief in immortality.

SIGNORA EMILIA: I like the first proposal. I want to fly about and see all the things in Heaven and Earth.

FATHER GIOVANNI: I understand the attraction in that.

DUKE LORENZO: The third viewpoint is attractive to reason, but a disappointment to those who anticipate the blessings of an eternal life beyond the sufferings of this world. This notions comes from Aristotle does it not, the soul as *entelechia*, the vital force that directs the flesh towards goals and purposes. Without this soul the body still lives but is devoid of meaningful purpose. I have seen this in men who have been struck on the head; they eat and breath and foul their breeches, but volition is absent.

DUCHESS YSABELLE: You are thinking of that horseman ... Marco? Who fell and was struck on the temple by a passing horse?

DUKE LORENZO: Marco is the one such, a fine man in his day. I still pay a pension to his family to care for him. But others too, struck by an evil blow in melee. I have seen many men laid out on the ground, and most recover their wits, but one I knew—a Scot acclaimed in the French court—was struck a grievous blow on the side of his helm and thereafter his hands shook so much he could not hold a tankard without spilling ale. Another struggled to find words—he could still write and comprehend, but his speech was bewildered. Some, like poor Marco, have to be cared for like children.

In other cases there is a loss of movement but no loss of acuity. You have met the count of Rigorno; his horse broke its leg in the hunt, he fell badly, and now he sits in a chair with wheels and servants move him from place to place. He remains as courteous and astute as any person.

DUCHESS YSABELLE: You are saying that the capacities we associate with the soul can be damaged by mace or sword just as the body can?

DUKE LORENZO: Or some connection between body and soul is disturbed.

SIGNORA EMILIA: Then tell me Father, if the soul is to wander about and witness far-off things, how do body and soul remain attached?

FATHER GIOVANNI: You may recall me saying, perhaps in our last meeting, about a notion that comes to us via the followers of Plato: that between any two things that have some communion there must be a third.

SIGNORA EMILIA: I recall this.

FATHER GIOVANNI: So between body and soul there must be a third thing. Let us view this matter as did the ancients: the Sphere of the Moon is closest to this world, and between Earth and Moon we find the elements—water, air, and fire—with fire being the finest and most subtle, and so it rises furthest beyond air and water. But even fire is not so fine as to reach beyond this terrestrial sphere, and so there is another essence, finer still, more subtle, a fifth essence, and many call it the quintessence. Others call it *aethyr*, which comes to us from Homer but now the word has philosophical connotations. Others still, meaning well but causing great confusion, call it spirit. It has even been called *eros*, because any communion between two things resembles love. Whatever it is called, it is the medium that communicates between the celestial spheres and this world.

Now the ancients saw an analogy between the communion of Moon and Earth and the communion of soul and body, which is why I said that the Moon ruled the lower parts of the soul. By continuing the analogy we say that the communion between soul and body is this fifth essence, or spirit.

SIGNORA EMILIA: So there is a tendril of this quintessence or spirit that fastens soul to body and stretches ere so fine as the soul ranges over all of Heaven and Hell, as did Dante with Virgil and Beatrice?

FATHER GIOVANNI: A tendril. A cord. A thread. There is a verse from the book of Solomon:

> Or ever the silver cord be loosed, or the golden bowl be broken, or the pitcher be broken at the fountain, or the wheel broken at the cistern. Then shall the dust return to the earth as it was: and the spirit shall return unto God who gave it.

Signora Emilia, some conceive of the link between body and soul as a silver cord, just as Solomon describes it. My lord, this verse also supports your observations. If the pitcher is broken it will not hold water. If the wheel is broken, the cistern cannot be reached. Solomon intends us to understand that if the body can no longer draw life from the spirit, it returns back to the dust from which it came.

But what if the pitcher is not entirely broken but it is cracked and leaks? What if the wheel is stiff and struggles to turn? Soul and body in fractured communication? These may be the maladies you describe?

DUKE LORENZO: Solomon eh? I will not dispute any matter with Solomon! He might command me to be cut in two pieces to prove his point. Or stop my mouth with his magic ring and torment me with spirits. But yes Father, as you say, fractured, like a cracked pitcher.

DUCHESS YSABELLE: A wise choice husband ... not to dispute with Solomon. I would like to mention a related matter: those who are moonstruck, those whose wits have been disordered by the rays of the Moon and talk nonsense, or harm themselves ... although some say it is devils that make people harm themselves, and not the Moon.

SIGNORA EMILIA: The aged are often moonstruck, forgetting their friends and family, wandering lost at night in their own homes, strangers to themselves.

FATHER GIOVANNI: When last we met we observed that this world is stubborn and implacable. It imposes its truths upon us and we are ruled by its necessities. The Sphere of the Moon rules differently: it suggests many truths and imposes none. It is fluid like the sea. It is disordered in the way that a dream is disordered—recall Pharaoh's dream, of cows eating cows, and grain eating grain, and all the wise men in Egypt could find no sense in it. The realm of the Moon is profligate, because every possibility is nourished, but it is resistant to reason. By contrast, this world is poor, because only some few of these possibilities are permitted to exist.

I would say that those who are moonstruck live in the plenitude of the Moon. They have forgotten Necessity, or have never understood it. They resemble fools when judged by the wisdom of this world, which follows the dictates of Nature.

DUKE LORENZO: It seems to me that that one might attribute many afflictions of the soul to the Moon, but they are so different they might not have the Moon as their universal cause.

DUCHESS YSABELLE: How so husband?

DUKE LORENZO: There are those who are normally sound of mind but who, on occasion, fall to the ground and writhe and lose all sense. Then they recover and are well again. It is written that Caesar was afflicted in this way, and he was a man of singular ability.

There are those who claim divine visions and prophecies, and stir up the common folk with talk of God's judgement, of pestilence and wars, and of disturbances in the affairs of nations. Are they prophets? Are they moonstruck? Or are they seeking attention and influence? Some are a harmless nuisance, but some are agitators and are taken before the magistrates.

There are those with a deficit of understanding who cannot grasp the detail of simple tasks and are called moon-calves or simpletons or lack-wits. They do not outrage our common sense with preposterous nonsense, and they are not at odds with our understanding of this world ... they simply fail to comprehend it.

There are habitual drunkards whose appetite for wine leads them to visions of serpents, and ants, and beetles, and they scream and rave. Are there more?

FATHER GIOVANNI: In our holy communities there are some who find an old horseshoe nail, scratch away at their skin, and proclaim that they have the marks of our Lord's crucifixion. Others are visited by saints and angels or by the Blessed Virgin, and cause a great furore. In some cases I have been called upon to assess testimony, to judge sanctity and character. These are difficult judgements.

DUCHESS YSABELLE: And how do you judge, Father?

FATHER GIOVANNI: Sanctity and character? A life of devotion and humility, a feeling of veracity, holiness perhaps. And yes, before you ask, there is holiness, and on occasion one can sense it.

DUCHESS YSABELLE: You have quite aroused my curiosity, Father.

FATHER GIOVANNI: A thing is holy when it is set apart from this world and becomes a receptacle for God. A church is holy. An altar is holy. The vestments of a priest are holy, and the rites and observances of the Church are holy. Some lives are holy and filled with divine grace. This is tangible to an interior sense—it is a convention among artists to display holiness with an aureole of light. Or was, I should say; the new fashion for verisimilitude in art does not sit well with ancient notions of holiness, and a halo that resembles a golden dinner salver is something I struggle to accept.

DUCHESS YSABELLE: But you have encountered this holiness?

FATHER GIOVANNI: I have, but rarely. I have encountered brothers and sisters in the Church whom I thought were excitable and confused. Were they not in the Church, I believe they would have been equally excited and confused about spirits, or witches, or portents, or planetary oppositions. Only rarely have I encountered holiness, but when I have, I found it humbling.

You visit the hospice at San Giovanni, my Lady; you must have encountered many maladies of the soul?

DUCHESS YSABELLE: I have Father. For the most part I see those afflicted with melancholia, who cease to care for themselves. The good sisters care for them in that hope that Christian charity will restore their spirits and they will no longer be tormented by Saturn and dark thoughts.

There are others who are excitable and disruptive and will not conform to the rule of the good sisters. These go either to the old lazar house at Montefalco—if they have family to pay for their care—or beg in the streets until the Bargello and his men eject them from the city.

And so they become outcast and travel from place to place. They are tormented by children and dogs, they must beg for charity, and they have no home or comfort. They do no harm unless they steal, and then it goes badly for them.

FATHER GIOVANNI: The Church provides care for as many as it can. One might argue that the Church is wealthy, so why can the Church not care for all the unfortunate? But wealth does not cure mad passions, baseless fears, and the delusions so common among the insane. These are a sore trial to care for in a place of calm and worship.

Some say the mad are tormented by devils and we should cast out these devils in the name of Christ. Not all of us are blessed with the power of Christ. And so we offer charity to those with an amiable disposition; some of these will take vows to become brothers and sisters, and if they are obedient to our rule then all is well. Those who disrupt the good order of a community are asked to leave. We are Christians, not warders. A community without order ceases to be a community.

DUKE LORENZO: Well said, Father! This country has been through many trials, with France, and Spain, and the Empire, all contending to take our birthright from us. The countryside has been trampled into mud by great hosts of hired rogues and blackguards from every nation. What the people of this city expect is good order ... and that the good order of the city should not be upended by those whose souls are in disorder.

SIGNORA EMILIA: It distresses me to hear of suffering and of those exiled from care and comfort. Are there no herbs or remedies to calm a disordered mind?

FATHER GIOVANNI: A physician might diagnose an imbalance of humours and employ the usual remedies—blood-letting, purging, and so on. Sometimes these remedies can bring some relief, but in my limited experience they do not provide a cure. Some herbal medicines—the juice of the poppy for example—have a pacifying effect but the relief is short-lived, and becomes less with each dose.

SIGNORA EMILIA: And so we should have communities with food and shelter where they can live, and not wander from place to place. It is a matter of wealth and family is it not? The wealthy care for their own; they find a secluded property and hire trusted servants. Families of lesser means pay the warders at Montefalco for a confinement that is barely Christian. Those with no means are left to fend for themselves.

DUKE LORENZO: The people believe that madness is a punishment from God. They will pay to increase the city walls and gates, but not to house the mad. But you are correct, there is a lack of Christian charity and I will address the council on this matter and solicit their views.

It seems to me, now that we have considered the matter, that each planet has the power to distemper and derange the soul. My dear wife has mentioned Saturn and the morbid gloom and lassitude it confers. I can see how Mars would lead to mania and violence, Jupiter to grandiose delusions, Venus to unseemly lasciviousness, Mercury to an intolerable mendacity. All these tendencies, taken to excess, disrupt the good order of our daily lives. The Moon, being closest, has the greatest power to disperse reason, and so takes the blame for all.

FATHER GIOVANNI: Indeed, my Lord, the Moon takes the blame for all. But she has her own power too, and it is a power of deceit, and concealment, and illusion. By the light of the Moon nothing is as it seems. There is a false appearance. We may be false to ourselves, imagining greatness in our features, in our speech, acuity, and influence. You will find that when Erasmus writes of folly, he writes not of the mad and moonstruck; he takes aim at the pervasive folly of all humankind. We are all in some way less than how we envisage ourselves; it is through vanity, arrogance, and self-deception that we conceal from ourselves what may be readily apparent to others—and is certainly apparent to God. We view ourselves, not with the clarity of sunlight, but in the ghostly half-light of the Moon.

Brandt also, in his *Ship of Fools*, exposes all that is coarse and ungodly. He makes it his task to show to us in satirical verse those things we choose not to see for ourselves. I will also cite Solomon, who teaches us that vanity and folly are paired. There is a universal folly; we are fallen from our original estate.

DUKE LORENZO: I do see that ... but we must live in the world as we find it, not in a world of human perfection as conceived by a poet. I have laughed at Erasmus and Brandt and seen the truth of what they say, but I have no power to reform human nature. Wife, we are far from our course and require your touch on the helm to bring us back.

DUCHESS YSABELLE: The Ship of Fools reaches her destination without master, compass, or helm.

DUKE LORENZO: And what might that destination be?

DUCHESS YSABELLE: The Moon! We will wave at the man in the Moon, and he will smile to see us abroad upon the starry deeps.

SIGNORA EMILIA: Madness indeed! This man in the Moon you speak of: Dante tells us it is Cain, exiled for kin-slaying, and finding no home in this world he lives upon the Moon. You should steer wide Ysabelle, steer wide.

DUCHESS YSABELLE: Then we shall steer wide—I will have no truck with Cain and his insincere smiles. We are in the full light of the Moon ... we must beware her rays and shield our eyes lest our wits be drawn out. Husband, shield your eyes!

DUKE LORENZO: I do! I do! This venture is worthy of Ulysses.

SIGNORA EMILIA: Father, while our helm struggles against the wiles of Cain and the tides of madness, I would like to return to the view that some believe the soul immortal and autonomous, having precedence over the body. I suppose that this is a venerable tradition, and many worthy ancients have held fast to it?

FATHER GIOVANNI: That is so.

SIGNORA EMILIA: If then the body is contingent and the soul is primary in its nature, the soul must have a power over worldly substance so that substance may be shaped according to the needs of the soul? And that the fifth essence, or *aethyr*, or spirit, that travels from soul to substance must possess the innate power to inform matter? To give it shape? To mould it according to the soul's desire?

FATHER GIOVANNI: Many have thought so. Is this not what occurs when the potter moulds clay? The mind conceives the form and so it is communicated via the spirit and hands; it is then verified via the eyes, body, and spirit working in harmony with the soul?

SIGNORA EMILIA: But if the soul exercises the body in a manner so marvellous, might it not work other marvels upon the world? Without the intermediary of hands and eyes?

FATHER GIOVANNI: By marvellous do you mean miraculous, as when Christ walked on water, turned water into wine, blasted a fig tree, multiplied loaves and fishes, and rose from the dead on the third day?

SIGNORA EMILIA: And now you have hobbled me, Father, for if I suggest that this is not what I mean you will ask me to explain and I do not feel adequate.

LIBER SPHÆRÆ

FATHER GIOVANNI: You wish to know whether the soul has an innate capacity for the miraculous that does not depend upon divine grace?

SIGNORA EMILIA: If I say yes, will you condemn me?

FATHER GIOVANNI: It is a difficult topic, a point at which the pagans and the Church diverge. You wish to know what autonomous power the soul possesses to work wonders? To command spirits? To summon winds, to blight crops, to speak to the dead, to discover secrets hidden since the time of Eden? You speak of magic, sorcery, witchcraft. Are these true wonders, or the works of evil spirits tempting the soul to perdition?

SIGNORA EMILIA: Your answer, if I read you right, is that there are ancient and reputable opinions on these matters, but that the Church condemns them ... and I should tread warily.

FATHER GIOVANNI: Let me circle around the matter that we may view it at a distance. There are three groups with which the Christian Church has been in contention from the earliest times ... and yet we have borrowed much of value from each group.

The first group includes those I first mentioned, the pagan philosophers of Greece, of Rome, and of Egypt, who tell us much about the celestial Spheres and how to draw down spirits into statues and the like. Many of the Church Fathers were educated in these traditions, men like Clement and Origen, and they came to the Church having first been educated in pagan beliefs and Greek philosophy. We must recall that even the saintly Paul was first a Jew—a Pharisee born of Pharisees—and a Roman, and he composed his epistles in Greek.

The Church values much that has come to us from the Greeks, ancient notions that can be found in the works of Dionysius, called the Areopagite because he was an Athenian judge, and in John the Scot, and of course in Aquinas. There is a struggle, a tension if you will, between how much of this thought is permissible and how much is to be condemned. This tension becomes most acute with the works of the Egyptian Hermes, called Thrice-Great, which have become a fashion among natural philosophers and alchemists and the like.

The second group is the Hebrews, an unfortunate people harried from country to country even though they are industrious and law-abiding. We have taken their sacred books for our own, and yet learn nothing from their Rabbis and little from their laws. And yet we hear that they possess secret books of Solomon and Moses and the angel Raziel that teach the secret names of God, names that command the angels; names and seals that move every power in Heaven and Earth.

The third group is the followers of Muhammad, with whom we have been at war since two centuries after the fall of Rome. We have from them much that is extraordinary in natural philosophy and medicine, from Averroes and Avicenna and many others. They have named the stars, and have marvellous books in which the virtues and powers of stars are disclosed, so that a man might work wonders or mischief according to his understanding of the hours, and the seasons, and the Mansions of the Moon.

DUKE LORENZO: You are saying that there is a magnificent banquet spread before us, with ingredients brought from the four quarters and prepared by the finest cooks, but we may taste but one small part of it? We may taste the venison but not the pastry, the meat but not the gravy?

FATHER GIOVANNI: Indeed.

DUCHESS YSABELLE: And why may we not taste the gravy?

FATHER GIOVANNI: Because the Church Fathers, having embraced the true faith, damned the gods of all other nations as devils. If you have read Augustine you will know that he has no good thing to say about the gods of Rome. When Paul writes in *Ephesians*:

> For we wrestle not against flesh and blood, but against principal-
> ities, against powers, against the rulers of the darkness of this
> world, against spiritual wickedness in high places.

he means that those temporal powers in this world that are set against the Church are allied with the fallen angels that despise God, and work to tempt our souls. The heart of the matter is that

Paul tells us that Satan is prince of this world. This is the meaning of John's vision, that there will be a great war and that finally all the powers of darkness will be put down to Hell and Christ will reign. I believe that this is the eventual answer to your question Signora Emilia: the soul, lusting after things it does not yet possess, may seek the aid of spirits ... but they will be false spirits.

SIGNORA EMILIA: But surely the angels are not false?

FATHER GIOVANNI: Some angels were false, and fell, and still retain some brightness. There is true gold, and there is the appearance of gold that excites fools.

SIGNORA EMILIA: Then I might then be damned for traffic with devils in disguise?

FATHER GIOVANNI: They seek to lure your soul into sin and so possess it on the day of judgement.

SIGNORA EMILIA: They shall not have it! If I am virtuous I might command spirits with holy names as do the Jews; as you say, they are industrious and law-abiding. And the wise and virtuous pagans—they cannot all be damned for meddling with spirits and statues.

FATHER GIOVANNI: Dante finds them in Hell. It is the outer circle to be sure, but it is a melancholy domain and there is little relief from gloom.

SIGNORA EMILIA: So he does. I had forgotten.

DUKE LORENZO: I am with the Signora Emilia on this matter. There are worse sins than a good soul calling out to good spirits for good purposes ... there are much worse sins, and I have had the misfortune to witness many. And what of Ficino and Pico, who say that there are natural affinities within the order of Nature that we may use to our advantage, and that these natural magics require no use of evil spirits and are divinely sanctioned.

DUCHESS YSABELLE: Husband, witness my raised hand! I am calling us to order. If we continue down this path we will seek to reform the Church; and Luther and Melancthon have already caused a sufficient uproar. Father, if it pleases you, would you kindly instruct us on these Mansions of the Moon.

FATHER GIOVANNI: Certainly, my Lady, I will recount what little I know. The twenty-eight mansions are named by the Arabs. Just as the Sun has a passage through the stars with twelve dwellings that we call the Zodiac, so the Moon travels through the stars and has twenty-eight houses. This teaching can be found in an ancient book called in the tongue of the Arabs *The Goal of the Wise*, but it is better known as the *Picatrix*.

SIGNORA EMILIA: How wonderful, the Moon visits her estates like a queen making a royal progress, and in each estate she is greeted by her stewards and servants, and banquets and entertainments are prepared. Except that her subjects are star spirits or demons or angels ... or I know not what.

DUKE LORENZO: That Jewish fellow Jacobus who brings silks from the East, he has taken the road from the Levantine coast to Damascus, which is some way across a barren land. In that clime the Sun is a burden and even a torment, but the Moon and stars are a great blessing. He told me that the people of those parts have given names to all the stars, and that even though the stars are beyond number they can name any star one points to, and the wise can state the virtue of each one, and how it assists the Moon in her travels.

FATHER GIOVANNI: Just so. Each Mansion is a boon for some ventures and a hindrance to others, so that when the Moon is in one Mansion it is good for a journey; when in another it is favourable to bring a suit before a judge.

SIGNORA EMILIA: You have studied this book of the Arabs, Father?

FATHER GIOVANNI: I have encountered manuscripts of indifferent quality, for it is a work much copied, passing from hand-to-hand many times over. Most copies are barely legible, having been copied so many times that the signs, seals, and names of spirits are beyond repair.

It is a book of mixed virtue, being in part a repository of fable and nonsense, and in other parts it echoes the Greeks. Some parts might be studied with profit, for there is much that concerns the workings of the World Soul and the commerce of the Spheres. Ficino states that anything of worth may be found in his *De Vita*, and he was greatly learned in these matters.

DUCHESS YSABELLE: Our goal is to comprehend the Spheres and so we should not neglect these Mansions, for the Moon possesses a potent power upon the things of this world. Where may we obtain this work?

FATHER GIOVANNI: When the late Duke Federico of Urbino assembled his renowned library, he possessed some books of this nature, translated directly from the writing of the Arabs by a famous Sicilian Jew called Moncada, who became a priest. Moncada could read their writing. The books were finely made and bound by Federico's own scribes.

DUCHESS YSABELLE: Father, it would be a favour to me if you would enquire as to the whereabouts of this *Picatrix*—or a similar book— in which the mysteries of Moon and stars are set forth.

FATHER GIOVANNI: Then I will write some letters, my Lady. Rare books such as these are prized by popes and cardinals, and Urbino has been picked over by the Borgia, by the Medici, and by the della Rovere. Who can tell what remains? I will write to the custodian of the library—it is no great distance from here to Urbino, perhaps we can locate a fair copy.

DUCHESS YSABELLE: My thanks, Father.

SIGNORA EMILIA: Ficino ... he was from Florence was he not?

FATHER GIOVANNI: He was well regarded by Cosimo de' Medici, who gave him a small benefice and purchased many manuscripts and books for him to translate out of the Greek. You may know that when Constantinople fell to the Turks, the Greeks fled and carried with them many rare things to sell.

From Ficino we have the gift of Plato in Latin, and also the followers of Plato—Plotinus, Iamblichus, Porphyry, Proclus—

who lived long after their master, and also the works of the Egyptian Hermes. Latterly Ficino became a priest ... I suspect that having been troubled and seduced by the arguments of so many pagan fathers, he feared for his soul.

Duke Lorenzo: He was widely discussed when I was a student, and I have his works in the library. I will seek them out.

Signora Emilia: Thank you, my Lord, I would fain study the lore of star beings ... and I will be virtuous and have no commerce with devils.

Father Giovanni: Then you should consult Aquinas. He admits that there is a natural magic where substances—stones, herbs, fine odours—possess an innate connection to some celestial potency and may be used to balance the humours in the body, and it is these legitimate and natural means that are used by physicians.

But any procedure that addresses a comprehending intelligence by means of writing, or supplications, by conjurations and orisons, by names and seals and images, this will summon a trickster spirit that will corrupt the soul. According to Aquinas, these spirits are mighty in the ways of deception and malice.

Signora Emilia: I will read Aquinas, Father, and fortify my soul with prayer and confession.

Duke Lorenzo: Well said! And now I must reveal a thought that might cause offence to my lady wife and to the good Signora. It is that the Moon offers nothing solid, nothing to grasp and hold. I am reminded of Proteus, the old man of the sea—Menelaus tried to hold him and he shifted from shape to shape. With the Moon, all is flux and change. There is false appearance, and we may believe that what we see is true when it is the case that we have lost our wits and are lost in delusion.

The Moon has no light, and so she clothes herself in the borrowed light of the Sun, filling the dark of night with a false glamour and shapes that are half-seen. She is the mistress of witches, and those who will not show themselves by day.

These things disturb me, for I am a man who enjoys an enduring world with a sense of constancy and depth. I know Luna is a goddess for women, and so I am loath to speak ill of her, and yet in the sphere of the Moon I feel lost, at sea, without Sun, or star, or compass to guide me.

Duchess Ysabelle: Oh Husband, you find that the Moon is fickle and inconstant, and her rays taint the souls of women. It is often said that women are ruled by the Moon, that women are subtle and fickle, that our affections ebb and flow with the tides, that we seek to charm and derange the wits of honest men with mysterious arts. We employ glamours; our appearance is artifice, and so we cannot be trusted. Why, perhaps we are all witches like Medea, who will chop our children in pieces to spite an inconstant lover?

Duke Lorenzo: I did not say that. Father, please observe that I did not suggest such a thing.

Duchess Ysabelle: Then hear this: if you seek constancy in life you will not find it in city walls, which are so often broken; or in laws, so often disregarded; or in wealth, so often squandered. You will find it in the hearts of women, who from the time of Eve have brought sons and daughters into this world and who have devoted their lives to the care of their families. Is there more constancy in life than this?

Duke Lorenzo: You have answered me well.

Signora Emilia: You are quite the advocate for our sex, Ysabelle! The Moon rides high above us and yet she has not sapped your wits!

Duchess Ysabelle: The Moon grants that we may use her power to charm the wits of men ... so that they walk the streets wearing fools' caps with asses ears, and cloth of motley sewn with bells, and yet they believe themselves lords and princes.

Sphæra Mercurii

Duchess Ysabelle: So many books!

Signora Emilia: Mercury is a quick and elusive spirit who darts from place to place ... but he is drawn to books like a mouse to cheese. We must wall him in with books lest he evade us and escape our comprehension.

Duchess Ysabelle: In that case we shall catch him quickly, for I see that we have all been industrious in the bookcases. Husband, kindly reveal to us what you have brought.

Duke Lorenzo: I have spent many happy hours. I thought to find such works of Ficino as I possess. This is the *Theologia Platonica*, and this the *De Vita Libri Tres*. This—most relevant for this evening's discussion—is a collection of books by the Egyptian Hermes that he translated out of the Greek. And you wife, you have before you a most extravagant volume.

Duchess Ysabelle: Emilia and myself have been studying the Arab book of starry wisdom that comes to us from Urbino. Father, our gratitude! Please assure the librarian that he is most welcome in this court should he choose to travel this way. This book is just as you said Father, a book of mixed virtue. In parts it relates the wisdom of Hermes, in other parts it is superstition of a low and unworthy kind. And you Father, what book have you brought?

FATHER GIOVANNI: This is merely a worn copy of Ptolemy, his *Tetrabiblos*. But I also have this.

SIGNORA EMILIA: Quicksilver! Pray spill some that we may pursue it! How did you come by it Father?

FATHER GIOVANNI: A goldsmith I know well, he is making a medal for the bishop. Quicksilver dissolves gold, and so all the floor sweepings from the workshop are saved and placed in quicksilver to recover the golden metal.

SIGNORA EMILIA: Restrain him with books! Another here! This agile spirit shall not evade us.

DUCHESS YSABELLE: Be not alarmed Emilia, see, we have made a prison for Mercury, and now that we have him, we can begin. Father ... I am sure you have been diligent in uncovering the nature of this spirit?

FATHER GIOVANNI: My lady, let me tell you what I have gleaned. Mercury is a wandering light that remains close to the Sun, so that he may be seen only at dusk and at dawn when the Sun is below the horizon. On account of this closeness and his speed of movement he was accounted the messenger or herald of the gods, charged with bearing messages to mortals, as he did when he bore the herb *moly* to Ulysses and saved him from Circe's enchantment.

This god is young and quick and glib, filled with a sly eloquence, as one might expect from a herald. He is quick not only in motion but also in comprehension and calculation. He bears a herald's staff, and on his head the round hat or *petasos* of a traveller. It is said that his winged hat and sandals were made by Vulcan, and his staff came from Phoebus, who is the Sun. As for the serpents, it is said that they were in dispute and he calmed them with his charmed staff, where they now remain.

Liber Sphæræ

There is a complication in the understanding of Mercury, for every race of people desires to possess some part of this God. We should perhaps give precedence to the Hermes of the Egyptians, for this god would seem to be the most ancient. This Egyptian Hermes is at times a man inspired by divine wisdom, and at other times he is an elder god named Tehuti or Thoth. He taught the alphabet and the art of writing, and the secrets of astronomy and mathematics and music.

The young Hermes of the Greeks is more cunning and wayward, a god of shepherds and herdsmen and travellers, and he devised the lyre from the shell of a tortoise. He will steal and he will deceive, as he did when he stole the cattle of the Sun and concealed them. He is a god of boundaries, of rights of way, of treaties. Of all the boundaries it is that boundary between life and death for which he is best known. He is a *psychopompos*, a guide who conducts the souls of the dead into the underworld. This god also rules the arts of divination by lots, by knuckle-bones and the like.

The Roman Mercury has some part of all of these things but is chiefly the god of merchants, of trade and commerce and markets, and is named for these things, so that when we say *mercato* we recall the provenance of his name. There is also the Mercurius of the alchemists, but that is another matter.

DUKE LORENZO: Mercury is a god for all who wish to sell us something; those who promise wonders with glib words.

DUCHESS YSABELLE: We would be poor indeed if we bought nothing. We would be as naked as Adam and Eve when they were exiled from the Garden.

DUKE LORENZO: Do you not find buying and selling distasteful, Signora? The buyer exaggerating every fault, the seller extolling the perfection of his cloth, or his oil, or his spices? All the haggling and shouting and yelling and filth? Markets are detestable places.

SIGNORA EMILIA: There is much to see, my Lord: tall heaps of spices and nuts, sweetmeats, pottery, bags and belts, cloth of every kind.

Sometimes there are jugglers and acrobats and those who pretend to the mystic arts. And people in all their varieties.

DUKE LORENZO: By the grace of God we have stewards to attend to these matters. I am content to leave the haggling to others.

DUCHESS YSABELLE: Oh husband, Saturn casts a ray upon your heart! You are downcast. Has a day in council blighted your view of humankind?

DUKE LORENZO: Yes, it has. I have spent too long in council. My day has been blighted by Mercury. Each man conceals the truth of his desires behind a profusion of words. They elaborate. They obfuscate. They prevaricate. They equivocate.

I must be outwardly calm, but inwardly I seethe like a kettle. Whom can I trust? How am I to divine their intentions? With knuckle-bones? Flights of crows ... or sightings of owls? Am I to consult a witch, as did Saul, or Pompey's son? It seems to me that Mercury is a god for rogues and scoundrels.

DUCHESS YSABELLE: I hear your complaint, Husband.

FATHER GIOVANNI: My lord, perhaps if I might read from Ptolemy. These are his words on the influence of Mercury:

> Mercury, alone, having dominion of the mind, and being in a glorious position, renders it prudent, clever, sensible, capable of great learning, inventive, expert, logical, studious of nature, speculative, of good genius, emulous, benevolent, skillful in argument, accurate in conjecture, adapted to sciences and mysteries, and tractable: but, when placed contrarily, he makes men busy in all things, precipitate, forgetful, impetuous, frivolous, variable, regretful, foolish, inconsiderate, void of truth, careless, inconstant, insatiable, avaricious, unjust; and altogether of slippery intellect, and predisposed to error.

As for vocations, he has this to say:

> For if Mercury governs action, to speak generally, he makes his subjects scribes, men of business, calculators, teachers, merchants, bankers, soothsayers, astrologers, sacrificers, and in general those who perform their functions by means of documents, interpretation, and giving and taking.

Duke Lorenzo: You see, Wife! The learned Greek agrees with me! Frivolous, foolish, careless, impetuous, inconstant! Foolish rogues with silver tongues and empty words!

Duchess Ysabelle: Husband, perhaps your judgement is disturbed by today's travails, for it seems to me that you are being most selective in your choice of words. In this matter you might contend with Mercury himself! Do we not admire the good Father who is prudent, wise, learned, studious, and indefatigable in his pursuit of truth? See, the words of Ptolemy can serve my purpose also.

Duke Lorenzo: I think perhaps the Roman Mercury offends me. The Egyptian Hermes is more to my liking.

Duchess Ysabelle: Then perhaps you can tell us what you have found in his books?

Duke Lorenzo: Then I will, and if there is a surly quality to my demeanour then I apologise, for it is not worthy of this company.

Ficino opines that these books of Hermes are ancient works; they precede the works of Plato and all the Greeks, and perhaps even the books of Moses. Here is what I have gleaned from this first book, which is named *Pimander*.

The *Pimander* tells how the world came into being. It explains how we are divided beings, one part coming from Nature and one part divine, and how the divine part descends into this world and is blinded by the passions arising from Nature, and so forgets what it is and whence it came—I believe we have discussed something of this sort.

The purpose of these books is to awaken the soul to the recollection of its divine origin. I perceive a reflection of this wisdom in Pythagoras, and in Plato, and in the teachings of the Stoa.

Father Giovanni: I agree my Lord, this is wisdom the Greeks learned in Egypt. It is said that Pythagoras was instructed by a priest of that country.

Duchess Ysabelle: And how did the world arise, Husband? See, now I task your recollection!

DUKE LORENZO: And it is sorely tasked, for this work is obscure. In the beginning there was an unformed watery chaos that shrieked and groaned in torment for it was without order. But there was also Mind, and within Mind there arose Thought, and there was the articulation of that thought in a Word, which the Greeks call *Logos*. God (who is Mind) uttered a word that, like a seed, impregnated the womb of unformed Nature. The elements divided, with earth and water tending downward, and air and fire tending upwards.

FATHER GIOVANNI: This is not so different from the first book of the *Bible,* that we call *Genesis*, which is to say, Beginning. And the book of the apostle John, where he tells us that in the beginning was the Word.

DUKE LORENZO: Now you say it, Father, I recall them both. I find this next part confusing ... then God formed a Craftsman (I know not why), and the Word rose out of Nature and united with the Craftsman, who made the Cosmos and its Spheres and overseers, and set it in motion. And the overseers are the spirits of the planets.

FATHER GIOVANNI: And this part resembles the *Timaeus* of Plato.

DUKE LORENZO: It does, and is perhaps its source, for the *Timaeus* was old when Plato took possession of it. Now it seems to me (the writing having more obscurities than I would wish), that God made a son, a Heavenly Man of vast stature, a son made in his own image (for I think this is the intent behind the use of the word "son", indicating a likeness). I assume this vast man resembles the Adam of our scriptures.

And although called "man" and "son", this great similitude to God had no sex, on account of being male and female united. This makes little sense in light of what follows.

SIGNORA EMILIA: I have a liking for it, my Lord. Some writings are intended as allegory and we must not be literal in our understanding.

DUKE LORENZO: A useful observation Signora, and it does remind me of an allegory told by Plato in his discourse called *The*

Symposium, in which he tells us man and woman were once conjoined in one body, and then torn apart, and spend their days attempting to find their lost half.

Let me continue. This divine son gazed through the Spheres of the heavens into the newly formed earth and water of Nature, and fell in love with the beauty of his reflection, and so united with Nature. In this fall Nature was impregnated with divinity, but the Heavenly Man forgot his origin.

This is how we came to be—at least, as Hermes tells it. Each one of us shares a portion of the Heavenly Man, and so one can say that we are all sons of Man. And this is why we are divided beings, having bodies comprised of water and earth, which come from Mother Nature; reason and mind come from the Heavenly Man and share the quality of the divine Logos. We are divine beings that have fallen into Nature and into ignorance.

DUCHESS YSABELLE: Thank you husband. And how is our ignorance to be repaired? How are we to be restored?

DUKE LORENZO: I believe (and here I conjecture), through knowledge and through contemplation, and through a rejection of that sensual pleasure which binds us to the grosser aspect of Nature.

SIGNORA EMILIA: This fall into Nature resembles the tale of Narcissus, does it not? Perhaps the story that Ovid relates is an allegory for us to interpret?

DUCHESS YSABELLE: I can relate to that tale Emilia ... falling into contemplation ... being oblivious of myself. How often have I lost myself in a book?

SIGNORA EMILIA: As have I. Or the petals of a rose. Or any flower, but a rose most particularly.

DUCHESS YSABELLE: Or a dog's nose ... am I the only person to be entranced by the perfection of a dog's nose? Perhaps it is the limpid eyes ... but lest we digress, let me recall this Hermes to see how well I comprehend him.

The Logos, which you likened to a seed, fertilises Nature and brings her to fruition, for without this seed she is in a disturbed and watery confusion that groans and shrieks? And if we, human-kind, are to return to our divine estate we should reject that part of our being that turns towards Nature and turn instead towards the purity of the Logos, towards the Thought and Mind of the Father?

DUKE LORENZO: I am sensing some antipathy.

DUCHESS YSABELLE: Not to you, dear Husband! Only to the popular notion, here essayed, that the nature of woman is defective, that we are too far sunk in water and earth for clarity and potency of thought, and that we should defer to the male on account of a man's natural affinity to the divine Logos, to the Thought and Mind of God the Father?

That the minds of women are lost in roses and dog's noses, and lack the natural reason that pervades the minds of men?

SIGNORA EMILIA: You have entirely captured my unease Ysabelle. Perhaps this Egyptian Hermes was secluded from women in some priestly enclave far, far in the desert, and had no women to challenge his wits?

DUCHESS YSABELLE: We must reach a better understanding on this matter. Father, can you tell us why reason is so adored?

FATHER GIOVANNI: I will try, my Lady. I would say that reason is the method whereby we organise our thoughts, so that we can distinguish sound opinions from foolish thoughts. We employ it when we plan for the future, when we explain ourselves to others, when we attempt to recruit others to our schemes and ideas, when we try to understand events.

DUKE LORENZO: When Hermes describes how the several parts of the Cosmos are brought into order and harmony, each part fixed into its ordained place, he views this as the operation of reason in the mind of God.

DUCHESS YSABELLE: Thank you Father, thank you Husband. Reason brings order to our wits so that we are not foolish, and in the same manner it brings order to the watery confusion that shrieked and groaned before the Cosmos? And this ordering of wits is most marked in men?

SIGNORA EMILIA: Ysabelle, if I may, I note that the Egyptian Hermes likens the ordering of the Cosmos to the work of a craftsman. It is in the crafts that we find a most excellent display of reason, for quality recommends method, and method demonstrates understanding. In a debate it is not always the best argument that prevails, for the audience holds its own opinions, but who can argue against a display of excellence in woodwork, or Venetian glass, or the art of the goldsmith? But ... and here is my point ... the masters of all crafts are men. Women are excluded, and so our quality is not demonstrated.

DUCHESS YSABELLE: But we demonstrate our quality in all the arts of spinning and weaving and sewing and tapestry and the like.

SIGNORA EMILIA: But it is womens' work and so deficient in value. Our excellence will not be acknowledged until we are admitted to guilds and to universities, where we may be the equals of men in crafts and in debate.

DUCHESS YSABELLE: But this will never happen for we are judged to be deficient in reason and best suited to domestic life.

DUKE LORENZO: Some would say that crafts are deficient in reason, that craftsmen have little understanding of what they do, that they copy the methods of their masters.

DUCHESS YSABELLE: Then Husband, tell us where will we find the best examples of reason?

DUKE LORENZO: In the works of great scholars ... students of Plato and Aristotle ... the Greek geometers ... Euclid.

SIGNORA EMILIA: I like your choice of Euclid, my Lord, for I am beguiled by the power of his arguments. His theorems have a surprising beauty ... the elements of reason are on display, and they are simple in conception and powerful in application.

But here is a counter argument. The cosmos that Euclid has chosen is small. It could not be smaller, for points and lines and circles are the simplest constructions—we may draw them upon the ground with a stick. His proofs are deductive, moving step by step from what is given to what is proven ... much as one might plan a journey from one place to another. Each step is small, for the power in the method is not the size of a step, it is the accumulation of truth. A step may summon any prior proof, for once a proof is made, it is more solid and enduring than stone. In this way is a House of Reason built, but it is confined to its initial matter—points, lines and circles—and nowhere within this method have I discovered divinity.

DUCHESS YSABELLE: Is there some matter in Euclid that is insurmountable for our sex? A path a man might follow but not a women? An aperture too narrow for our hips? Is there a puzzle so sublime that it remains out of reach of our meagre comprehension?

SIGNORA EMILIA: Let me show you reason, Ysabelle. I say 'a needle is sharp' and you say 'sharp things make holes' and so I say in reply: 'then a needle makes holes'. I say 'all dogs bark', and you say 'barking is frightening', and so we assert that all dogs are frightening. This is reason.

DUCHESS YSABELLE: But not all barking is frightening. Some is merely irritating.

SIGNORA EMILIA: These are philosophical dogs and they bark philosophically. If I say barking is frightening, then it is frightening.

DUCHESS YSABELLE: So reason is a game of words? We pretend something is true so that we may pretend that something else is true?

SIGNORA EMILIA: Unless our reason is practical, for then it concerns the things of this world, and we may consult the world to discover whether we have understood it correctly.

DUCHESS YSABELLE: And philosophical dogs, do they have reason?

SIGNORA EMILIA: They have prudence. I find prudence in all animals, for they seek out what is good for them, and they are fearful of harm.

DUKE LORENZO: An interesting argument Signora. You view reason as an adjunct to our existence in Nature?

SIGNORA EMILIA: I do, my Lord. We use reason in every simple task. There is no better way to comprehend reason than to place limits upon a young child, for they protest every command vigorously, and they are best tamed with explanations.

DUCHESS YSABELLE: That is so true, Emilia. They are wayward and ready to quarrel about any small matter. Forgive us husband, we have wandered far from your *Pimander*.

DUKE LORENZO: That is a matter of no consequence—this subject intrigues me. And yes, I have seen how reason is absorbed into the souls of children ... although in my case I did not discover prudence until after my father died. Signora, you are less in awe of reason than many scholars I have met.

SIGNORA EMILIA: As a woman I must examine this reason and discover why it is so admirable. If there is a gate guarded by angels and I am not permitted to pass through, then I must discover it.

DUKE LORENZO: And have you discovered it?

SIGNORA EMILIA: I am uneasy when there is a debate about things that are not of this world. Let me explain, my Lord. A word, a noun, resembles a finger that points; we may follow the finger and find the thing it points to. Children learn this quickly; they are not yet two years old and they disregard the finger and look to where it points.

Scholars use words that point beyond this world. They argue about Original Sin, or the Trinity, or Truth, or Virtue, or Justice, or Beauty. This would not matter if they agreed, but they do not, and every man has his own notions.

We do not experience Truth, Virtue, Justice, and Beauty; we experience true statements, virtuous people, just laws, and beautiful art. It seems to me that these are empty words, not a suitable matter for discourse. To take a word out of this world makes for a Babel of misunderstanding and contention. Reason requires an understanding of a matter, an understanding of entities and their relations, of causes and their consequences. I am not competent to reason about navigation, or architecture, or artillery, for I have no understanding of tides or arches or gunpowder. And yet some feel able to argue about whether a new-born babe is depraved by the sin of Adam and Eve.

FATHER GIOVANNI: I see that Aristotle had a daughter Signora, but we should not deprecate philosophy. The scholar wonders what is true, and uses reason to uncover truth. Perhaps you wonder what is the root matter or substance of Truth, in what earth is it planted; Plato would answer that Truth is God.

SIGNORA EMILIA: Ah, now I see my error Father. I require tangibles and so I plant my tree of reason in the ground of Nature, whereas Plato plants his in God. This arises from my womanly affinity to earth and water, whereas Plato, having the body of a man, rises to the realms of air and fire.

DUCHESS YSABELLE: I agree, Emilia, your reason is the wrong kind of reason. It is wicked reason, fallen reason, natural and practical reason. You have eaten the fruit from the Tree of Knowledge, as did Eve.

Father, it seems to me that the Signora suggests that reason requires tangibles whose attributes we may comprehend. If this is so, then in what manner is reason divine?

FATHER GIOVANNI: How are we to be virtuous unless we make prudent choices?

DUCHESS YSABELLE: That is an excellent answer. Very particular, but I accept that we should aspire to virtue, and if we are to choose between actions we should choose wisely and not foolishly.

FATHER GIOVANNI: Also, it is through scripture and theology that we comprehend God.

SIGNORA EMILIA: But does not reason require something that is a given, something that is known to be true, and from that one may infer further truths? I learnt this much from Euclid.

FATHER GIOVANNI: You seek for incontrovertible truth, Signora? The truth that you require would be works of the Holy Spirit communicated through saints and prophets.

SIGNORA EMILIA: But some works are truer than others, Father.

FATHER GIOVANNI: Do you suggest that scripture is not divinely inspired, Signora?

SIGNORA EMILIA: Only that theologians are famously contentious on every subject and lack agreement on canonical texts, free will, sacraments, calendars, salvation, celibacy, saints, indulgences, festivals, the Eucharist, purgatory, original sin, predestination, the Trinity, and the nature of the Incarnation. Did I neglect any point of contention Ysabelle?

DUCHESS YSABELLE: You neglected to mention one issue of total unanimity, which is the role of our sex in the Church. St. Paul writes that we should defer to men—I expect this is on account of our turbulent and watery natures, our shrieking and groaning, and our devotion to matters of common sense, to inconsequential practical reason.

SIGNORA EMILIA: Ah, yes, women in the Church. On this one issue theologians are famously in agreement. Protestant or Catholic, they would sup together on this one issue. St. Paul does not mention the tumult of our womanly natures specifically, but it is clearly implied, and he must have encountered women exhibiting the wrong kind of reason and found them tedious.

FATHER GIOVANNI: You are correct Signora, the methods of Euclid achieve divergent conclusions when applied to Scripture. You are also correct when you say that words may mean different things to different people ... when their meaning is not grounded in the world of sense.

It is not all acrimony in the world of theology however. If you have been following the sessions of the Council of Trent, then you will know that the Church will approve the Vulgate as divinely inspired, down to every dot and tittle. Here is some priestly convergence for you.

DUKE LORENZO: I expect this is to forestall the Protestants, who imagine that by learning Hebrew and Greek they might find superior readings and so outflank the Church of Rome?

FATHER GIOVANNI: The Church of Rome has long had precedence in Latin. Why meddle with other tongues?

DUKE LORENZO: Yes, one should build on strength and not on weakness. Occupy the high ground. With every new *Bible* the Protestants sunder into smaller sects. They are rebuilding Babel.

FATHER GIOVANNI: Very amusing, my Lord, a new Babel indeed. The Protestants will scatter into mutual incomprehension, war upon each other, and leave us in peace.

SIGNORA EMILIA: I have a question concerning Babel, Father. It relates to scripture, and the several tongues in which it is written.

FATHER GIOVANNI: Please proceed Signora ...

SIGNORA EMILIA: When God cursed the builders of Babel for their presumption, there was a sundering. Those who had acted as one became a multitude without common speech, and have remained so. First they had one speech, then they had many ...

FATHER GIOVANNI: Indeed.

SIGNORA EMILIA: And when Adam and Eve ate of the forbidden fruit there was another sundering, a falling-away from God. They saw that they were naked. They were driven out into a world of pain and death and sin.

FATHER GIOVANNI: Yes.

SIGNORA EMILIA: And when God spoke and said 'Let there be light' and he saw the light was good; and He separated light from darkness ... and He said 'Let there be a firmament in the midst of the waters, and let it divide the waters from the waters'. The Word sundered the unity.

FATHER GIOVANNI: That is an interesting view.

SIGNORA EMILIA: Forgive me Father, this day my head is filled with questionable thoughts. I struggle with my words that I should not be condemned for foolish opinions.

FATHER GIOVANNI: It is not heresy to have thoughts—I have many I would not own to. It is only heresy if you preach against the doctrine of the Church.

SIGNORA EMILIA: Then I will say it: we are fallen away from God many times over, and with every fall our speech is corrupted and made inferior. How can Holy Writ be holy when our speech is so fallen and inferior? First there was the Word that caused a multitude of separations, of light and dark, of Heaven and earth; and then there was the speech of angels spoken in the Garden, (which must be inferior to the Word of God lest angels be able to make new worlds); and then there was the speech of the Fall (which is the speech of a fallen world), and then there are the multitudes of uncomprehending tongues that came after Babel. And then there is Holy Writ, where we find Greek and Hebrew—and now the Vulgate in Latin.

DUCHESS YSABELLE: I see you have acquired the rudiments of godly reason, Emilia.

FATHER GIOVANNI: Indeed she has, and the question is proper. In what manner is the Holy Writ holy when it is written a speech so fallen away from the first tongues of creation? And now the Church endorses the Latin Vulgate as Holy Writ, even though the tongues of scripture are Hebrew and Greek. In answer to your question I will observe that words by themselves do not yield up truth without a comprehending intelligence. It is the reader who, by the grace of God, discovers truth—we might observe that the words of scripture resemble seeds buried in dry ground, and it is the descent of the Holy Spirit that makes them fertile, so that they bear fruit.

I will add to your observations. It is not only our speech that is fallen away from God ... it is our blighted and sinful comprehension that removes our awareness of the divine. We speak a language of separations. Let us examine the parts of speech.

Nouns are situated: on the table, under the chair, before me, behind me, above, below, inside, outside. Events have a place in time: before, after, soon, later, yesterday, at the full Moon. Verbs declare the order of creation, for people have more verbs than animals, animals more verbs than plants, and plants more verbs than stones. For the most part our daily speech reflects only the natural and fallen world in which we find ourselves.

SIGNORA EMILIA: Just so, just so! Our speech is limited by our comprehension! Everything is fallen into separation; we see things in space and time, and we are overwhelmed by entities and causes and consequences. We see only surfaces; we cannot see hearts or souls or kind thoughts. Our speech is fallen into darkness.

How do we depict plants? We have so little understanding of their lives, for in our eyes they merely grow, and flower, and die. They have so few verbs! And poor stones! In our eyes they do nothing. What if they are holy and we do not see it! Perhaps the angels see that they are holy. Father, can we recover the speech of angels?

FATHER GIOVANNI: First you would require the faculties and comprehension of an angel. Then you might speak as you comprehended.

SIGNORA EMILIA: Ysabelle, we must study stones and discover that they are holy! Then we shall be as angels!

DUCHESS YSABELLE: Any stones, or particular stones?

FATHER GIOVANNI: Plato asserts that God is both the Good and the Beautiful. You should study the most beautiful, and the best.

DUCHESS YSABELLE: Those considered precious? Rubies, sapphires, emeralds, amethyst …

SIGNORA EMILIA: Indeed … we must leave now for Rome. The Pope and cardinals have all the best stones in Italy.

DUCHESS YSABELLE: I will instruct the grooms. The maids must prepare our finest dresses.

FATHER GIOVANNI: You jest, my Lady, but I know cardinals who would approve this theology.

DUKE LORENZO: God blesses them with abundance. Their wealth is a sign of divine grace.

FATHER GIOVANNI: Indeed, my Lord.

DUKE LORENZO: Returning to our fall into pain and death, the Book of Hermes would have us rise up through the Spheres, divesting ourselves at each Sphere of the celestial garment wrapped around us during our descent into this world. In this manner we may return to the ninth Sphere and perceive the pure forms of the divine. The fall of the divine man into Nature would be reversed, and we would then possess a faculty of comprehension superior to all the angels, for we are made in the image of God. And having attained the comprehension, we might recover the forgotten speech, as you said Father.

DUCHESS YSABELLE: And how might this elevation be effected? Did I ask this already?

DUKE LORENZO: We must hold fast to the Truth, which, as you have said Father, is God. But there is more, and here the teachings are vague.

It seems that we are blinded both by the passions of the body of flesh that comes from Nature, and by the workings of the Spheres, through which we are imprisoned in Time and Fate. Nature has captured us, but it is the overseers of the Craftsman who hold us fast and obstruct our vision of the infinite.

Perhaps the spirits or daemons of each Sphere can be subjugated with holy names—I have heard men speak of such things.

FATHER GIOVANNI: There are teachings of this nature. In their refutations of heresy, Ireneaus of Lyons and Hippolytus describe sects that taught secrets for the mastery of the rulers of the Spheres— signs and seals and names—so that the soul might be liberated. But these are rank heresies.

The story told in Scripture is that we are made in the image of God, but the Father and Mother of our kind were tempted into disobedience by the evil power of Satan. Christ died on the cross to save us from this sin, and free us from the oppression of all the evil powers of this world. They are already defeated, yet they do not know it.

SIGNORA EMILIA: And is there a secret tongue for harassing daemons and ordering them about?

DUCHESS YSABELLE: This book of the starry wisdom of the Arabs that we have from Urbino, has signs, seals and names.

SIGNORA EMILIA: But these are more for the purpose of drawing down the power of a star to chase away scorpions and serpents—a goal with which I am fully in accord, and might even consider if I was beset by serpents and scorpions. But what of a lost speech of angels, forgotten after the Fall? If God is Truth, is the speech of angels a speech in which there are no lies, and there is no concealment, and truth is revealed with every utterance? And daemons cower and fly in fear for they cannot abide truth?

DUCHESS YSABELLE: There is sense to that, for Jesus tells us that Satan is the Father of Lies. And yet Satan told his first lies in the Garden, and he was but recently fallen, so perhaps the speech of angels was already a vehicle for untruth.

FATHER GIOVANNI: And it is said that he seduced a third part of the angels away from God before he seduced Eve into breaking God's commandment, so we cannot place our trust in the speech of angels. Signora Emilia, what you said concerning separations, that is the essence of it. When things are drawn apart they become estranged, so that light is in conflict with darkness, and darkness conceals from the light. When there is estrangement and concealment, then we have lies.

DUKE LORENZO: And so we return to today's council, where all are estranged, and all are presenting a false face for the better purpose of defrauding each other with ingenious lies and insincere promises.

DUCHESS YSABELLE: Husband, I think you know full well that mendacity is a certainty in a fallen world ... and we cannot repair it by fretting. Let me see whether we can compose our discussion into something more harmonious and seek the positive in Mercury.

I understand that Mercury rules that part of human nature in which we most differ from the beasts of this world. Is that so Father?

FATHER GIOVANNI: If you mean our varieties of speech, which we inscribe in books so that others may read our thoughts after we are dead, then no beast can do this. We make reports that others can read, and so we know what takes place in Paris, or Geneva or Rome—no beast can do this. It is true, a report may be false, but if we are wise we learn whom we can trust. And merchants can make accounts and contracts so that they may trade in great quantities of goods. Beasts must content themselves with what is at hand.

DUCHESS YSABELLE: Thank you Father. I will add that through speech we can explain our thoughts and feelings and so reveal the hidden part of the soul that is obscure to others. If a dog snaps and is ill-tempered, I cannot know what has roused its ire—it may be ill or in pain, I do not know. And Emilia, while it is true that animals are often prudent, they receive no instruction in prudence and they provide none, nor can they explain what is prudent or foolish. Is that fair?

SIGNORA EMILIA: It is fair. Whatever wisdom cats possess, they have not been willing to share it with me. What is more, it seems to me that any creature in possession of exemplary wisdom would not require nine lives.

DUCHESS YSABELLE: Indeed! Mercury also rules those who buy and sell, those whose presence in the marketplace causes you so much disquiet husband, but who supply us with food and spices and silks and so many other fine and useful things.

DUKE LORENZO: The occupation of a noble is to be noble. The occupation of a merchant is to argue from daybreak to sundown over the price of a horse. There is no end to yapping, weighing and measuring, contracts, bills of exchange, attorneys, scriveners, and the transport of goods from place to place. And disputation, for which purpose they engage troupes of lawyers to worry the magistrates with vexatious claims. But, as you say, they arrange the transport of Occident and Orient to our doorstep, and so I should not complain.

DUCHESS YSABELLE: You should not complain, dear Husband.

FATHER GIOVANNI: It seems to me that Mercury rules our freedom, for there is no freedom without agreement—our neighbours guard our boundaries and they might become our enemies should we neglect to honour them. Boundaries, treaties, agreements belong to Mercury. And jurisprudence, for there can be no justice without the formulation and articulation of laws. Those who demand freedom without agreement are ruled by the contentious spirit of Mars and are forever at war, whether in the field, or in the courts, or in the streets.

DUKE LORENZO: And here we have the history of Italy, for our cities pretend to worship the spirit of concord and agreement with one hand, and purchase armies of rude mercenaries with the other. France, Spain and the Empire envy our wealth and so our cities are riven with intrigue, faction and betrayal. Treaties are signed by day and broken by night. Our worthless treaties are composed by Mercury and tossed into the fire by Mars.

DUCHESS YSABELLE: Husband, you have a horror of double-dealing.

DUKE LORENZO: You know that I do. There is no honour in it. Deceit is an act of power—as you said Father—the spirit of Mars prevails. The weak, the powerless, the knavish, those without principles or honour or scruples, they practice deceit because it permits them to work their will upon the forthright and the honourable.

DUCHESS YSABELLE: And it is widely said that women are weak and have no power, and so we must weave a spell of words to charm the minds of men ... do not deny it, Husband, I read the thought! It is a commonplace that women are deceitful, filled with guile. Poor men, ever at the mercy of womanly wiles.

But the charm of words is not the sole province of knaves and women. Let us step back and take a different view, for while words may charm and deceive, they may be used honestly and to good purpose.

Would you say that it is better to rule by compulsion, by means of harsh laws and severe punishments, like those of Draco of Athens? Or is it better to win the hearts of your subjects?

DUKE LORENZO: You are leading me by the nose ... you wish me to say that it is better to win hearts.

DUCHESS YSABELLE: And how might one do that?

DUKE LORENZO: By debate and eloquence, by reason, by argument made public, by listening to delegations, by engaging the common self-interest of the broad mass of people. Or as Aristotle declares, by *logos*, by *pathos*, and by *ethos*.

DUCHESS YSABELLE: And so, if we do not wish to be tyrants, you must practice the rhetoric you learnt in Padua to win the assent of those you rule. You may proclaim new laws, but you do so knowing that the guilds, the councils, the magistrates, the Church, the bankers, and the captains, have been persuaded by your eloquence, and will hopefully be true to their word and not speak or act against you.

DUKE LORENZO: Hopefully? Hopefully true to their words! Should we not require 'certainly'? Or 'definitely'? Or 'absolutely'? There was a time when oaths were sacred. In a world where people are not true to their word it is much less tiresome to be a tyrant. I should be a tyrant. As a tyrant I have only to bribe the captains and the magistrates ... and purchase some more hangmen.

FATHER GIOVANNI: My lord, you are much admired for your enlightened rule.

DUKE LORENZO: But you must admit that Mercury does test our wits and try our temper.

SIGNORA EMILIA: He does not like to be caught; see, he ever slips through my fingers.

DUKE LORENZO: Silvery and slippery as a fish, almost as slippery as an advocate. Father, are there any men further removed from truth than advocates?

FATHER GIOVANNI: Only cardinals, my Lord. And tailors.

DUKE LORENZO: Very droll Father, very droll. I might add troubadours, poets, and lovers. It seems to me that words are like a fog, or a smoke made to hide the movements of soldiers: words obscure what is real and true.

I detest the liar because he seeks to conceal the truth from me. How can a ruler be wise or prudent when all he surveys is a pretence, a weave of deception and evasion, of flattery and concealment. If God is truth, then truth is the light that uncovers deception, while lies are the darkness that conceals.

FATHER GIOVANNI: These words are akin to the words of Jesus in Gospel of John, almost to the word:

> Everyone who does evil hates the light, and will not come into the light for fear that their deeds will be exposed. But whoever lives by the truth comes into the light, so that it may be seen plainly that what they have done has been done in the sight of God.

DUCHESS YSABELLE: See, you are quite the cleric, husband.

DUKE LORENZO: If only the world possessed clarity, if only there was light where now there is so much obscurity. This devious Mercury of the Romans has more than a little of the Devil in him.

FATHER GIOVANNI: Mercury is a potent spirit in a world so mixed and contrary in its nature. It is small wonder that so many people seek to possess this god. Some say the two serpents intertwined on the caduceus or magic rod of Mercury represent contraries brought into reconciliation. The Logos not only brings chaos into order, it must stabilise the contraries that fumed and roiled before the utterance of the Word.

SIGNORA EMILIA: Father, if I might intrude, if one serpent is the wicked serpent from Eden, the serpent that leads us into sin, is there then a good serpent that leads us into virtue?

FATHER GIOVANNI: Why, yes, Jesus compares himself to a serpent in John, in a passage where he speaks to the pharisee Nicodemus. He alludes to the book of Numbers, where Moses places a serpent on a staff.

There are some who place a serpent on a cross as a symbol of Christ's mission in this world, as a sign that, should we repent of our sins, then there will be forgiveness. The serpent on a cross is also found in books on alchemy, but its meaning is unknown to me.

DUCHESS YSABELLE: A serpent on a cross! That seems perverse to me.

DUKE LORENZO: It does.

DUCHESS YSABELLE: Of a sudden I feel weary.

DUKE LORENZO: Do you wish to conclude? Perhaps it is the fault of this library—it has brought slumber to many.

DUCHESS YSABELLE: No, no, we are not done.

SIGNORA EMILIA: Perhaps it is the nature of this Sphere to exhaust us, like a conclave of clergy splitting hairs over whether we are to be saved by good works, by sacraments, by faith, by grace … or that salvation is beyond our power to influence … because our destiny is chosen from the making of the world.

FATHER GIOVANNI: God preserve us from the heresies of John Calvin! Signora Emilia, what you say is true, there is a wearying quality to Mercury. How we are wearied by speeches and debates! By agendas and points-of-order, by motions and counter-motions, by amendments and corrections, and by the interminable contributions of the pompous.

DUKE LORENZO: How I am wearied by windbags! Apologies, pray continue Father …

FATHER GIOVANNI: There is an implicit tension in every utterance: I say a thing, it demands a response, an affirmation or denial, spoken or unspoken. Those affirming are opposed to those denying, and like a tumult of heaven and earth the lightning flickers twixt sky and ground and thunder rattles until we have men-at-arms laying waste to cities. Even in such good and courteous company we still sense the antinomies, the contraries, we are pulled one way and another.

DUCHESS YSABELLE: Perhaps it is that. Husband, you were wearied even before we began?

DUKE LORENZO: I was indeed wearied, and it is just as you say Father, there is a wearying quality to speeches. It is not only that each person feels his outlook is uniquely valuable … I am wearied by the posturing, each man acting as if it would be a deadly affair of honour to disparage some ludicrous nonsense. I must be courteous to fools enamoured with their own words. And there are some who delight in picking apart notions simply for the pleasure of it, like a cat tossing a mouse! For me it is a duty, for them it is entertainment. Tell me my good wife, are women in conclave so tedious?

DUCHESS YSABELLE: If you ask whether there are women who are loud, garrulous, opinionated and easily offended, then yes. Do we quarrel, and are there tears and factions? Yes. Are there deadly hatreds? Most certainly. However, as we have so little power in civic affairs, as we are burdened by so many insignificant tasks, and as we receive so little applause for what we do, we value close companionship and we delight in small talk. Is that fair Emilia?

SIGNORA EMILIA: Yes, we delight in small talk. But I also observe that since the time of Adam women have been relieved of the primary purposes of speech (which are the naming of God's creatures, the formulation of doctrines, the administration of sacraments, opinions on angels, devils, Hell, sin, and purgatory, negotiation of marriages and dowries, the execution of wills, and the persecution of heretics) so, in moments of boredom, we must employ our ingenuity in the persecution of each other. We can be most subtle.

But for the most part, small talk is the means by which we adhere to each other and I find it is only wearisome when I am wearied from other causes.

I have the opinion that it is not talk itself that is wearisome ... why, these conversations are delightful. It is arrogance, pomposity, bombast, pretence, grandiloquence, flattery, all the gross affectations of manner—these are wearisome, and in this I will offer you my sympathy, my Lord. We are wearied by affectations because as one person puffs themselves up, so we are deflated in turn.

DUKE LORENZO: Well put, Signora Emilia, that, exactly that: deflated. And puffed-up windbags, yes, like birds when they fluff-up and preen themselves. Mercury, god of windbags. Would you say that Father, an airy spirit? God of windbags?

FATHER GIOVANNI: He does possess wings, my Lord, on cap and sandals, and flies between heaven and earth. I would agree, an airy spirit.

DUCHESS YSABELLE: You must not disparage spirits with insults, Husband. What if we are invaded by serpents and scorpions and must banish them? What if we grow stout and must seek out a tailor who is a paragon of flattery? And what if (and I tremble at the thought) we oppose the most gifted of advocates and have need to humble him? What then if Mercury glowers at us and turns his face from us because you have called him a god of windbags? We shall be distraught! How we shall despair!

SIGNORA EMILIA: He must do our bidding if we capture him and put him back in his flask. Did you know this, Father, that the people of Araby confine spirits in flasks? And they must grant us wishes?

FATHER GIOVANNI: So they do! It is written that Solomon did exactly this with his magic ring.

SIGNORA EMILIA: He had a magic ring?

FATHER GIOVANNI: It was a gift from the Lord and it gave him power over all the spirits.

SIGNORA EMILIA: But we can confine this Mercury on the table without a magic ring. I see you have a goose feather.

FATHER GIOVANNI: We can use it in the manner of a brush to persuade Mercury towards the edge of the table. I have a small card that I have folded to guide this subtle spirit into the mouth of the flask. If it please you, deploy the feather and I will hold flask and card.

SIGNORA EMILIA: Now that Mercury is fallen into Nature he is not so nimble. Slippery, elusive ... but there, we have him.

FATHER GIOVANNI: Yet goldsmiths say that when he is heated by fire he ascends invisible and scrambles the wits of men. They go quite mad.

SIGNORA EMILIA: Mercury is enraged at being confined in Nature and like a cat released from a bag, he tears at them.

Sphæra Mercurii

DUCHESS YSABELLE: Father, what is our next Sphere?

FATHER GIOVANNI: It is the Sphere of Venus, my Lady.

DUCHESS YSABELLE: Pleasure and beauty, that will be a pleasant relief.

SIGNORA EMILIA: And doomed love affairs. Dido and Aeneas. Paris and Helen. Jason and Medea.

DUKE LORENZO: Wine and good food.

FATHER GIOVANNI: In moderation, my Lord, lest we summon Dionysus. As for feasting and banquets, these are in the province of Jupiter, and we ought to defer that pleasure.

Liber Sphæræ

Sphæra Veneris

DUCHESS YSABELLE: So many books again. I did not think we would greet Venus with books ... see, I have brought roses, and with them the perfume of roses.

FATHER GIOVANNI: I approve of your roses, my Lady. As for this old book, is only my Ptolemy—we found it of some use when discussing Mercury.

SIGNORA EMILIA: I have brought poets, because love is so often the occasion for poetry and poetry expresses our understanding of love. This is Ovid, famous for his advice on love. This is Catullus ... each time I read of poor Lesbia's sparrow, I weep. And of Sappho, some fragments. Oh, and Petrarch. I find him a bore, but compendious in the matter of doomed and tragic love.

DUKE LORENZO: Petrarch a bore? That is an opinion to consider. For myself I have brought Ficino's *De Amore*.

DUCHESS YSABELLE: Husband, how you value your Ficino!

DUKE LORENZO: Yes I do. He was well regarded when I was a student and I purchased many of his works.

DUCHESS YSABELLE: Then do you wish to commence with Ficino?

DUKE LORENZO: As our subject for today is the sphere of Venus, I think it would be fitting for a woman to commence. How many of us thought to bring roses?

FATHER GIOVANNI: You speak wisely, my Lord.

DUCHESS YSABELLE: So be it, I will commence ... let your minds imagine that there are soft breezes and scented airs. The evening star shines bright. There are sweet sounds of music; nymphs sing of love and beauty. Winged cupids spread a carpet of rose petals, and, stepping down from a gilded chariot drawn by sparrows, Venus in gorgeous raiment attends our discourse. She finds us cowering behind a palisade of books, and swiftly departs ... oh, do not look abashed Emilia, I jest.

SIGNORA EMILIA: A jest that speaks the truth. Venus loves luxury and gaiety, music and laughter, happy faces flushed with wine, the fertile bloom of gardens, paths strewn with petals, lovers' trysts ... I have I been wearing a widow's drab for too long and I see that my gaiety has departed. I foolishly sought to reveal some part of Venus by weeping over Lesbia's dead sparrow.

DUCHESS YSABELLE: Not foolish! Venus brings us love and tears both, and often more tears than love. Let us hear Catullus.

SIGNORA EMILIA: Are you certain ... *Lesbia's Sparrow?* There will be tears. Now I feel ashamed, I should not spoil our conversation with my indulgence.

DUKE LORENZO: Please Signora, I know the poem, it moves me too. It is fitting that Venus should be welcomed both with roses and tears.

FATHER GIOVANNI: I would hear it Signora. As for tears, they are a daily accompaniment to confession and repentance, and sometimes I weep myself.

SIGNORA EMILIA: Let me find my kerchief. I must compose myself. I will begin:

O mourn, you Loves and Cupids,
and all men of gracious mind.
Dead is the sparrow of my girl:
sparrow, darling of my girl,
which she loved more than her eyes;
for it was sweet as honey,
and its mistress knew it as well as a girl knows her own mother.

Nor did it move from her lap,
but hopping round first one side then the other,
to its mistress alone it continually chirped.

Now it fares along that path of shadows
from where nothing may ever return.

May evil befall you, savage glooms of Orcus,
which swallow up all things of fairness:
which have snatched away from me the comely sparrow.

O wretched deed! O hapless sparrow!
Now on your account my girl's sweet eyes,
swollen, redden with tear-drops.

There Venus, now you have my tears, tears shed for all the little creatures that steal our hearts. How we love them, and how we are inconsolable at their loss!

DUCHESS YSABELLE: And so we are. And yet, and forgive me for this observation ... I wonder whether Catullus is peeved that his love-making is to be postponed and so he mocks Lesbia's sorrow with an overblown sense of tragedy?

SIGNORA EMILIA: I was so distraught at her poor sparrow that I failed to see that. Now you have said it, I recall how often Catullus exercises his wit at the expense of others.

FATHER GIOVANNI: You remind us that there are many kinds of love, and that Lesbia's grief for her sparrow was doubtless sincere. Also that Catullus, for all his clever poems, was a man devoted to personal pleasure and carnal love. A peevish irritation would not be out of character.

SIGNORA EMILIA: I like Catullus for his unsparing honesty, even when he reveals the strife and selfishness that accompanies passion. There

is a little poem of his, barely a scrap, I have marked the page ... here
...

> I hate and I love. And if you ask me how,
> I do not know: I only feel it, and I'm torn in two.

I think Catullus desires Lesbia beyond reason, but she is self-willed and he hates that he has no power over her ... but even more he hates that he has no power over his own feelings.

DUKE LORENZO: An unhappy soul indeed, Signora! Love and hate, the twin poles of feeling. We move towards, or we move away. I recall that this is a philosophy espoused by Empedocles, who proposed that we reside in a realm of love and strife. There is a continuous motion of parts where some parts are bound by love and other parts thrown apart by strife. Is there any feeling that does not, either literally or figuratively, comprise attraction or repulsion?

DUCHESS YSABELLE: Indifference?

DUKE LORENZO: But indifference is an absence of feeling.

DUCHESS YSABELLE: I suppose that is true. So we move towards those things that will benefit us, and avoid those things that will harm us. And if a thing is pleasant and makes us happy we say that we love it, and if a thing is unpleasant and hurtful we say that we dislike it, or fear it, or hate it.

DUKE LORENZO: And all feeling is some variation of these impulses.

DUCHESS YSABELLE: Then what of jealousy or envy?

DUKE LORENZO: We desire something another possesses; we simultaneously love what they have and hate that they have it.

DUCHESS YSABELLE: Very subtle.

SIGNORA EMILIA: What of grief, my Lord?

DUKE LORENZO: The loss of something beautiful that we love?

DUCHESS YSABELLE: And surprise?

DUKE LORENZO: Aaah ... but surprise has no duration and instantly becomes delight or fear ... or some other feeling, such as disgust or anger.

DUCHESS YSABELLE: Then anger. What of anger?

DUKE LORENZO: Anger is protective. We are aroused by something that assaults our sense of propriety, that disturbs the harmony of what we value and love.

DUCHESS YSABELLE: So we move towards something we do not love?

DUKE LORENZO: Ah, touché, my thesis is contradicted.

DUCHESS YSABELLE: It is an interesting thesis. For myself I wonder whether love and hate are more interwoven than Empedocles imagined, and not so much in opposition. So often love turns to hate, and sometimes hate into love, just as Catullus suggests. What of those people whose hate consumes them and so they attempt to destroy those whom they hate? Where there is a furore of spite in their hearts that overwhelms reason? Hate can bind as much as does love.

SIGNORA EMILIA: Yes, I see this in Catullus. When he cannot have Lesbia he slanders and mocks her, and yet his spite is founded in desire.

FATHER GIOVANNI: The soul is fallen and is divided between good and evil impulses. A part inclines towards God, and a part towards the Devil. The part that inclines towards God contains nourishing and beneficent feelings, and the part that inclines towards Satan contains malevolence and violence.

SIGNORA EMILIA: I can subscribe to this notion Father; the human soul is a battleground of conflicting impulses. When we are provoked we can incline towards evil with all our hearts. The most poisonous thoughts fume out of our abyss. Tell me, have we travelled too far from Venus?

FATHER GIOVANNI: Not in my view Signora. Was there ever a human love unmarked by tears or anger? By a tumult of feelings? And sometimes by terrible deeds?

SIGNORA EMILIA: That is so Father. I have one more poem to share if I may. I sought to find poems about love that were not written by men. I wondered: why do so many men have so much to say about love? Perhaps Venus places a stamp upon their souls, so that a phantasm of Venus pervades their thoughts ... an unrequited passion ... I am thinking of Petrarch's love of Laura, and Dante's love of Beatrice. They reach out to this phantasm by poetic invocation, but outside of poetry their passion is fruitless and arid, for their love was never reciprocated in life, and the poor girls are long dead.

This love is less a passion and more a construct of the poet's imagining. As for Ovid, he may be the acknowledged master of love—within the company of men at least—for he is irreverent and clever, but he maintains a distance from the tumult of feelings that tear us to pieces.

I have here a fragment of Sappho, renowned throughout antiquity.

DUKE LORENZO: Let us hear it Signora.

SIGNORA EMILIA: This is the love of a woman, a love that stops the mouth and the heart:

> That man to me seems god-like
> For he sits facing you
> Listening to your sweet voice
> And the tempting laughter
> That trembles my heart.
>
> Even a glance at you
> Cleaves my tongue; my mouth is stopped
> A subtle fire brushes my skin
> My eyes go dark, my ears thrum,
> Sweat breaks forth, cold,
> And I tremble, shake,
> More pallid than dead grass.
> Like unto death I am.

DUCHESS YSABELLE: I like this, Emilia. It reminds us that love is not an effusion of flowery talk, or riding about on noble quests. This is love where it is a malady of the flesh, and skirts on the edge of madness. There is no prudence in this love, it is a violence done to the soul ... by Cupid with his bow and arrows of fire, just as the ancients describe.

SIGNORA EMILIA: It is indeed a violence done to the soul. You will recall the love of Dido for Aeneas: when Aeneas sailed away from Carthage she heaped his possessions into a great fire and in her madness she burned herself to death. And the madness of Medea, who murdered her own children to spite Jason for his unfaithfulness.

I have here the *Heroides* by Ovid, in which women who were treated unjustly write letters to their lovers ... there is Dido to Aeneas, Medea to Jason, Ariadne to Theseus, and many more. I am always saddened by poor Ariadne, abandoned on Naxos by Theseus.

DUCHESS YSABELLE: She thought to purchase his affections with a ball of twine?

SIGNORA EMILIA: When you say it like that ...

DUCHESS YSABELLE: I suppose it was mindful of Ovid to consider that a woman might feel aggrieved.

SIGNORA EMILIA: I love to hear their voices ... even though all the voices are spoken by Ovid.

DUCHESS YSABELLE: Indeed. Emilia, you have Petrarch there before you. His *Triumph of Love* numbers all those famed for loving too well or unwisely.

SIGNORA EMILIA: Yes, I have it here. The poet describes the God of Love leading a triumphal procession in the ancient Roman manner, of all those taken captive by love. His list exceeds the patience of most people, but let me see. Poor Ariadne, abandoned by Theseus. Helen, who was bewitched by Venus so that she adored the Trojan Paris, and left Greece to be with her lover. Pygmalion, who adored a marble statue. Orpheus, who travelled to Hades to bring back Eurydice and lost her again. Dante and Beatrice. Narcissus, who loved his own image and was drowned. Cleopatra, who charmed both Caesar and Anthony. Samson, beguiled by Delilah, the Philistine woman.

Why, Petrarch summons all of antiquity, real and imagined, to his procession ... but I do not find Sheba and Solomon, a love celebrated in joy—and not in doom and despair.

FATHER GIOVANNI: There is indeed a bright and wholesome quality to the *Song of Songs*:

> Let him kiss me with the kisses of his mouth;
> for your love is better than wine.

SIGNORA EMILIA: Father, it is the most exquisite song of love! It has a woman's touch ... I know that it declares itself to be the song of Solomon, but I cannot imagine the great Solomon writing in so free and sensual a manner. He is quite sombre and grave in his *Ecclesiastes* and abundantly prudent in *Proverbs*—I cannot imagine him abandoning his kingly manner. Do you think that Solomon wrote each part, or that the voice of the bride was written by Sheba? A man did not write every part, of that I am certain, there is the voice of a woman in it.

FATHER GIOVANNI: It is a puzzling text, a work of several voices, and perhaps Sheba sang her parts to Solomon. Did you know that it is one of the most holy books among the Hebrews?

SIGNORA EMILIA: Is that so?

DUKE LORENZO: That is contrary to expectation. I thought it little more than a song of love and pleasure. How did you discover this Father?

FATHER GIOVANNI: The Church Father Origen offended his bishop and was exiled from Egypt, and so he travelled to the Holy Land to live among the Hebrews, where he made the acquaintance of some of their teachers. He was told that there are great mysteries concealed within this work, but they are forbidden to speak of them.

DUKE LORENZO: And you can throw no light on this matter?

FATHER GIOVANNI: The Jews of Ferrara have a monstrous large book called *Zohar* that expounds on secret matters, but it is written in Chaldean, an ancient tongue of the East, and few are able to read it. Only scholars of the *Talmud*, their work of law, possess the learning to read this *Zohar*, and fewer still can comprehend it. They call this learning Cabala, which means a secret teaching passed by word of mouth.

DUKE LORENZO: I have heard of Cabala. Giovanni Pico of Mirandola made a great noise about it, asserting that it revealed hidden mysteries of scripture. And the *Song of Songs* is a part of this Cabala?

FATHER GIOVANNI: That is my understanding. Origen, of whom I spoke, was so swayed by the opinion of the Jews that he wrote a commentary on the *Song of Songs*, reading the love of groom and bride as an allegory. This is why we say that the Church is the bride of Christ, for Christ is the groom who comes for His bride.

I am reminded: St. Bernard of Clairvaux, of blessed memory, also wrote famous sermons on the *Song of Songs*, although there is more in his sermons concerning the love of God that any particular understanding of Solomon.

DUKE LORENZO: Then I will seek them out. Tell me Father, how do you understand the difference between love and lust? According to the Church, lust is a sin, but love is not.

FATHER GIOVANNI: Ah, an interesting question, my Lord. You recall that I have spoken of the parts of the soul.

DUKE LORENZO: I recall your discussion of the parts of the soul. We are divided beings, with a part inclining towards Nature and a part inclining towards God. Why, I expounded on this myself from the *Pimander* of Hermes.

FATHER GIOVANNI: Just so. Each part of the soul loves in its own way. The nutritive soul loves to eat and drink. The sensitive soul aches for coitus, and is much given to ambition and status, and to quarrel and strife. The rational soul loves knowledge and seeks understanding. The immortal soul seeks to unite with God.

You ask about lust ... lust occurs when the soul is overwhelmed by passions arising from Nature, dominating the soul with carnal thoughts. Lust is selfish, having no concern for another. Love is different matter ... love occurs when the rational and immortal parts of the soul recognise the image of the divine in another.

DUKE LORENZO: You have echoed Ficino! You have read *De Amore*?

FATHER GIOVANNI: Many years ago, my Lord, and I recall but little
... a banquet held in Florence in memory of the *Symposium* of Plato?
Many speeches on the subject of love?

DUKE LORENZO: That is it!

DUCHESS YSABELLE: Husband, you cannot disguise your enthusiasm
for this work; perhaps you will be generous and share it with us?

DUKE LORENZO: Now you task me! It is abstruse, I picture the
scheme in my mind and yet my tongue struggles to give shape to
it.

DUCHESS YSABELLE: But some outline? I would love to hear your
thoughts on this matter.

SIGNORA EMILIA: As would I, my Lord.

DUKE LORENZO: The core of the subject matter is the thoughts of
Socrates as recorded by Plato, and it seems Socrates was instructed
by a priestess named Diotima. All this is further related by Ficino
and his learned friends in Florence, so we have the matter at some
distance ... and now at a greater distance still as I explain it to you.

SIGNORA EMILIA: A priestess, my Lord! Instructing Socrates?

DUKE LORENZO: Indeed Signora, and greatly revered by Socrates.
Let me collect my thoughts and begin at the beginning. According
to Plato (and the many advocates of Plato), all things flow forth
from God as if from a spring of pure water. Now we say that God
is One, and by that we mean that God is not composite or divided.
Also, we say that God is eternal and omnipresent, and by this we
mean that God exists outside of time and space. God is One, eternal
and omnipresent.

At one step removed from God there is a level of being that is
no longer singular—one might imagine a drop of lemon juice added
to milk, so that the milk separates. This is the Mind or Intelligence
or Thought of God, and although it is still beyond time and space,
it appears to our minds as a plurality, as many beings. We might
imagine these thoughts as gods, which would be heretical, or as
archangels, which would cause less concern.

Then there is a level that is within time and subject to change, and so we say it has motion—beginnings and endings—and this is the level of souls, the souls of men and women.

Souls require bodies, and bodies exist within Nature, which is bounded both by time and space. Lastly bodies are composed of the four elements. Thus we have five levels of being: God, Mind, Soul, Nature and Matter. The One becomes Many. Am I being suitably lucid dear wife?

DUCHESS YSABELLE: Indeed. There is a hierarchy of being that depends for its origin upon God and is removed from unity as it falls into time, space and matter.

DUKE LORENZO: That is the nub of it. We are far removed from God. Our organs of sense perceive the world of the elements, a world bounded by space and time. If we are to seek for truth, beauty, justice or goodness we will not find them in Nature because Nature is in continuous flux and change. The soul, seeking truth, must turn away from Nature and regard the eternal forms in the mind of God.

We know that people love beauty: the proportions of a face, the grace of a dancer, a harmony of voices, the colours of a garden. This is beauty in Nature, and this beauty is temporal and subject to decay—like the withered rose, or the broken lyre of Socrates.

So rather than pursue the ephemeral we might seek for beauty out of Nature, beauty within a soul, beauty that we perceive as virtue and goodness. This is your point Father: seeing an image of the divine in another.

FATHER GIOVANNI: That is it, my Lord. We have spoken previously of how we are made in the image of God. Some imagine by this that God must have arms and legs. However, one can find a deeper meaning in this: the image of God is goodness and truth.

DUKE LORENZO: Thank you, Father ... and here is a key point of Ficino: that beauty is the perception of goodness, and we seek beauty because we seek goodness. We seek goodness because our souls wish to revert back to God and unite with our seed in the mind of God ... our angel or our star as it were.

This is the philosophy of love as taught by the priestess Diotima to Socrates: love is our desire to possess beauty, and beauty is the exterior form of goodness and truth. Love is incompleteness and poverty, a lack of what we desire to possess, and all desire is rooted in our desire to revert back to God. Now I am done, I have expounded Ficino as well as I am able.

DUCHESS YSABELLE: Clearly expounded ... and yet I feel this is a most austere and philosophical outlook on our most defining passion. Is there nothing more to Love than a deficiency, an unfulfilled need? Can we not speak of Love unless we can see God in the soul of another?

FATHER GIOVANNI: My lady, we arrived at this point by examining the difference between love and lust. We have spoken of love, so now let us speak of lust, of passions that are not wholesome. These are the sins, where desire and deficiency are most visible, pernicious, and to the detriment of all. As you will know, the sins are Greed, Lust, Wrath, Sloth, Gluttony, Envy, and Pride. Here we find love directed towards the self. Where these sins exist there is no common purpose, no compassion, no fraternal love, and no love of God. St. Bernard had this to say, and I recall it most particularly:

> There are two evils that comprise the main enemies of the soul: a misguided love of the world and an excessive love of self.

SIGNORA EMILIA: A soul in distress seeks to soothe itself with comfort and diversion.

FATHER GIOVANNI: It does Signora, and it will pour vials of wrath upon any who stand in its way. Have you attempted to take a meaty bone from a dog?

SIGNORA EMILIA: Only once Father. Even cats, normally so amiable, will bare their teeth and growl and hiss.

FATHER GIOVANNI: That is my point: they revert to wildness. We like to believe that we are better than these creatures, but the animal soul within us will snap and growl when it is deprived of what it desires. Perhaps this will answer you, my Lady; if we love and do not see God, then perhaps we only regard ourselves.

DUCHESS YSABELLE: Thank you Father. I understand what you say, and yet there is a hesitancy in me. Let me think on it.

FATHER GIOVANNI: I should add that we must provide for the needs of the body. I do not hold that we should live in the desert wastes, feed off locusts and honey, and dress in the skins of animals. We all require some comfort and diversion lest the spirit of Saturn enter our souls and we become dour and melancholy.

    The difficulty is right measure; the golden mean between extremes, the point at which the desire for comfort becomes sloth, greed and gluttony, and where self-love turns into envy, pride and wrath. We can grow to love evil desires. It is here I diverge from Socrates and Plato and Ficino. Evil can engage all the powers of the soul in pursuit of its goals. There are evil loves. We have spoken of this already.

DUKE LORENZO: I am persuaded, Father. I have contemplated the savagery of the sack of Rome by German mercenaries in the pay of the Emperor Charles. It is clear that men revert to animals when there is no justice to restrain and harry them. In my heart I desire to agree with Plato—that no evil descends from Heaven, that evil is but a matter of ignorance—but my common sense concurs with your wisdom.

FATHER GIOVANNI: No words can encompass the savagery of the sack of Rome. However, we have strayed from Venus into the Sphere of Mars, and I am at fault.

DUCHESS YSABELLE: Thank you Father, I was beginning to hear the voice of Venus protesting that Mars was a poor husband and a worse lover. Can we return now to roses and perfumes lest she depart?

SIGNORA EMILIA: We should not offend this goddess. Her son bears sharp arrows, and they sting and burn.

DUCHESS YSABELLE: We should not. I have a question concerning love. We have talked of loss, and doomed love, and poor Dido, and needy desire, and lust, but what of the love that requires nothing in return, that fills the heart to bursting and overflows ... a love that shines forth unwavering, like the Sun. There is no emptiness in a mother's love. It is abundant.

FATHER GIOVANNI: Perhaps that is indeed the love of the Sun. It was said by the pagans that the Sun is the invisible God made manifest in this world.

DUCHESS YSABELLE: I did not think of that. Emelia?

SIGNORA EMILIA: Perhaps each Sphere has its own love. The Moon, a love of wildness and hunting; Mercury, of words and knowledge; Venus, a love of pleasure and coitus; the Sun, a love of growth and life; Mars, a love of powder and shot and fortifications, a protective love of family and city; Jupiter, a love of banquets and prosperity and civic institutions; Saturn, a love of wisdom and prudence and wealth. As a mother I love my children like the Sun, and protect them like Mars.

DUCHESS YSABELLE: Can we truly say that a soldier loves the machineries of war? Or that a dried-up stick of a scholar loves anything besides bedtime and a sound sleep? Is this love?

DUKE LORENZO: I will speak up for soldiers. I have known men who relished conflict, who sought battles. And yes, a man can love a sword or a bow ... and certainly a horse of war or a hunting dog. Gun crews delight in their work and wager which crew will first breach a wall. Never have I seen men work with such devotion. Their guns are named and often blessed. Mars fosters many strange passions, but I think we must call them love.

FATHER GIOVANNI: I will speak for scholars. Yes, books are indeed loved with a passion, and great passion goes into their making. The love of script and decoration, the love of bindings and gilding, each book is akin to the chapel of a saint. It is also true that scholars like bedtime and a sound sleep, for how better to prepare the mind for a new day of study?

SIGNORA EMILIA: You are saying that a passion that we may compare to love drives men and women to strange purposes, so that they give their lives to devising new weapons, or books, or arts, or music, or clothing.

DUKE LORENZO: Indeed, indeed—Ficino makes this very point, Signora, that no thing of beauty, no work of art, no composition of music, would exist without a mind to bring it to birth, that without love there would be no beauty in this world. It is love that makes the mind fecund, and the mind gives birth to novelty and invention.

DUCHESS YSABELLE: Perhaps men wish to take for themselves the superior role in this matter of love and creation, and leave women to wipe the noses of their sons and daughters?

DUKE LORENZO: You doubt that there are many kinds of love?

DUCHESS YSABELLE: I have no doubt that there is a power of attraction that entangles the destiny of all things. That there is a creative power within the soul that can imagine a novelty and give it shape. One must possess passion to overcome the difficulties of creation and one must have passion to develop a mastery of a medium, and so we admire the work of painters, poets, sculptors, jewellers, musicians, and many others. They create from within themselves.

There is also something else I feel inside me, something I call love ... and it is not these things. A long-dead Greek decides that one word is sufficient for all occasions because philosophers agree it is simpler not to multiply entities ... and I am required to agree? I think not.

DUKE LORENZO: Then tell us about your love?

DUCHESS YSABELLE: Not yet husband, not yet. First I wish to hear what another dead Greek has to say about Venus. Father, I would be much indebted to hear the words of Ptolemy.

FATHER GIOVANNI: Firstly I will say that Venus is known by astrologers as *Fortuna Minor*, for she manifests pleasant and agreeable circumstances. Secondly I will say that there is much here to take issue with. These are the words of Ptolemy:

> When Venus rules alone in a position of glory, she renders the mind pleasant, good, luxurious, copious in wit, neat, cheerful, fond of dancing, jealous, abhorring wickedness, delighting in the arts, pious, decorous, healthy, happy in dreams, affectionate, beneficent, compassionate, refined in taste, easily conciliated,

tractable, and entirely amiable : but, if contrarily posited, she renders the mind careless, amorous, effeminate, timorous, undiscriminating, sordid, censorious, insignificant, and ignominious.

DUCHESS YSABELLE: I see, when Venus is well-disposed we have the perfect courtier, and when her aspects are ill-disposed we have a woman.

FATHER GIOVANNI: Reading between the lines, one might discern an element of that. If we are to interpret Ptolemy in a charitable manner, then either sex can be courtly, and either sex can be poorly-aspected. I say this with confidence, for among clerics of the meaner sort, one encounters those for whom Ptolemy here would provide the perfect testimonial.

DUCHESS YSABELLE: Let us be charitable then. The well-aspected sons and daughters of Venus are most agreeable and life would be dull without them. I think I recall ... affectionate ... beneficent ...

FATHER GIOVANNI: ... compassionate, refined, easily conciliated ...

DUCHESS YSABELLE: Thank you Father. Those with the gift of Venus are agreeable because they direct their affections outwards and enjoy amity and concord. And if one was to find a person disagreeable it might be because they differ from Venus in being arrogant, selfish, inconsiderate, self-important, over-opinionated, easily-offended, and demanding. I could go on, but the good St. Bernard mentioned an excessive love of self. What I am doing is describing how this might appear.

FATHER GIOVANNI: Such people can be tedious and exhausting, and wear away at our feelings of Christian charity.

DUCHESS YSABELLE: Just so. They have little love for others, and not only do they demand our time and energy, they do little or nothing to salve the injury to our sense of self-worth. As you say, our feelings of Christian charity are strained and we might struggle to love our neighbour. Do you ever struggle to love your neighbour Father?

FATHER GIOVANNI: On occasion I have the greatest difficulty. I find I must step back from my feelings and attempt to understand what

circumstances led to such a person. It is often the case that the person has had to struggle against adversity since childhood; their nutritive soul has been ill-fed and harshly treated and resembles a feral cat that hungers incessantly and knows no affection. Perhaps I find it easier to love someone when I observe that they have been ill-treated by life ... they know not what they do.

DUCHESS YSABELLE: They know not what they do ... so true. Who would continue to be disagreeable if they knew what they did? In fullness, knowing the injury done to others? And those of us who pretend to understand love must know what we do. We must examine our conduct towards others, observe the hurts and injuries we cause, and root out from our souls carelessness, indifference, and self-love. Here is your answer Husband: my love is knowing what I do.

DUKE LORENZO: Would that you had spoken to Socrates and his friends, for our understanding of love would be much improved.

DUCHESS YSABELLE: But we are no longer pagans and our understanding comes from the words of Christ. The good Father has taught me these things.

FATHER GIOVANNI: [nods humbly]

SIGNORA EMILIA: It seems we have come some long way from the passion that drives people mad, so that they do wild and intemperate things.

DUKE LORENZO: You speak truly Signora, I was thinking the same, that a single word does the work of many horses. This is the fault of philosophy, going from some particulars to a generalisation and then marching forward to a universal. Somewhere along the way we lose sight of where we began.

FATHER GIOVANNI: We can indeed blame the Greeks, and not only for philosophy. They had many words for love. When scripture speaks of the love of God, or when we are told to love our neighbour, they would use *agape*. Those feelings of affection and familiarity between friends and family might be termed *philia*. The love of parents for children they might term *storge*, and the self-love of vanity, pride and arrogance they name *philautia*. As for the mad passion that leads to wild and intemperate actions, this they call *eros*.

SIGNORA EMILIA: And speaking of mad passion, you must know that our court is riven with gossip, people whisper of a scandal—I will name no names, nor do I wish to hear any—but this also falls within the province of Venus. The names of good families are besmirched, peerless women are maligned with false gossip, brothers and uncles die in defence of honour.

Cupid's arrow is a fearsome weapon. The staff of Mercury calms warring serpents, the arrow of Cupid is often the instigator of disorder.

FATHER GIOVANNI: I do like this notion of Mercury and Cupid being twin spirits, one communicating order through the divine word, the other bringing tumult and change due to the innate attractions between things. There is an elegance to the notion.

DUKE LORENZO: And Ficino has more to say on this, although I am loath to burden us with more philosophy.

DUCHESS YSABELLE: I will hear it willingly.

DUKE LORENZO: I have marked a small passage:

> But why do we think that love is a magician? Because the whole power of magic consists in love. The work of magic is the attraction of one thing by another because of a certain affinity of nature.

By this he means natural magic, the means by which the wise can work wonders by understanding which herb or stone or sound attracts the occult virtue of a planet. But he also includes a magic of daemons such as the pagan Greeks and Egyptians understood it. Here, another passage:

> ... the works of magic are works of nature, but art is its handmaiden ... The ancients attributed this art to daemons because the daemons understand what is the inter-relation of natural things, what is appropriate to each, and how the harmony of things, if it is lacking anywhere, can be restored ... daemons are

magicians through understanding the friendship of things themselves.

DUCHESS YSABELLE: This recalls that Arab book of starry lore we had from Urbino.

FATHER GIOVANNI: I suspect that Ficino may have had it on his desk—or at least, a book like it.

DUKE LORENZO: Ficino tells us that the rites of love resemble those of magic: supplication, devotion, offerings, deeds, sacrifices, orations, and poems. These weave a magic web around the beloved. The rites of magic, much condemned, resemble those of love, and cast a net around an outcome that it might be brought within the grasp of the magician. The magician learns the use of affinity or sympathy and becomes like a lodestone.

SIGNORA EMILIA: These are seductive doctrines, my Lord.

DUKE LORENZO: Indeed, and now I am the lodestone, leading minds astray.

FATHER GIOVANNI: A valid point, my Lord, as you may recall that Ficino was accused of heresy before Pope Innocent. It is more prudent to discuss the doctrines of the ancients as literature, history or curiosity than to discuss them as if they were a plausible philosophy. There is (or was) a German travelling the cities of Europe named Agrippa, I have mentioned his name before, and he goes much further than Ficino in discussing the occult philosophy of Nature. I think perhaps his wanderlust keeps him ahead of the Inquisition.

SIGNORA EMILIA: Have you met him Father?

FATHER GIOVANNI: I heard him lecture in Pavia. He is (or was, I know not whether he still lives) a prodigy of learning, and could recite the ancients from memory—in this he resembled a walking library. He was also extraordinarily quarrelsome and contentious, and I doubt that his understanding of the Spheres extended far into that of Venus, for he could be quite disagreeable. I would have more respect for these advocates of ancient philosophies if one could admire their lives.

Sphæra Veneris

Signora Emilia: The temperament of Mars and Mercury conjoined?

Father Giovanni: Just so, with Sagittarius rising.

Duchess Ysabelle: Father, we are all becoming quite astrological, I do hope we will not be burned.

Father Giovanni: As I have said, my Lady, it is not what one knows or believes that is the issue; it is what one proclaims to be true, in public, and before hostile witnesses. Our next Sphere is that of the Sun, and it is here that our faith will meet some challenges, and we must be prepared to encounter them.

LIBER SPHÆRÆ

SPHÆRA SOLIS

DUCHESS YSABELLE: Father, it is wonderful to see you in good health again!

FATHER GIOVANNI: My Lord, my Lady, Signora; yes, I am somewhat recovered. I had a tertian fever, fierce at times. Now I am frail but once more in possession of my wits. I blame my journey to Rome. I must have breathed the pestilential air from a marsh along the route.

DUKE LORENZO: Foul air is ever a hazard of travel. When I travelled from Rome to Naples a third of our company was sorely stricken by fever ... as you will know, the air of the Pontine marshes to the south of Rome is often fatal ... fortunately your journey did not take you through those parts. I am most glad to see you.

FATHER GIOVANNI Thank you, my Lord. After being racked by chills, this warm sunshine is most welcome.

DUCHESS YSABELLE: I thought the loggia would be suitable for today's conversation ... there is shade from the heat of the sun, and we can admire the garden in the sunlight. The world becomes so much clearer in the sunlight.

FATHER GIOVANNI: It does. I can scarcely read by candlelight; letters blur, my eyes grow weary, but in the Sun I can see as I did in my youth.

SIGNORA EMILIA: And flowers are so bright; there is no other colour to match them ... unless we also count butterflies ... and birds ... and ... I see my thought was poorly conceived but the sentiment accurate, that the Sun reveals the glory of Nature.

DUCHESS YSABELLE: That it does. And there are few fair things that thrive in the dark ... shadow is a place for mould and mushrooms, spiders and scorpions, innumerable flying things that bite and cause lumps and itches, mice, rats ... the dark is a place for thieves, spies, plots, and treacheries hid from the sight of honest folk.

When the Sun shines all malice flees into the shadows. And it is of the Sphere of the Sun that we will speak today. I see that we are all clutching at some small item. Husband, what is that small pouch in your hand?

DUKE LORENZO: See, some golden florins I borrowed from the treasury. I understand that gold is the metal that best embodies the essence of the Sun, as it has no corruption in it and remains pure and untouched by any hazard of earth, water, fire and air.

SIGNORA EMILIA: Apart from mercury, my Lord, mercury seeks to unite with gold. You told us so Father ...

FATHER GIOVANNI: That is indeed the case—mercury will devour these coins. With a little heat the mercury flies away and the gold remains as it was, in full measure, and without stain.

DUKE LORENZO: So unless there is a hazard involving mercury my florins will remain bright as minted?

DUCHESS YSABELLE: The greater hazard to your coins may be our architects and masons, who also wish to unite with gold and demand it in abundance. The chapel of Santa Chiara has a man on a scaffold pasting gold leaf over the carvings, and burnishing them to an extraordinary brightness. A profligacy of florins I fear, and a sacrilegious horror to Protestants.

FATHER GIOVANNI: But all paid for by the silk merchant Calvini, who must have done something reprehensible to be so stricken by this impulse of piety. And the gold is spread thin of course, beaten out into a tissue.

DUCHESS YSABELLE: Of course, spread exceedingly thin ... all our florins are spread exceedingly thin. Emilia, what sunny treasure do you conceal in that clay pot?

SIGNORA EMILIA: Honey! I plundered the kitchens and brought forth this portion from a comb of honey.

DUCHESS YSABELLE: Ah, of course, bees love the Sun.

SIGNORA EMILIA: I swear it smells of the Sun, Ysabelle ... the flowers collect sunbeams, the bees decant them into little wax chambers, and it is there that bees grow. I declare that bees grow out of sunbeams.

DUKE LORENZO: Very good Signora. Bees from sunbeams ... hahaha ... the olden kings of France had bees upon their banners, they are an ancient mark of kings.

FATHER GIOVANNI: 'Thy lips, O my spouse, drop as the honeycomb: honey and milk are under thy tongue; and the smell of thy garments is like the smell of Lebanon.'

DUKE LORENZO: What is this verse, Father?

FATHER GIOVANNI: The verse is from the *Song of Songs*. The sweetness of honey reminds us of divine love.

DUCHESS YSABELLE: In that case I will taste some of your honey. Mmmm ... it is glorious. I taste lavender ... Father, be so kind as to tell us what is written upon that scroll you clutch so firmly.

FATHER GIOVANNI: It is a prayer to the Archangel Michael, who, as the most radiant of the angels and the foe to all darkness, is reputed to be the angel of the Sun. I will read it first in the Latin as I have it upon my scroll:

Sancte Michael Archangele, defende nos in proelio; contra
nequitiam et insidias diaboli esto praesidium. Imperet illi Deus,
supplices deprecamur: tuque, Princeps Militiae Caelestis,
Satanam aliosque spiritus malignos, qui ad perditionem
animarum pervagantur in mundo, divina virtute, in infernum
detrude. Amen.

And now I will offer my version in the common tongue, and
forgive me if I stumble:

Saint Michael the Archangel, defend us in battle. Be our protection
against the wickedness and snares of the devil; may God rebuke
him, we humbly pray; and do thou, O Prince of the Heavenly
Host, by the power of God, thrust into hell Satan and all evil spirits
who wander through the world for the ruin of souls. Amen.

According to scripture, Michael is the angel sent by God to
keep Satan within his appointed bounds. He will meet Satan and
all the hosts of Hell at the End of Days to vanquish and bind them
for all time. This is told by the divine John of Patmos in his *Revelation* of things that will come to pass.

DUKE LORENZO: Amen to that. And he is truly the angel of the Sun?

FATHER GIOVANNI: He is. His likeness is set upon high places that
he might ward this world from evil. He brings healing too, and
here is a curious thing: he has acquired some aspects that were once
the province of the pagan god Apollo.

SIGNORA EMILIA: I greatly desire to talk about Apollo.

DUKE LORENZO: And we shall Signora, we shall, but first I desire to
know what secret thing my good wife has brought. You have seen
our secrets, Wife, now pray show us your own secret.

DUCHESS YSABELLE: I do have something in this silk pouch. Let me
undo the laces ... there, here are tears and chunks of golden frankincense, the sap of some tree that grows far away in the land of the
Arabs.

DUKE LORENZO: Ah, frankincense! Tears of gold ... how curious!

DUCHESS YSABELLE: Yesterday I went to the chapel of Santa Chiara
to approve the design of the new altarpiece, and the air was filled
with the scent of this resin. You may recall that in the chapel there

SAINT MICHAEL THE ARCHANGEL, DEFEND US IN BATTLE.
BE OUR PROTECTION AGAINST THE WICKEDNESS AND SNARES OF THE DEVIL;
MAY GOD REBUKE HIM, WE HUMBLY PRAY; AND DO THOU,
O PRINCE OF THE HEAVENLY HOST, BY THE POWER OF GOD,
THRUST INTO HELL SATAN AND ALL EVIL SPIRITS
WHO WANDER THROUGH THE WORLD FOR THE RUIN OF SOULS.
AMEN.

C.A.L 2022

is a monstrance ... a reliquary in the form of a great golden Sun containing a lock of the blessed saint's hair.

As I stood there it occurred to me that our forebears have sought out for each sense what they considered to be most holy. For our eyes it is gold and the light of the Sun; for taste it is wine and bread; for the ears it is plainsong and prayer; for the nose it is frankincense ... and so I requested some resin from the deacon.

SIGNORA EMILIA: Shall we send to the kitchen for some charcoal?

DUCHESS YSABELLE: This incense belongs to our blessed Santa Chiara and I will return it to the chapel tomorrow. Father, have I done right? Or wrong?

FATHER GIOVANNI: I am certain the holy Chiara will not miss her incense for a single day. But if you mean to ask whether frankincense is to the Sun as gold is to the Sun ... and as sunflowers are to the Sun ... and bees and honey are to the Sun ... then my answer is yes.

The ancients made lists of these affinities, of how a plant or stone or perfume in this lower world resonates in sympathy with a Sphere in the upper world, and how one might use such substances to draw down celestial influences. Agrippa has recorded many such affinities in his troublesome book on occult philosophy.

DUCHESS YSABELLE: And we use these affinities still in our churches?

FATHER GIOVANNI: In outward appearance only. When last we met I said that we might encounter some challenges to our faith. This is one such, for the Church has taken many things from the pagans and then forgotten from whence they came. Frankincense was traded among the people of the East long before the time of our Lord, and burned in temples, just as we do today.

DUKE LORENZO: The Protestants assert as much, accusing us of idolatry. They have been answered quite ably by theologians of the Holy See. We do not worship statues as did the heathens. We do not worship the Sun. We honour and worship our Lord, whom we *liken* to the Sun.

FATHER GIOVANNI: Admirably explained, my Lord! When the prophet Isaiah describes the coming of our Lord he has this to say:

> Arise, shine; for thy light is come, and the glory of the Lord is risen upon thee.

> For, behold, the darkness shall cover the earth, and gross darkness the people: but the Lord shall arise upon thee, and his glory shall be seen upon thee.

He compares the coming of our Lord to the rising of the Sun, but he does not speak of the literal light of the Sun! He speaks of the light of truth and life, and the darkness of ignorance, and of sin, and of death.

DUCHESS YSABELLE: We are more subtle than the pagans, and more subtle, it would seem, than the Protestants.

SIGNORA EMILIA: Forgive my intrusion: we have gold and frankincense. Should we have myrrh?

FATHER GIOVANNI: Oh, well-observed Signora! The three gifts of the oriental kings to the infant Christ? Perhaps we should. Frankincense honours the son of God, the priest and prophet who came into this world to redeem us from sin. Gold is a tribute suitable for a king, for 'Christ' means anointed, and Jesus reigns in Heaven as king ... and was mocked by the Romans as King of the Jews.

Myrrh reminds us of one who was embalmed and wrapped in a shroud and set into a rock-hewn tomb; it is an ancient means of purification and signifies rebirth from the dead.

The heathens observed that the Sun is born into this world as a child at dawn, that he rules the heavens as king at midday, and he dies in the West and goes down into the tomb. So we have frankincense, gold and myrrh.

SIGNORA EMILIA: So once again, Christ is likened to the Sun. The three wise men of the East foresaw all that would take place during Christ's ministry, and honoured him in their heathen way?

FATHER GIOVANNI: There is much in this vein, perhaps too much for a close study by the faithful. Perhaps you know that the Emperor

Nero commissioned a bronze statue of himself? It was named the 'Colossus of Nero' and stood thirty paces high. It showed him with a solar crown.

SIGNORA EMILIA: He desired that Romans should see him as the Sun?

FATHER GIOVANNI: In those days a man might imagine himself a god. His successor Vespasian, who was no friend to Nero, had the face remodelled and it became the Colossus of the Sun. Later it was removed to the site of the Flavian Amphitheatre, the ruin that we now call the Colosseum, for it was named after the statue. There was an excellent reason for placing the Colossus by the amphitheatre: the god of the Sun moves across the sky in a chariot drawn by a team of four horses, a *quadrigae*, and so the Sun became the god of chariot racing.

DUKE LORENZO: You jest!

FATHER GIOVANNI: And the Moon has a chariot drawn by a pair of horses ... but that is a digression. As we have chosen to study the Sphere of the Sun, I would like to mention some history that has intrigued me for many years. We began when we talked of gold, frankincense and myrrh, and how these were the gifts of the wise men of the pagans. Few will talk about these matters, but I will talk about them now and I hope you will not doubt my judgement in doing so.

There is an argument that our Christian faith would not exist in its current form but for the Roman Sun god. I will recite it if I can gather my thoughts.

DUCHESS YSABELLE: Please do, my understanding of those times is is poor indeed.

FATHER GIOVANNI: Thank you, my Lady. How to begin? The gods of old Rome were twofold: firstly, the gods of the household, the *lares* and *penates* and *genii*, and secondly, the gods of the state, such as Jupiter and Mars and Vesta. Sacrifices to the household gods would be made by the *pater familias*, and sacrifices to the gods of the state were made by officials, the *sacerdotes publici*, appointed from ancient noble families.

The Empire grew, and the city of Rome began to take second place to the cities of the eastern seaboard of the Mediterranean. There were many of these cities, founded along the rivers and coast of Anatolia, the Levant, and of course the great metropolis of Alexandria in Egypt. In the East there were ancient cities too numerous to count. There was trade, and where is much trade there is great wealth.

Now, where there is wealth there must be taxes; and where there are taxes there must be governance and census taking, and innumerable officials fussing over ledgers, and swarms of tax collectors, and of course there must be legions ready to guard these wealthy provinces from the grasp of the enemies of Rome: the Persians and the Palmyrans and the Nabateans ... and even the Jews, who greatly resented the Romans, and warred against them until they were broken and dispersed during the reign of Hadrian.

These eastern provinces were a great prize to Rome, so much so that Constantine moved his capital to the old Greek colony of Byzantium on the Bosphorus, where the sultan of the Turks now has his palace. It was renamed Constantinople, and the language of the Eastern Empire became Greek, and not Latin.

The earliest Christian congregations were founded among these cities of the East, as we know from Paul's letters: Ephesus, Philippi, Colossae, Corinth, Galatia, Thessalonika ... more are named by John in his *Revelation*, where he addresses the seven churches of Asia (which are in Anatolia).

You will wonder what the gods of the traditional Roman family and state had to do with the Eastern Empire, and the answer was: very little. The empire had outgrown the customs and rituals of its founding city, and the citizens of Rome were confronted by the ancient gods of the eastern provinces, brought to Rome by its own citizens. People who had once been enemies or foreigners were now Romans, and paid taxes, and served in her legions.

DUKE LORENZO: Now that you have explained it, all this is plain enough Father ... children outgrow their clothes.

Signora Emilia: And forget and neglect the customs and fashions of their grandparents.

Father Giovanni: They do, and in this manner the Romans prayed to new gods, and there were many. Isis, and Magna Mater, and Mithras, and Semiramis, and Cybele, to name but a few. The Jews kept to their God as they have always done. A small number found comfort in the Christian faith, which, as you know, comes from the Holy Land.

Now, about two centuries after the coming of our Lord there was a city in Syria named by the Greeks Emesa, but now the Arabs call it Homs. In this city was a family, wealthy and powerful, and the male line were priests of a god they named *Il Gebal*, a god of the Sun. This family had two accomplished and educated daughters, the elder named Julia Maesu and the younger Julia Domna.

To keep this story short, the future emperor Septimus Severus cast his eyes upon their wealth and married the younger sister Julia Domna, who bore two emperors, Caracalla and Geta. The elder sister, who was an accomplished schemer, accumulated vast wealth and influence and so promoted her young grandson to emperor. This boy chose to be called Elagabalus.

Duke Lorenzo: Elagabalus! Never was a youth less suited to the task of governing an empire.

Father Giovanni: Once I thought so, but now I will be generous and say that his talent for leadership led the empire in a new direction. He had been raised and trained as a priest of the Sun and he announced that all the gods of Rome would be worshipped as aspects of a single supreme god he named *Sol Invictus Elgabal*, and in future all the official sacrifices of the Roman state would be directed towards this Syrian god.

Duke Lorenzo: And so he was murdered for it.

Father Giovanni: There was some impatience with emperors in those days, my Lord—both of his uncles were assassinated, and also his cousin. After his cousin was murdered there was a year of six emperors, and each one of them was murdered. We should not judge Elagabalus too harshly for the fact of being murdered. He was young and naive and unaccustomed to the ways of Rome. But he sowed a seed.

The Roman emperor and state required divine sanction from a god who was widely recognised in every part of the empire, and most particularly, in the East. Fifty years later the emperor Aurelian reflected upon the notions of Elagabalus, and so *Sol Invictus*, the Unconquerable Sun, became the god of the Roman state.

DUCHESS YSABELLE: And this bears upon our Christian faith?

FATHER GIOVANNI: It does, my Lady, most directly. The emperors of that time were, for the most part, warriors. They gave their allegiance to gods who brought them success. The emperor Constantine the Great first gave his allegiance to the Sun god *Sol Invictus*, but he had a great victory under the sign of our Lord, and so he gave his support to our Church. I doubt that he cared greatly which god brought him victory; after all, according to long Roman tradition, he was a god himself.

In the chronicles of the time it states that Constantine erected a stupendous column of porphyry forty paces high, and on that column a depiction of Apollo with Constantine's own face, and around the head, seven rays of the sun. The rays were said to be made from nails from the Cross of Christ.

A gambling man might observe that Constantine was betting on two horses, and appealing to two constituencies, the Christians and the pagans. An untutored commoner of that time might struggle to understand how the new Christ god of the Emperor Constantine differed from the Sun god of Aurelian or Elagabalus.

DUKE LORENZO: So there is a path that leads from Elagabalus to Constantine, and to the untutored eye *Sol Invictus* might resemble Christ in his glory.

FATHER GIOVANNI: Then, and for centuries afterwards. It is an awkward point to express, my Lord, how the ignorant might mistake one for the other, but yes, one can argue that Elagabalus opened the door to our faith. But whether the door be open or shut, who can stand against the will of God?

DUCHESS YSABELLE: Perhaps it was the one true God who moved
Elagabalus and not his heathen Sun god.

FATHER GIOVANNI: Well said, my Lady. This is why I urge that we
do not judge others too harshly, for God moves in ways that may
be a mystery to us. The heathen Elagabalus may have been an
instrument of God's will.

DUCHESS YSABELLE: Well, I must confess that my faith is undisturbed
by the revelation that a citizen of old Byzantium could not tell and
did not care whether a statue represented Constantine the Great,
the Sun god, or our lord Jesus Christ.

FATHER GIOVANNI: There is a more to it than that, my Lady, as the
Protestants aver. They make a great fuss about the calendar and
the date of our Lord's birth at the winter festival of the Sun. They
maintain that the Church of Rome is but the paganism of the
Roman Empire. And that praying to the statues of saints is idolatry.

DUCHESS YSABELLE: But we know that the saints reside in Heaven
and intercede with Christ, while pagan idolatry is devil worship.
I do not understand how they can be so in error. Let us not spoil
our discussion with Protestant nonsense. Emilia, you have been
silent.

SIGNORA EMILIA: I did not wish to divert your discussion. As prepar-
ation for today I aspired to be diligent and discover something
about the god Apollo, whom I thought to be the Sun god of the
ancient world.

I searched through Homer and Ovid and Hesiod and other
ancient writers and I discovered countless stories that left my
thoughts in a tangle: Apollo was a deadly archer, he was a healer,
he brought plagues and pestilence, he was a herdsman, he was a
musician, he was a beautiful youth, he granted the gift of prophecy,
he was companion to the Muses.

It seems that the Sun god was Helios, and he rode across the
sky in a chariot drawn by a team of four horses, just as you have
said Father. I cannot place Apollo in the scheme of things.

FATHER GIOVANNI: I have wondered about this myself, Signora. Helios, or Sol, was indeed the Sun god, a Titan, part of the ancient order of things before the gods of Olympus. Apollo and Diana were children of Jupiter, and Jupiter supplanted older gods such as Helios and Hekate with his own children.

As for Apollo, I can say that the religion of the Greeks was unlike that of our Church of today, where one faith prevails over all of Italy. Each city had its own temples and gods, and each temple had its own priests, and priests like to tell stories and claim some uniqueness for their shrine. This is why the god Apollo has a multitude of titles, as if there was a multitude of gods fused into one by later storytellers. But one important title is Phoebus, which means bright. He is a god of many bright and beautiful things. I think that 'bright' may be the key to understanding.

SIGNORA EMILIA: Phoebus! Ah ... yes ... god of all things bright and beautiful! Indeed, I see that now, two gods born as twins, Diana and Apollo, both archers. Diana rules over the night and all that is wild, a god for those who live in forests and mountains and commune with nymphs and dryads.

Apollo is a god for the daytime, for all things that flourish and grow in the light of day, a god for men who are both beautiful and cultured, who live in elegant cities and spend their hours composing songs and poetry.

DUKE LORENZO: Oh, an excellent characterisation! Not a god of the Sun so much as a god for everything in which the qualities of the Sun are manifest—reason and eloquence, proportion and elegance, harmony and balance. Goodness and beauty ... did we not discuss that beauty is the exterior form of goodness?

DUCHESS YSABELLE: You did, and you have on several occasions, when you were extolling the views of Plato and Ficino and others who see the stamp of goodness in all things according to their closeness to God. I am less certain of this; I have known people who were ideally formed and beautiful to look upon, but who possessed little goodness.

I know of others in whom piety, love, and charity are equally blended and yet they come from a rough peasant stock and the Sun has not gifted them with much in the way of fine features or bodily grace. So you see ... I have encountered beauty without goodness and goodness without beauty. Beauty is an outward circumstance, goodness is in the heart.

DUKE LORENZO: Beauty is a circumstance?

DUCHESS YSABELLE: An agreeable arrangement of parts, agreeable according to the fashion of the day ... all women know this. A fashion comes from the French court and it is copied throughout Italy. Fashions that were once acclaimed are given to the maids.

Women are born with whatever form and features the good Lord sees fit to grant us. If we are fortunate and considered fair then we are praised ... and if we are not fair then we must hope for an extravagant dowry. We resemble flowers, for we bloom and wither ... and poets extol the bloom of youth, not the withered petals of old age. Even flowers that all judge to be beautiful are subject to fashion and taste. Emilia, do we not harass the gardeners?

SIGNORA EMILIA: Oh, we do, we do! Cut this rose ... no, not that one, it is past its best, this one here! Take cuttings from this plant, it is superior to the others. This plant is vigorous and well-formed, save the seed. There is little in Nature that cannot be improved to suit our taste. My lord, I believe you do likewise with horses, choosing sire and dam for superior qualities in the foal.

DUKE LORENZO: What you say is true, horses are bred for a purpose. The hunter finds beauty in one horse, the farmer or coachman in another—as you say wife, an agreeable arrangement of parts, so that one horse is bred to be quick and agile, another, placid and strong.

Socrates makes an argument about a lyre: when it is well-made and tuned it produces harmonious and beautiful sounds. When its parts are not so arranged, it is discordant. This agrees with your argument that beauty is an arrangement of parts. And yet the lyre is not a work of Nature. It is the skill of the maker and the musician that reveals a beauty that would otherwise be hidden. Although they may be subject to the distress of time, the world would be a poorer place without roses and lyres.

SIGNORA EMILIA: Ysabelle, even if beauty in this world is transitory and subject to opinion, we still give thanks to its author, whether that author be God or some person of peculiar genius.

Can we not say that some people are the authors of beauty and some the authors of ugliness? The authors of beauty desire to display in this world the beauty they find in their hearts. The authors of ugliness despise the beauty that others have made.

DUCHESS YSABELLE: Perhaps this was my meaning when I said goodness is in the heart. I am confused! So many that seem fair are spiteful and self-regarding—roses are fair but they have sharp thorns! Others who have not been well-used by life are filled with charity and kindness.

SIGNORA EMILIA: I think we are in agreement when you say that goodness comes from the heart. The beauty of this world is corrupted by Nature, but its source is good. Father, have you not said that we are made in the image of God, and so have some capacity for goodness and beauty in our works?

FATHER GIOVANNI: Indeed I have, and while I agree that the beauty of this world is transitory, we can redeem some part of Plato by observing that the higher part of the soul that desires to create a better and more beautiful world derives that impulse from God, for it recollects the forms of Beauty. As for the authors of ugliness, they have evil in their hearts, and devils at their ears.

DUKE LORENZO: I find within me an impulse to make our world more fair and pleasant. I look out at the city from my balcony and I have a notion of what is good and beautiful: that buildings are in good repair, that aqueducts and fountains are flowing, that roads are well laid, that churches are pious and provide succour to the poor, that there are hospitals for the sick, that the magistrates provide justice and are not corrupt, that the city watch is both awake and on duty, that the guards practice in the field (and are not drunk and gambling in their barracks). Even that gardens are well tended.

I see that goodness and hence beauty come from my desire—and the desire of all righteous citizens—to make a better city. A city that serves the needs of its citizens, not only in function but in form. Beauty is not merely a circumstance or accident, it is conceived by a will that acts upon the world to make it more beautiful.

Is this not what we might expect from the Kingdom of Heaven? That everything is as fine and good as it might be?

DUCHESS YSABELLE: Father, you must answer this, I insist!

FATHER GIOVANNI: Must I, my Lady? Well, here are my private thoughts, and you may dispute with them. There are many depictions of Christ in Majesty, as ruler of Heaven and Earth. Often they are placed over doorways into cathedrals—there is one such in Chartres in France that I found memorable. Also the fresco by Buffalmacco in the Camposanto in Pisa ... no doubt you have seen it.

We can imagine that Christ the King is, at the very least, as dutiful as our Duke in minding the fountains and aqueducts in the Kingdom of Heaven ... but this is not what we are shown. We are shown a scene of Christ on a throne surrounded by saints and fathers. It appears motionless and eternal. There is no depiction of aqueducts and magistrates and hospitals. Indeed, there is no more evil, so no need of magistrates, and no more sickness, so no need of hospitals.

I find this places a strain upon my imagination, for where there is no lack, there is no industry, and so we find the blessed saints on thrones with nothing to do. You have observed this yourself Signora, that when we are purged of contention and have a clear view of God's eternal truth we may become somewhat decorative.

Hell on the other hand is depicted in abundant detail, and functions with efficiency. The devils, outcast from Heaven for their wilfulness and unruliness, take delight in many menial tasks. They are model citizens of a model community, and in their selfless devotion are as much to be admired as monks sworn to the rule of

St. Benedict. We find this also in Dante: Hell is a place of efficient industry, Heaven a place of music and lyres.

To my shame and discomfort I find I am unable to place much credence in these visions of Heaven and Hell.

DUCHESS YSABELLE: Father! You can say this even though the vision of John shows us the Lamb of God, and the throne, and the elders, and saints, and angels.

FATHER GIOVANNI: My lady, the fault is mine. I have no doubt that our Lord will come again and everything that is broken will be made whole; that there will be a great cleansing of evil, and that we will suffer death no more. But I also doubt that it is within my power to imagine how this might come to be. I find that all artists have struggled in the same way. I do not feel bound by the works they have imposed upon us, even though they meant well.

SIGNORA EMILIA: If I may comment, my Lord ... picking up a loose thread, your view of the city from the balcony ... it seems to me that we possess a sense of unrealised goodness, a practical aspiration to improve every aspect of life. When you stand upon a balcony and imagine a more beautiful city with happier citizens, I wonder whether some impulse from the Sun brightens your inner eye that you may see more clearly into the future. The Sun makes us bright and bold. This is prophecy of a kind, but not the riddles and enigmas of Delphi ... a more accessible gift of clarity and possibility.

DUKE LORENZO: Signora, I do feel some of that. All who lead must imagine a world of possibility. We must look for a path into the future, for others depend upon us. A general imagines how he will prevail in conflict; the statesman imagines a treaty and a lasting peace; a duke such as myself must foresee a path to greater prosperity ... for citizens may gripe and complain about every manner of thing, but they will be happy with a more comfortable bed, mutton for dinner, and woollen cloth from Flanders.

But to lose that view of a better tomorrow ... it is like being lost in the dark, stumbling about.

SIGNORA EMILIA: And equally bad or worse, one may view the future with certainty and yet be powerless and ignored, as was Cassandra, daughter of Priam. She was blessed with true prophecy by Apollo, and then cursed not to be believed.

DUKE LORENZO: A cruel fate, to foresee the fall of Troy and the death of one's kin and yet have no power to change the course of events. And yet even when cursed, who would choose to see less clearly? To have foresight extinguished? To walk in darkness while the Sun shines? Who would wish to be foolish instead of wise? Is not wisdom a kind of foresight that the foolish lack? Yet how often are the wise ignored by the young and foolish, and mocked for their foresight and prudence?

SIGNORA EMILIA: Now that you have said it, I would always prefer foresight to foolishness, whatever the cost.

FATHER GIOVANNI: To see oneself clearly and to see one's place in the world clearly? To have a larger view? I have spoken this thought to myself, thinking it might be a grand thing to be wiser and see the world more clearly.

In confessional I find this is not so. People hide from themselves and blame others. They do not want insight and clarity. Most people would not wish to be wiser if it meant guilt and misery.

SIGNORA EMILIA: You mean that wisdom requires that we encounter truths that we might not wish to encounter?

FATHER GIOVANNI: We cannot be wise if we do not know ourselves, and the Sun searches out all the dark places. We must witness our evil and sin, and we must judge and forgive ourselves. We must repent.

Our Lord witnesses all the evil and sin in this world and yet He still loves us and still finds forgiveness for us. Is that not remarkable?

DUCHESS YSABELLE: That is the essence of our faith: admitting our sins, and praying for repentance and forgiveness. I begin to have a sense of what the Sun offers to us. Do we wish to be small, and live life in the shade with a shuttered view, or do we wish to be larger and see further? Are we to be mice, living in crevices and sneaking about in the dark? Or are we like that spirit of fortitude that stops the mouths of lions?

This *Invictus* of the Romans, it means invincible or unconquerable does it not? This is courage that encounters the vicissitudes of life and is not blunted or cowed. This is the clarity that sees what lies ahead, and does not turn away. This is how our Lord faced his death at the hands of the Romans. And if one is humble, repentant and courageous, one can accept any clarity of sight that is offered by the Lord.

DUKE LORENZO: An admirable speech! Indeed the Sun brightens what is dimly seen, and in like manner it removes all the impediments of doubt and fear that cloud the mind.

SIGNORA EMILIA: Bravo Ysabelle. I will drink a toast to that. I will leap up and stop the mouths of metaphorical lions if I can be a greater person.

FATHER GIOVANNI: I also concur ... although I am not so courageous as I would wish to be. There is some wisdom in knowing that. I sense that the Sun has penetrated our hearts. Our opinions have become bold and colourful.

SIGNORA EMILIA: This is so ... brighten my sight O Lord! I would rush the gates of Heaven and proclaim myself ...

DUCHESS YSABELLE: And disturb St. Peter with noise and theatricals?

SIGNORA EMILIA: The Sun demands that we shine brightly!

FATHER GIOVANNI:

> Neither do men light a candle, and put it under a bushel, but on a candlestick; and it giveth light unto all that are in the house.
>
> Let your light shine before men, that they may see your good works, and glorify your Father which is in heaven.

DUCHESS YSABELLE: Oh Father, you have quite caught the moment!

FATHER GIOVANNI: And yet I must express caution. The brighter the sunlight, the darker the shadow, so that we have an eternal contest between Michael and the Serpent ... or Apollo and Python for that matter. The sun bestows an exuberance, but it is like a glamour. Even our Lord went into the grave and for three days his light was extinguished.

DUCHESS YSABELLE: Father, I am confounded ... you have quenched our high spirits.

FATHER GIOVANNI: Forgive me, my Lady. There is a pattern to the moods that the Spheres bestow upon us. The Sun invigorates with exuberance and daring, but it is oft followed by melancholy.

YP: You have encountered this?

FATHER GIOVANNI: Many times, my Lady, many times ... in the confessional, and when giving the rites of the Church to the sick and the dying. People recall their days in the Sun and mourn the passing of their hopes and dreams. They believed they were the authors of a bold new world, but their moment passed, their noontide faded, and their Sun went down into the west. The strong become weak, the vigorous become lame, the industrious watch as their children squander their wealth.

Great families are eclipsed. We have seen this with the Visconte— no sons, no heirs, and so the Sforza possessed Milan, and now they too are gone. There are larger powers in this world: the Wheel of Fortune, the threads of Fate, the temptations of the Devil, and the will of our Lord.

DUKE LORENZO: So there is falseness even to the Sun? It paints the world in brightness but, as you say, there is a glamour, a false appearance.

SIGNORA EMILIA: It cannot be entirely false, my Lord, for the world grows green and abundant under the Sun, and we prosper.

FATHER GIOVANNI: Indeed, not a falseness, it is simply not all those things that we might wish it to be.

DUKE LORENZO: But it shows us futures, makes us bold to accomplish them, and yet they are undone.

FATHER GIOVANNI: It does not promise us eternity. Spring and summer at most. Only our Lord Jesus can promise eternity. Those heathens who worshipped the Sun worshipped a false god, a deceiving god—'he takes his seat in the temple of God, declaring himself to be God'—just as the blessed Paul declares.

DUCHESS YSABELLE: Do you suggest that the Sun is a deceiver?

FATHER GIOVANNI: My lady, I believe the blessed Paul refers to the emperor of Rome, I will add my own view if I may ….

DUCHESS YSABELLE: Please do Father.

FATHER GIOVANNI: The apostles and the early fathers of the Church were beset by enemies of many kinds and so they were vigilant. From without they were opposed by emperors who declared themselves gods, just as Paul states. From within they were corrupted by false prophets and messiahs and heretics of every kind, and so they warned against false men.

Even today Christendom is threatened by the armies of the Turk, and by a northern multitude of Protestant heretics who probe and riddle the Bible to find whether the day of the Lord is at hand and how Rome is Babylon and how his holiness the Pope leads us all to Hell.

It seems to me that all this turmoil occurs under the same Sun and that the Sun favours no party.

DUKE LORENZO: Wise words Father, wise words, the Sun is the least of our troubles … and I recall that in the first book of the *Bible* it states that God made the Sun and Moon and stars and saw that they were good.

DUCHESS YSABELLE: I am much relieved husband, I could not abide living under the light of a false god.

SIGNORA EMILIA: The Sun that warms our day and bathes this garden in a singular and beauteous light is not false. We do not dignify a lie. We are not deceived by the warmth of a summer's day.

FATHER GIOVANNI: There is an ancient tradition concerning the Sun that I would recite, even knowing that it will not quiet your unease. With your permission?

DUKE LORENZO: Father, you are a fount of arcane curiosities, and as I am curious I will hear it.

147

FATHER GIOVANNI: It is this. According to the ancients, perhaps the followers of Pythagoras, each planet is in sympathy with a number. For Saturn it is three, for Jupiter it is four, for Mars it is five, and for the Sun it is six. Now the same ancients formed squares from these numbers; for the Sun they made a square of six times six numbers, that is to say, thirty six numbers in a grid, with each number from one to thirty six occurring but once.

    With some ingenuity it is possible to arrange the numbers so that each row and column adds to the same number, and in the case of the Sun it is one hundred and eleven. The sum of all the numbers in the square is six hundred and sixty-six.

DUCHESS YSABELLE: The number of the beast! John the Divine reveals this number in his vision of the End of Days!

FATHER GIOVANNI: It is but a curiosity of arithmetic, the sum of numbers from one to thirty six.

DUCHESS YSABELLE: You have indeed stirred the pot, Father, and now I am disposed to believe that the arch-fiend has taken possession of the Sun and dazzles our minds with glamours and delusions and false doctrines. We must pray to St. Michael to oust the devil and put him down and shackle him for all time.

SIGNORA EMILIA: Ysabelle, the Arab book of starry wisdom we borrowed from Urbino ... these squares were in it. They are part of the lore of the Heavens according to Greeks and Arabs and misguided clerics who desire to conjure spirits from mouldy old books. The Sun is good, and scripture tells us it is good. Indeed, you said yourself that unwholesome things of the night cannot abide the light of the Sun.

DUCHESS YSABELLE: Father, you are quite wicked to alarm me so. Let me hear more about how the Sun is good.

SIGNORA EMILIA: Apollo has the company of the Muses, who are women of the highest accomplishment and inspire those who seek greatness in art and philosophy.

DUKE LORENZO: And can you name them all, Signora?

SIGNORA EMILIA: Indeed I can, for I have sought their company since childhood. Calliope, Erato, Polyhymnia, and Thalia cultivate the varieties of poetry. Euterpe is accomplished in music, and Terpsichore in dance. Clio recalls and celebrates the lives of those gone before, and tells their tales to the music of a lyre. Grave Melpomene shows us how great lives fall into error and are ruined, while sombre Urania instructs us in the mysteries of the Spheres and may be present with us even now.

DUKE LORENZO: Bravo, Signora, excellent, we are honoured to have such learning in this company. And the Muses you favour most?

SIGNORA EMILIA: Thank you, my Lord, these would be Euterpe and Terpsichore, for in better times I loved music and dance. But in moments of melancholy, when I ponder my place in this world, Urania speaks wisdom to me.

DUKE LORENZO: And should we all seek guidance from the Muses?

SIGNORA EMILIA: We should, for great poets have no shame in calling upon them. Hesiod has left us a great oration to the Muses, and he tells how he received a poet's staff from the goddesses of Helicon. Dante calls upon the Muses each time his voice falters, and he names them 'Ladies of the Heavenly Spring'.

Am I wrong in thinking that there is a power of mind superior to reason that comprehends whatever is adjacent to God?

DUKE LORENZO: So the Greeks believed ... Father, your thoughts?

FATHER GIOVANNI: They called it *nous*, the direct apprehension of divine thought, and yes, superior to reason.

SIGNORA EMILIA: So we must be humble in our work and call on higher powers to aid us when we seek to create a new thing that only God has seen, something He wishes to be revealed through us. We should quiet the voice of reason and draw our thoughts from the Heavenly Spring. Who can doubt that Dante was blessed by the Muses and granted a divine voice in showing us *Inferno*, *Purgatario*, and *Paradiso*? I do not doubt it.

DUCHESS YSABELLE: Nor I.

SIGNORA EMILIA: Father, when you spoke of the parts of the soul you said that each of us has a guardian spirit among the angels, a spirit that some believe is a part of the soul not yet revealed to us?

FATHER GIOVANNI: I do recall saying something of the sort. In earlier times this spirit was known as a genius or daemon, and Socrates spoke with such a spirit. Today it is more politic to speak of an angel ... the difference is moot, for both are intermediaries of God ... we are merely splitting hairs over words. Sometimes they are called ministering spirits, and sometimes tutelary spirits, for they instruct and guide us.

SIGNORA EMILIA: So when a poet calls upon the Muses, he gives his mind over to some higher voice.

FATHER GIOVANNI: So I imagine, but I cannot say for certain, because my inner voice contains little of rhyme or rhythm.

DUCHESS YSABELLE: Father, I am sure your inner voice speaks of divine mysteries.

FATHER GIOVANNI: When my inner voice has occasion to speak it mumbles indistinctly, as if eating bread and cheese.

DUCHESS YSABELLE: Father! Your modesty is noted and commendable but not credible. Emilia, I see that an inner voice is prompting you!

SIGNORA EMILIA: It is, it is! I begin to see how our threads of discourse unite. I would like to share these thoughts.

DUKE LORENZO: We are eager to hear them.

SIGNORA EMILIA: When we spoke of the Moon we discussed how the Moon ruled the lower parts of the soul, and the Sun the upper parts. The beasts are ruled by the Moon, and they devise little that we consider ingenious or beautiful. Perhaps a web, or a nest, but we do not seek out the wolf, or fox, or any beast of the field for mastery of stone, or wood, or precious metal. They leave no images; they do not portray nature or scripture or themselves. They do not entertain us with songs of ancient kings and queens. The realm of the Moon is mute, and she presides over wild hills and forests, where the only sounds are those of the wind, the waters, the

howling of wolves, the hooting of owls, and the murmurings of nightingales.

For this reason the sages of old proposed that we have within us some part of the Sun, an inner Sun, a faculty more bright and expansive than the Moon. Is this not so Father? A brightness, seeing clearly?

FATHER GIOVANNI: It is a principle of medicine that soul and body mirror the Cosmos. So yes, Moon and Sun.

SIGNORA EMILIA: Thank you Father! Those parts of understanding that are ill-perceived by the beasts (having but the inconstant light of the Moon to view their interior realm) are lit to a fuller understanding by the Sun within us. The faculty of language is revealed, and all the arts and accomplishments of the Muses. In this bright light of understanding we see what is good and evil, and make laws so that we may live harmoniously.

DUKE LORENZO: And we may also foresee the future and recall the past. Indeed, our inner sight reveals a great vista.

SIGNORA EMILIA: And we see possibility. When we look out upon a wilderness we desire to bring it to order that it may flourish in great variety. We seek to govern the wild beasts and make them obedient. Our light reveals much to us that was hidden.

FATHER GIOVANNI: It is written that when God formed all the beasts of the land and sea and sky, He did not name them. He brought them before Adam to see how he would name them, for even God did not know. And Adam knew their names, for he was the master of this world and he possessed a light of understanding.

SIGNORA EMILIA: Yes, that is my meaning. The Sun illuminates our interior realm so that we feel that we are masters of this world.

DUCHESS YSABELLE: Men are seduced by this brightness. They feel like gods, and demand to be worshipped. But we are not gods, and so I mistrust this light.

SIGNORA EMILIA: I understand your unease, Ysabelle. Where there is light there is dark. Where there is truth there is lie. I see some truth in what you say, that when our inner sun is too bright its light is a partner to darkness.

FATHER GIOVANNI: Perhaps in the first days of Eden our light was singular, but no more, for we have tasted the forbidden fruit of good and evil and are now exiled into a world of sin.

DUCHESS YSABELLE: Father, you have expressed it exactly ... in a fallen world we should not trust the Sun as an image of goodness. The Sun is fallen too. The Sun in the sky may be bright but he does not convey understanding. The Moon may instil madness, but when dawn breaks, her fools are not wiser under the light of the Sun.

We mistrust the Moon because she is inconstant, varying from day to day, but the same is true of the Sun; he rises, he sets, he retreats to the south in winter and advances towards the zenith in summer. We seek for an image of what is eternal, but the Sun comes and goes.

And so I view the Sun as I view many people who make claims upon my trust. Is a smile sincere or is it false? Am I to be cozened? Am I to be mocked behind my back? What if the Sun does not care to have me in his world of elegance and beauty, for I am lacking in accomplishments—Husband, you have witnessed the French court, is it not a nest of vipers?

DUKE LORENZO: It is a nest of vipers. There is a false appearance that dazzles the eye, a glory of magnificence and splendour, but the gold—and there is a great deal of it—is spread very thin.

DUCHESS YSABELLE: Did the pagans who worshipped *Sol Invictus* worship the false brightness of Lucifer? Is this why Michael must ever struggle for possession of the Sun?

SIGNORA EMILIA: These are troubling thoughts Ysabelle. In this doubling of the Sun you are reminded of Christ and anti-Christ?

DUCHESS YSABELLE: I am. The sack of Rome has been an unimaginable horror to us all ... how could the Emperor Charles fall so far into iniquity as to permit the rape of the Holy City? And fill his army with cruel men, followers of the false priest Luther? Are we at the End of Days long prophesied? How many prophecies are already accomplished? How many seals of the great scroll are already undone?

FATHER GIOVANNI: I think we should be cautious in interpreting these terrible events. The history of Italy is one of broken alliances, betrayal, and cruelty. There has been no end to it. The immediacy of events is shocking, but the trend is unbroken from ancient times.

DUKE LORENZO: I agree with you, Father. The student of history will find that the Pope has played the statesman and general for centuries. I am reminded of the city of Palestrina, which was razed to the ground twice, the first time on the orders of Pope Boniface, and the second time on the orders of Pope Eugenius. We can weep for Rome, but the papacy is not innocent. Those who field armies and act the general will be subject to the Wheel of Fortune.

DUCHESS YSABELLE: That such terror and rapine and desecration should be considered a part of our inheritance is no comfort. How does Italy still stand? How can beauty prevail against this mad impulse to rend what is beautiful?

DUKE LORENZO: It seems to me that we have arrived at that border where the business of the Sun ends, and the business of Mars begins.

SIGNORA EMILIA: In that case we must fortify our souls and sharpen our blades.

SPHÆRA MARTIS

So may all your enemies perish, Lord!
But may all who love you be like the
Sun when it rises in its strength.
Judges 5:31

DUCHESS YSABELLE: Today we have come together to discuss the
Sphere of Mars. I feel apprehensive, for he is a rude and immoderate
god, all swagger and arrogance. I fear he will bring dissension
among us.

SIGNORA EMILIA: Perhaps you are recalling the Greek god Ares from
the *Iliad*, where we learn that he is indeed a dolt. Homer tells us
it was wise Athena who drove Ares from the field, and carried
winged Victory upon the palm of her hand.

DUCHESS YSABELLE: Then perhaps I am recalling Ares. Or perhaps
not—our *condottieri* seem to enjoy trumpets, and drums, and

fanfares, and parades, more than they enjoy fighting. So is Mars not all arrogance and swagger?

DUKE LORENZO: Mars was well regarded by the Romans and accorded great dignity. They told how the twins Romulus and Remus were fathered by Mars. The city was founded by the sons of Mars.

DUCHESS YSABELLE: And the sons of Mars brought war to the entire world.

DUKE LORENZO: Or peace. Rome brought an end to the warring and feuding between minor states, so that a greater prosperity was possible.

FATHER GIOVANNI: There is some truth to that, my Lady. Many regions were subject to incessant warfare, neighbour against neighbour, tribe against tribe, before the Romans brought the world to order.

DUCHESS YSABELLE: And yet I am not comforted by the thought of legions bringing the terror of fire and siege so that they might impose their notion of a common good. The Hebrews were never comfortable with Roman notions, were they Father?

FATHER GIOVANNI: They were not, and so they were dispersed from the Holy Land, and the emperor Hadrian forbade them to enter Jerusalem.

DUCHESS YSABELLE: And the Romans crucified our Lord.

FATHER GIOVANNI: They did, and they persecuted and martyred many saints before accepting our faith.

DUCHESS YSABELLE: And so I think we should be wary of Mars—he is savage and forbidding, and he will bring dissension upon us.

DUKE LORENZO: Wife, you are wise as always.

DUCHESS YSABELLE: Husband, you ease our debate by flattering me ... but I am wise to this, just as you say. However, I depend upon you to guard us from the spirits of Mars. I see you have brought your sword.

DUKE LORENZO: I have brought my sword. It has been resting in its scabbard for many years, and I had hoped it might never see daylight again. I do care for it however, and oil the blade, for it is, in this age, the mark of a gentleman, and a gentleman must ever guard his honour or be despised and outcast.

SIGNORA EMILIA: Have you ever defended your honour, my Lord?

DUKE LORENZO: Once, Signora, when I was a student, I fought over some trifling matter. At that time we were as prickly as hedgehogs, determined to find insult and eager to prove our worth. It did not help that we drank too much. They say that Mars is fiery, not only on account of his ruddy appearance in the night sky, but also on account of the fiery passion that is kindled in any affair of honour and violence.

SIGNORA EMILIA: And were you injured, my Lord?

DUKE LORENZO: Some inconsequential scratches—I have had worse when hunting. In those days we fought to first blood, not wishing to be charged with murder and so outcast from our studies. We were devoted to our maestros, usually some tavern bravo who swore to reveal to us deadly strokes that none could parry. To refuse a challenge was unthinkable. There was no place in Christendom so remote that one might live with the disgrace.

FATHER GIOVANNI: But I understand that it is possible to refuse a challenge with honour, my Lord?

DUKE LORENZO: Indeed, in the company of grown men of known and established quality one might refuse. One can dismiss a challenge that reflects badly upon the challenger—foolish and intemperate words spoken while in one's cups for example. An honourable man, once sober, will admit that he spoke hastily and unwisely. There is a meeting between parties, a public reconciliation, so that all will agree that the matter has been resolved with honour.

Also, one can dismiss a challenge by a knave or an inferior. But if it is a challenge between equals, and if it concerns a matter of substance—the honour of a lady for example—then it must be accepted. There cannot be the smallest suspicion of cowardice.

FATHER GIOVANNI: As you know, my Lord, the Church does not countenance duelling. Both parties are excommunicated and if a man dies, he will not receive a Christian burial in consecrated ground.

DUKE LORENZO: I do not wish to give offence, Father, but in this matter the Church resembles a toothless dog. It barks loudly, but rarely bites.

FATHER GIOVANNI: That is also true, my Lord. We are Italians, and a question of honour becomes a family matter. Every cousin will search out his sword and sharpen its blade, and every uncle in the Church will consult with his bishop.

DUKE LORENZO: Oh indeed, and when I was young and intemperate there was comfort in knowing that I could number two bishops and a cardinal in my immediate family.

SIGNORA EMILIA: A man is respected for his willingness to defend his honour, the honour of his family, and the honour of any woman he favours. A woman is honoured for her chastity. I see here the quintessence of Mars and Venus.

DUKE LORENZO: It has always been thus.

DUCHESS YSABELLE: Women depend upon their menfolk to challenge foul gossip. It is a sombre thought that a husband, a brother or a cousin might risk death because of a baseless slander.

SIGNORA EMILIA: It is a grave responsibility, and so we must guard our conduct at all times. We must seek our companions in women of irreproachable virtue.

DUCHESS YSABELLE: And men of irreproachable virtue—it is well that the good Father is present with us, for we do not need gossip and drawn swords.

We digress, but it seems to me that we have grasped an aspect of Mars: an eagerness for conflict ... an abhorrence of weakness or timidity ... a combative tendency where there is a hazard of injury or death.

DUKE LORENZO: An eagerness for conflict? Among the young, I agree, this is evident. Many who have seen battle and stood in the blood of other men become less eager. Reason takes the place of passion. An old soldier looks for strategy, scouting and spies, the location of good water and supplies of fodder, the condition of horses, and the state of the ground. War is, after all, an exercise in practical reason. The Romans taught us this: organisation, discipline, good practice, and terrifying punishments.

SIGNORA EMILIA: What punishments, my Lord?

DUKE LORENZO: Men were beaten to death by their own comrades. For a Roman it was preferable to die in battle than to lose a weapon (for cowards would cast away their weapons when they fled the field).

To prepare my mind for this discussion I have been reading the Greek Polybius, specifically his history of the wars with Carthage. He speaks of many other matters, including details of how the Romans organised their legions, how they marched, how they camped. I was intrigued to read about Hannibal and his elephants, for Polybius spoke to living men who crossed the mountains with Hannibal's army.

SIGNORA EMILIA: I have never seen an elephant, my Lord.

DUKE LORENZO: Nor I, Signora.

FATHER GIOVANNI: Ercole D'Este had an elephant on one of his estates near Ferrara. I saw it once, as large as a house. Also some great cats with spots. I doubt that the elephant still lives—they are unhappy beasts when they are forced to live alone.

DUKE LORENZO: And they are not born for our climes; Hannibal brought his beasts across the Alps, but they were exhausted from the rigours of the march, and almost all died during the winter.

SIGNORA EMILIA: An elephant in Ferrara! I was born too late, all greatness has passed from the world.

FATHER GIOVANNI: We must locate another. I hear the Pope desires an elephant for his menagerie.

DUCHESS YSABELLE: And now we digress beyond all bounds. Elephants indeed! Emilia, I feel sure you have brought some token of Mars for our education.

Signora Emilia: I have! I had originally intended to bring blood, for blood reminds us of Mars on account of its redness and its association with war and violence. I placed some drops of blood on a kerchief, but I found it distasteful, as if I had been mopping a nosebleed. Then I thought of bringing a phial of blood, but that would require a physician to achieve a pointless result, for we know what blood looks like—we hardly need a reminder.

    Finally I recalled that I am entirely blood—as a small scratch will prove—and I need only exhibit myself. So, behold! If I am provoked to anger I will become flushed and appear martial. My Lord, may I borrow your sword?

Duke Lorenzo: Indeed, Signora—but this is no carnival piece, so beware.

Signora Emilia: Thank you, my Lord, I will be cautious. Now I strike a pose ... thus ... and I look fierce (as I do when a groom mistreats a horse) and I hold the sword ... thus ... as I have seen men do, and I demand satisfaction from some knave who has given me mortal offence. Is this Mars, or do I remain Venus?

Duke Lorenzo: Your stance is bold and resolute—that cannot be feigned.

Father Giovanni: Undoubtedly Mars, Signora.

Duchess Ysabelle: A sharp sword is a powerful argument, Emilia!

Signora Emilia: Excellent! It is my belief that it is not our sex that makes us Venus or Mars; it is the fire in our blood and the temper in our hearts that makes us bold. Whether I am to be accounted a master of the sword is another matter ... but do I know the parries ... see ... *prime, seconde, tierce, quarte*. And I am judged a fair shot with a hunting bow.

Duke Lorenzo: I have watched you hunt, Signora.

Signora Emilia: War, as you have said, my Lord, is a matter of practical reason. If one can master the subtleties of dance or music, then one has the capacity to master a sword. I have no ambition to do so; this was merely to demonstrate, for my own satisfaction, that

I can set aside Venus when the occasion arises and call upon Mars to guide me, that the spirit of Mars is not exclusive to men.

DUKE LORENZO: And Mars is present Signora. I think we are approaching the heart of this matter. It is easy to be misled by the trappings of Mars, the martial aspect of arms and armour, of trumpets and parades, the strutting and swagger. These are things that men do to fortify their spirits, for men may seem strong outside when they quiver inside.

I have seen men given to bravado waver and fluster in the heat of battle, pleading the wisdom of retreat, while quiet men with no trace of affectation stand firm and implacable in the face of mortal danger. It seems to me that the essence of Mars is boldness in the face of adversity, a resolve that stands firm, or advances, and does not give in to despair.

FATHER GIOVANNI: Like a galley that makes way against tide and wind.

DUCHESS YSABELLE: Very good Father, and some craft have but few oars and struggle against the waves, while others have many oars and cut a path through an inclement sea.

SIGNORA EMILIA: And some, like Elizabetta in the kitchen, have but one oar and travel in circles.

DUCHESS YSABELLE: Alas for poor Elizabetta, who returns to the place from whence she began and has forgotten why she set out. Elizabetta's birth was not blessed by Mars but by Venus ... and the power of Venus does not lie in making way against hostile tides. Elizabetta has a pleasing face and a sweet smile. Mars goes forth with clamour and strife, Venus stands still and all things come towards her.

SIGNORA EMILIA: Vulcan made a girdle for Venus that rendered her irresistible. We spoke of this previously, of Empedocles and his philosophy of Love and Strife: Venus is Love and Mars is Strife.

Also Ficino and his view that love is at the heart of all magic, for love draws together those things that are separate. Venus resembles the lodestone that draws iron towards it.

DUKE LORENZO: An interesting comparison. But, if we set aside Venusian girdles and the mysteries of magic, history is dominated by Mars.

SIGNORA EMILIA: Unless, like Helen, one has a face that launches a thousand ships. Venus took the part of Paris and Helen, and although the Troy fell, she brought her son Aeneas to Italy and so the history of Rome began.

DUKE LORENZO: Very astute Signora, my argument is confounded. I mean that men must make their way in this world, that some martial vigour is necessary. And history admires martial men such as Alexander and Caesar.

DUCHESS YSABELLE: So, if the object of your desire does not come towards you, in the manner of Venus, then you should march out and seize what you desire?

DUKE LORENZO: I mean having a goal, and not being daunted by adversity. And besides, the strong have always taken from the weak. In the histories of the Greeks and Romans there is one universal, which is the desire for plunder and slaves. I see this clearly in Polybius.

DUCHESS YSABELLE: And what if one is not strong? How can a woman approve a world in which the sack of cities, the defilement of women, and being sold into slavery is considered the sport of warriors? You cannot imagine the terror we—the Signora and my other companions—felt at the sack of Rome, that the Holy City could be so violated.

SIGNORA EMILIA: It is so, my Lord. We were sick with fear.

DUKE LORENZO: That was an infamous episode in the history of Italy. I feared that we would be obliged to assist the Florentines and so become embroiled in an affair that defied all sense. We were fortunate to be out of the line of march.

DUCHESS YSABELLE: When I was young I imagined that our Christian faith had made a better world, that good had triumphed over all the old evils, that the human spirit had been reformed and rectified in the ways of God. That thought sustained me, and I

could dismiss evidence to the contrary. How wrong I was! So our fears were not merely womanly vapours and imaginings?

DUKE LORENZO: Your fears were not vapours or imaginings. The Wheel of Fortune turned in our favour, and in this instance our city was fortunate. Italy is once again a battleground for greater powers, and I mean France, Spain and the Empire. Perhaps even the Devil, for the Church is divided in its loyalties and cardinals war upon each other.

FATHER GIOVANNI: Indeed, my Lord, one cannot ignore the fact that the outrage that led to Rome being despoiled began as a dispute between princes of the Church, a squabble over titles and appointments ... worldly ambition writ large ... all the ancient antagonisms of Italy coming to the fore: a Colonna cardinal in league with the Holy Roman Emperor leading a Spanish and German army against a Medici pope allied with France ... and the poor people of Rome ravaged by the worst dregs of humanity.

DUCHESS YSABELLE: The sack of Rome was infamous, the work of the Devil. We sought to reveal the spirit of Mars. It seems that we have done so, and in my mind he remains an uncouth spirit. Father, I have forgotten all courtesy—I have not invited you to show what you have brought for us.

FATHER GIOVANNI: My lady, whether the moment arrives early or late the result is the same. I have brought this symbol.

DUCHESS YSABELLE: What is this ... I recognise it.

FATHER GIOVANNI: It is the *Chi-Rho*, my Lady, an ancient sign of our Lord.

SIGNORA EMILIA: It is the *Chi-Rho* Ysabelle, see, the letters *Chi* and *Rho*, from the Greek, *Christos*.

DUCHESS YSABELLE: You know that I have no Greek, Emilia.

SIGNORA EMILIA: And this sign speaks to the nature of Mars? A puzzle! Let me see ... it was the sign given to Constantine that he would win a great victory against a false emperor and so he instructed his army to paint it upon their shields.

FATHER GIOVANNI: Indeed, that is the story. This is the sign that conquered.

SIGNORA EMILIA: You imply that in this sign our Lord triumphed over the power of Mars?

FATHER GIOVANNI: That was my thought, Signora. From the earliest times the Romans gave their allegiance to Mars and Jove. Then Constantine fought under the sign of our Lord and triumphed. From that day our Christian faith was allied to the fortunes of the Empire, so that there is now but one God and one faith in all the kingdoms of the West.

DUCHESS YSABELLE: My mind follows the logic of this, but my heart is confused. On one hand I understand that the one true God should conquer all false gods … but Jesus taught us to love our neighbour. Christian piety requires that we obey God's laws, attend to our fallen natures by acquiring virtue and confessing our sins, perform good works among the sick and poor, and love God with our heart, soul and mind. There is nothing of war and conquest. Father, are you able to explain this for me?

FATHER GIOVANNI: You are correct, my Lady. The early Christians lived in peace and turned the other cheek as our Lord instructed. They loved each other, and forgave their tormentors. They thought that our Lord would come again within the span of their lives and that there would be a new world of righteousness. There would be a great and final war, and evil would be put down for all time, just as John describes in his vision of the End of Days.

But the time of our Lord is not yet come, and as the apostle Luke records, 'But of that day and hour no man knoweth, no, not the angels of heaven, but my Father only'.

Many believe that the final days are at hand. There is a mania among the Protestants for reading the *Bible* and numbering the words and calculating the days, but in truth, as our Lord declares, no man knows when the trumpets will sound in Heaven and the dead will rise. Until that day we must live our lives as best we can. We must bring the Lord's words to everyone: to the poor and to the wealthy, to the meek and to the bellicose. Where there is evil in this world we must attempt to reform it. If it moves against us we must counter it. So it was that our Lord give a sign to the soldier Constantine for the greater good of our faith.

DUCHESS YSABELLE: May I keep this sign Father? I will pray for understanding.

FATHER GIOVANNI: I will ask a scribe to render a fair version—this is but a scribble

DUCHESS YSABELLE: If you would. I will pray that our Holy Father may triumph over the heretic knaves and ruffians that threaten our cities.

FATHER GIOVANNI: My lady, perhaps you would be interested to hear the song that Moses sang to praise the Lord for the destruction of Pharaoh and his army beneath the waves of the sea?

DUCHESS YSABELLE: I would. Do you have it?

FATHER GIOVANNI: I do. I foresaw this moment. I have it written on this paper ...

> Then sang Moses and the children of Israel this song unto the Lord, and spake, saying, I will sing unto the Lord, for he hath triumphed gloriously: the horse and his rider hath he thrown into the sea.
>
> The Lord is my strength and song, and He is become my salvation: He is my God, and I will prepare Him an habitation; my father's God, and I will exalt Him.
>
> The Lord is a man of war: the Lord is his name.
>
> Pharaoh's chariots and his host hath He cast into the sea: his chosen captains also are drowned in the Red Sea.
>
> The depths have covered them: they sank into the bottom as a stone.
>
> Thy right hand, O Lord, is become glorious in power: thy right hand, O Lord, hath dashed in pieces the enemy.
>
> And in the greatness of thine excellency thou hast overthrown them that rose up against thee: You sent forth Thy wrath, which consumed them as stubble.

There is a deal more in a similar spirit, but I think this suffices.

DUCHESS YSABELLE: Moses exults that God has destroyed his enemies. He feels no pity for their plight, only pride that his God could work such destruction.

FATHER GIOVANNI: And before the drowning of Pharaoh the Angel of Death had taken all the firstborn of Egypt. And every son of Egypt had a mother who mourned for him. This should excite our pity, but we are told that Pharaoh was hard of heart, and the people of Israel suffered under his rod.

DUKE LORENZO: If the mercenary knaves that sacked Rome had come our way, and if by some divine grace their army had been dispersed and slaughtered, I would have exulted like Moses. The mothers of the heretic slain could have wept oceans of salt tears and still I would have praised God for our deliverance.

DUCHESS YSABELLE: Now that I consult my feelings, I know that I too would have been filled with joy at such a deliverance. Father, is it wrong that I agree with my husband in this matter, that we should pray for the destruction of such enemies? It feels wrong to do so, and yet I cannot bear the thought of our city being ravaged. It is my duty to protect our women and children.

FATHER GIOVANNI: It is not wrong that you should pray for deliverance from evil. Why, our Lord instructs us to do so in the prayer that he taught his disciples. Those very words: deliver us from evil.

DUCHESS YSABELLE: And yet God did not spare Rome from the German heretics. I am certain our Holy Father must have prayed for deliverance. The prayers of the Roman people must have reached the ears of some saint—we have so many saints—and still they were given over to the heretic dogs.

FATHER GIOVANNI: I have no answer, my Lady. The people of Israel suffered many such tribulations, as when the temple of Solomon was ruined by the armies of Nebuchadnezzar and the people taken away to Babylon and exile. The Second Temple was desecrated by the Greek Antiochus, who placed a statue of Zeus within it and sacrificed pigs on the altar. The Temple was finally destroyed by the Roman Titus, who burned Jerusalem and took its golden treasures to Rome.

SIGNORA EMILIA: So we can pray for deliverance from the allies of Satan but God might turn his face from us. Tell me, my Lord, what might have occurred if we had been in the line of march, if the Emperor's army had reached our walls?

DUKE LORENZO: It does not bear contemplation Signora, but as you ask, I will inform you.

As you may know, there is an ancient rule of war that a city taken by storm will be sacked. This is a reward for the besieging soldiers, who must undergo the many hazards and terrors of storming walls and breaches. During a sack there is no law, and soldiers are permitted any malice against the inhabitants. A commander might order that every living thing within the walls be slaughtered, as Joshua did to Jericho. In the days of ancient Rome a general might order the slaughter of the old and young so that they might not be a burden on his army, and sell into slavery every person of a useful age.

During a sack soldiers are so drunk they are hardly different from wild animals. They become insane with lust and greed. Their soldiering pay is a pittance, not worth the hazards of war, so what they seek is plunder and treasure. Citizens are tortured into revealing their valuables. Churches are stripped. No law, human or divine, has power during a sack. The recent sack of Rome lasted many months until there was no one left to torture, and plague took hold of the city.

Now, unless there is personal animosity, a besieging general might wish to avoid the cost of a siege, or the horrors of a sack. There would be a negotiation, an exchange of messages. The besieging commander would explain that if his troops should storm the walls he must, according to long tradition, permit the city to be sacked. He would then present the alternative—the payment of an enormous and ruinous sum of money to compensate his troops, a garrison of his own soldiers, a governor of his own choosing, and finally, that leading members of the city must go into exile.

There might be executions. This is typical, but circumstances vary greatly. Men of honour might negotiate a lenient surrender and part friends—it is sometimes better to win allies than bring desolation to a beautiful city. Sometimes a commander fears his troops will mutiny if they are not permitted to plunder a city.

In answer to your question Signora, we could not have held out against the army of the Emperor. They were too many, and they had siege cannon. I would have been forced to surrender the city to save it from worse. Foreign soldiers, probably Spanish, would have occupied the city, a law unto themselves. I have not been a friend to the Empire and so I and my family would have had to go into exile ... I know not where. A bitter prospect.

DUCHESS YSABELLE: But where would we go, Husband? You have not spoken of this ... had you planned this far?

DUKE LORENZO: Our options have been reduced by recent events. The Emperor now owns most of the North. Many of our allies have surrendered. There is still Venice, but my father warred against them and they owe me no favours. The Kingdom of Naples is in the hands of the Empire and so is barred to us. Rome is now a wasteland of poverty and plague. Perhaps the Papal States, but then we must deal with the ancient families of Rome—Colonna, Farnese, Orsini and other families— who will recall quarrels and feuds going back to the days of my great-grandfather.

I had thought we might find refuge in France.

DUCHESS YSABELLE: France! And are we owed favours in France?

DUKE LORENZO: We are not owed favours in France, but neither are there ancient enmities.

DUCHESS YSABELLE: And how would we live? Our properties would be forfeit, our rents would go towards funding the Emperor Charles. He would rule Italy with our income.

DUKE LORENZO: Our wealth is not all in strongboxes and property. I have investments with the Medici bank—it is the modern way.

DUCHESS YSABELLE: And how would we arrange this exit to France?

DUKE LORENZO: My brother Giacomo—his wife Anne has a brother who is something in the Church near Avignon.

DUCHESS YSABELLE: Something in the Church? Is that the best we can do? I am certain I can discover some better accommodation with the French!

DUKE LORENZO: I know that you can—your family has many kin in France. I did not mention this matter because we are currently in no danger, and had I sought your aid you would have thought the situation more threatening to us than it has been.

DUCHESS YSABELLE: That is exactly what I would have thought. But now that our weakness in the face of heretic armies is established, I will make the effort to find a future home should we need one. And what of our friends and servants, we cannot abandon them?

DUKE LORENZO: Nor should we. I will look into this also. We must preserve all those under our care, whether citizens, servants, family, or friends. Forgive me Father, forgive me Signora, I seek your discretion, our weakness is exposed. Our ancient allies are dispersed, or bought, or under foreign rule. Milan did not hold, neither did Florence, and Rome is ruined. We are one small duchy, grist between the millstones of the Holy Roman Empire on one hand and the French on the other. But God be praised, fortune has spared us. Italy is once again catching its breath and may not return to uproar and chaos in our lifetimes. We must not alarm the citizens … and yet we must exercise foresight and prudence.

FATHER GIOVANNI: I am accustomed to silence, my Lord.

SIGNORA EMILIA: My silence is also assured, my Lord.

DUCHESS YSABELLE: Mars has brought us to this, just as I thought he might. I woke happy, now I am afraid. He is a wicked god.

SIGNORA EMILIA: He is the god of men who violate women and murder their children.

DUCHESS YSABELLE: He is! Well spoken Emilia! We have heard that under the rules of war soldiers are granted this license, and may exercise it in any manner they choose.

SIGNORA EMILIA: And then they may choose to celebrate it, as the Romans did, vaunting that Mars raped a Vestal virgin while she slept, and in this manner became father to Romulus and Remus. And they celebrated the abduction of the Sabine women when they could not find wives. What a glorious thing, to violate women who have neither strength nor arms, and then to recall and celebrate that day in the sacred calendar!

DUKE LORENZO: Those were rude times. At least the Romans acted well in the rape of Lucretia.

SIGNORA EMILIA: Forgive me for disagreeing, my Lord. It seems to me that if Lucretia had been a baker's wife, or a seamstress, there would not have been an uproar. It was the dishonour done to a noble family that caused revolt. It was the honour of men that was impugned. Men could regain their honour in making war and ousting a corrupt king; poor Lucretia could not. That is why poor Lucretia killed herself.

DUCHESS YSABELLE: And now we are at odds. Spirits of Mars surround us just as I said they would. Emilia, well said, and I agree, but we should not pursue this. These spirits feed off contention, do they not Father?

FATHER GIOVANNI: They do. Where there is fear there is anger, and where there is anger words are spoken that are not easily unsaid. My lady, Signora, you are correct to fear Mars; even our Holy Father had to flee the heretics. His Swiss guard was slaughtered. There are mighty devils in this world.

But what does Dante have to say about the sphere of Mars? Why, he exhibits the blessed spirits of warriors of the faith, men who stood against the infidel: Charlemagne and his paladin Roland and the like. Noble Christian warriors. And what of those who uphold the law, for there is no law without Mars. You have studied law, my Lord, perhaps you would be kind enough to speak on this matter?

DUKE LORENZO: There is indeed no law without Mars. You are familiar with our Bargello, who keeps order in the streets and knocks on the doors of those who must answer to the law. I appointed him many years ago. He was a captain of Swiss mercenaries who fought for my father. He is sober, diligent, courageous, and keeps good order among our constables. I watch him carefully, and meet with him routinely, and I do him every honour, for he is of that species of man who values respect and favour more than gold, and who gives his loyalty to those who value his worth.

Without law we would have no industry, wealth, or community. Each race of people gives first place to its lawgivers—Solon in Athens, Lycurgus in Sparta, Moses among the Jews—and many others. It is a matter of observation that people obey the law most diligently when they fear it. Pious exhortations to do good are all very well, but the law and its officers are more effective. What do you say, Father?

FATHER GIOVANNI: At the end of days there will be sheep and goats, and woe to the goats—we have discussed this. There are laws in Heaven and laws in this world.

DUCHESS YSABELLE: And whom should we honour for our laws, dear Husband?

DUKE LORENZO: The Romans of old had a large hand in our secular law, and the Church in our moral law.

DUCHESS YSABELLE: A strange conjunction, the children of Mars and the Kingdom of Heaven.

DUKE LORENZO: Roman law is sound, for they had a thousand years to improve it. We owe a debt to the Emperor Justinian, who ordered a great study and compilation of Roman law as it existed in the late Empire, law that was adapted to the customs and needs of a great multitude of people.

DUCHESS YSABELLE: I did not know that.

FATHER GIOVANNI: Justinian was a good Christian who built the greatest church in the Eastern Empire, the Church of the Holy Wisdom ... but alas, it is a church no more, for the Turks have it and use it for their own worship. Justinian was zealous in the persecution of pagans and the forbidding of blood sacrifices.

Dᴜᴄʜᴇss Ysᴀʙᴇʟʟᴇ: That is a recommendation at least. So I suppose we must praise Justinian for his laws, even though he was a Roman of sorts. And I concede the point about the administration of law and the Bargello and his men. I see that Mars may be tolerable when governed by law and confined by civil powers to do no harm to honest citizens. But when Mars is given licence, he is Satan himself.

Dᴜᴋᴇ Lᴏʀᴇɴᴢᴏ: We are in agreement. Now our disputes are done, Mars does not hold us in thrall.

Dᴜᴄʜᴇss Ysᴀʙᴇʟʟᴇ: I have heard that sorcerers command wicked spirits using swords. Your sword must terrify the spirits of Mars lest you prick them.

Sɪɢɴᴏʀᴀ Eᴍɪʟɪᴀ: They have witnessed a woman armed and resolute. I will prick them worse than a wild rose! I will be Athena and put them to flight! Ysabelle, you have not told us what token of Mars you have brought.

Dᴜᴄʜᴇss Ysᴀʙᴇʟʟᴇ: For I have not been asked until now! Why, I have brought my husband, who shields us all from the wickedness that besets Italy.

Dᴜᴋᴇ Lᴏʀᴇɴᴢᴏ: Ha! You have not had a good word for Mars.

Dᴜᴄʜᴇss Ysᴀʙᴇʟʟᴇ: But I have a good husband, and you have been a soldier.

Dᴜᴋᴇ Lᴏʀᴇɴᴢᴏ: Yes, I have been a soldier.

Sɪɢɴᴏʀᴀ Eᴍɪʟɪᴀ: Tell us of your soldiering, my Lord. If you will.

Dᴜᴋᴇ Lᴏʀᴇɴᴢᴏ: I have little distinction as a soldier. My father was another matter … he led our city on the side of Florence during the war with Venice. He gave me command of a troop of light horse to scout around our march and to harass the enemy as they went about collecting food from the countryside.

A memory lives in my mind, and I recall it often. It is not a noble memory. We happened upon a group of foragers who were loading a cart with grain, and hams, and wine, and chickens, from a farm. They were mercenaries come up from Naples to fight for Venice. They had used the women badly, bloodied the nose of the farmer, and had made good progress along the path to being entirely drunk. They heard the thunder of hooves and tried to flee, and we rode them down and killed them all.

I marked a man and chased him as he fled … the horse leapt a fence, it was all a blur, he turned, stumbling, and I struck him full on the face with my sword. That is my memory, the look of terror in his eyes as my sword came down, and the feeling of horror that I had done such a thing. I was not Achilles; this man was not Hector. The poor fellow stood no chance against a galloping warhorse. In that moment I understood that, for all his faults, this man was the child of a mother in Naples, a mother who would never see her son again.

SIGNORA EMILIA: Now I wish I had not asked, my Lord, that you have had cause to recall such an ill memory.

DUKE LORENZO: I am glad you asked, Signora. Men in their cups brag incessantly about war. Often it is about japes and pranks; saddle straps loosened, noble lords falling face-first into horse dung, famous women of ill-repute, extraordinary loot, all the various ways in which men glorify the tedium of campaign.

But some men enjoy killing, and believe that all men should enjoy killing, and talk of little else. It is my observation that most men do not care to kill. Most men would sooner plough fields, cut timber, feed their families, carve stone, raise churches, and minister to the poor. How do you feel about Mars, Father?

FATHER GIOVANNI: That true courage is being resolute and firm in one's faith when confronted by an evil power, as were the holy martyrs of the Church.

DUKE LORENZO: So we might discover some quality of Mars even in saints?

DUCHESS YSABELLE: Perish that thought!

FATHER GIOVANNI: Forgive me, my Lady, but if we are to say that steadfastness in adversity, and being courageous and resolute even unto death, are marks of an admirable soldier, then we must recognise these qualities in our holy martyrs, even though they never held a sword or a pike.

SIGNORA EMILIA: Many holy martyrs have been women, who held fast to their faith, such as the blessed St. Catherine, who was put to death most cruelly. And have I not demonstrated that a woman can be martial? With sword and stance and firm visage?

FATHER GIOVANNI: You did Signora, and we all concurred. In truth, courage or fortitude has been judged a cardinal virtue since the time of the Greeks. Aquinas has much to say on this matter. I agree, Mars appears to be a cruel and bloodthirsty villain, but we might recall Michael warring with Satan and observe that there are two sides to conflict: that of righteousness, and that of evil. We might find in Michael a part of Mars that we can admire. That is how Dante views it. I recall those admirable Swiss in the Papal Guard who gave their lives to protect our Holy Father ... like Roland at Roncesvalles.

DUCHESS YSABELLE: So Mars may be tolerable or even admirable when he is bound by law.

DUKE LORENZO: The Romans had many laws and institutions to bind their generals and restrain their ambitions.

DUCHESS YSABELLE: And were they restrained?

DUKE LORENZO: In part; their laws were well conceived and executed. But when a man is exceedingly wealthy or popular he fancies that he can ignore the law, or make new laws to favour his own ambitions. When Caesar crossed the Rubicon with his army he broke the law and completed the destruction of the Republic.

SIGNORA EMILIA: So wealth is a friend to Mars, and an enemy of law and justice, for a man of sufficient wealth can purchase as many generals, and as much popularity as he desires.

DUKE LORENZO: For the most part I believe this is so. Many princes are now owned by their bankers. I believe the Fuggers own much of the Holy Roman Empire.

FATHER GIOVANNI: They exchange loans for monopolies, my Lord. It is a new kind of taxation; instead of the Emperor repaying interest and loan, the people are forced to buy from the Fuggers at monopoly prices. In this way the Fuggers evade laws on usury, and the Emperor can pretend that he has not raised taxes.

DUKE LORENZO: It is iniquitous. Perhaps we can thank the Fuggers for the army that sacked Rome.

DUCHESS YSABELLE: Are we owned by bankers, Husband?

DUKE LORENZO: I borrowed money for the new city gate.

DUCHESS YSABELLE: Which will not be proof against cannon.

DUKE LORENZO: It will not be proof against *large* cannon. The townsfolk find comfort in walls and gates.

DUCHESS YSABELLE: I wish they found more comfort in almshouses and hospices ... but they do not like to imagine themselves in old age. This has been most stimulating ... it seems that Mars is not so much the fearsome spirit I thought he might be. He has masters.

SIGNORA EMILIA: The god we should fear is Pluto, god of wealth. He keeps a large dog with three heads at his gate, to snarl and bark at intruders. Should we fear the dog, or should we fear the master who feeds him?

INTERLUDE

SIGNORA EMILIA: Ysabelle, if I may, a moment of your time.

DUCHESS YSABELLE: Please come in, be seated, it is always a delight to see you. I hope all is well.

SIGNORA EMILIA: I am all a-flutter. I lie awake at night, sleep does not come. My thoughts are a tumult, they jingle and jangle like a conclave of fools.

DUCHESS YSABELLE: Your heart is a-flutter? What is the cause of so much unease? An unwelcome marriage proposal? I have heard nothing.

SIGNORA EMILIA: I am reflecting upon myself, Ysabelle. Am I too forward? Am I an unruly woman? My husband said I was unruly. I would not wish the Duke to find me unruly.

DUCHESS YSABELLE: I recall your husband as having uncharitable opinions on many subjects.

SIGNORA EMILIA: A seed, once planted, grows by itself.

DUCHESS YSABELLE: But we should not nourish weeds. Unruly? Departing from his notion of womanhood? Riding? Dogs? Reading? Your dislike of needlework? Having an opinion on many subjects? Speaking out of turn?

SIGNORA EMILIA: Do I really? Speak out of turn?

DUCHESS YSABELLE: You do not. You are forthright in you opinions, as am I. What I meant was ... I thought your husband intolerant of your voice. Any opinion of yours was an offence to his ears.

SIGNORA EMILIA: I desired to be a good wife. I did not imagine I would be disregarded and diminished.

DUCHESS YSABELLE: You were a girl, he was your senior by some fifteen years, and he was not by nature a kind man. Industrious, capable, forceful in his opinions, and not kind. Is that a useful perspective? You were meek when he first encountered you, but you grew rapidly in learning and comprehension. Perhaps he desired that you remain meek and unlearned?

SIGNORA EMILIA: Your husband has several years advantage in age.

DUCHESS YSABELLE: I was older than you when we married, and my husband has never disregarded my voice.

SIGNORA EMILIA: Ah.

DUCHESS YSABELLE: I was fortunate ... we were fortunate. We had a private understanding before we married. You were fortunate in one sense: your husband's indifference to you was so complete that he left you to do as you pleased. You had a horse, and a groom, and dogs, you could ride with hunts, you could employ tutors, you had the use of several collections of books, including our own.

SIGNORA EMILIA: We had some friendship while we hunted together. It was his passion, he would talk of little else. But while I carried and tended my daughters we saw little of each other, and he grew impatient with me.

DUCHESS YSABELLE: But today the issue is not your husband, but mine?

INTERLUDE

SIGNORA EMILIA: If I may explain. You may find me foolish, my concerns childish. I feel ill-at-ease. Men are tutored for public life and are instructed in rhetoric and grammar. They study works on the arts of persuasion—Cicero in the first instance—and are tested in public debate. Some are instructed in law and statecraft, others in philosophy. Even those with less learning go to war and meet in council, and are familiar with the rhythm of debate. They learn when to speak, when to be silent, what is implied but unspoken, what is widely understood. Men are accustomed to address each other on matters of consequence.

Women are kept from these things: from council, from law, from war, from study, from all seniority in the Church. How childish we must seem. Yes, we may talk of trifles ... how pretty the roses are this spring; do I prefer the *galliard* or the *pavane*; whom is the greater hero, Orlando or Rinaldo; is Orlando Furioso long-winded and tedious; how can the sonnet be improved ... but what if there is to be a new law? Does anyone solicit my opinion? I am of no consequence in this matter, no more to be consulted than a child or a horse.

DUCHESS YSABELLE: You fear that my husband humours your opinions out of courtesy?

SIGNORA EMILIA: He is too practised at courtesy to reveal his thoughts, but he must judge me as he judges others. I fear that as we address matters of consequence, I will seem both forward and foolish.

DUCHESS YSABELLE: Let me reassure you, my husband does not find you foolish. He remarked that you remind him of Isabella d'Este.

SIGNORA EMILIA: Isabella d'Este! You jest! Perhaps he was being flippant?

DUCHESS YSABELLE: He was not being flippant, so put your mind at rest.

SIGNORA EMILIA: When last we met, and we spoke of Mars, I was afraid, not only for myself, but for my daughters. I was angry that some day I must instruct them about lust and evil men. It is just as Father Giovanni said, where there is fear there is anger, and where there is anger, words are spoken incautiously. I felt that I might go beyond the bounds of courtesy and cause offence.

And now we will speak of Jupiter, and I must struggle not to berate the world with my feelings and opinions.

DUCHESS YSABELLE: I understand that you might feel so with Mars, for I share your fear and outrage ... but why Jupiter?

SIGNORA EMILIA: We must speak of power, and custom, and law, which are the substance of all society. The law is a great power, power that is granted to some, and denied to others. In this matter, how can I tame my mind and bridle my tongue? Law is made by men for the convenience of men. Mars does violence to some women, but Jupiter does violence to all women. First we are governed by our fathers, and then we are married and sent off to be governed by our husbands. We are denied all but the meanest forms of employment. We may govern ourselves only if we wish to be wretched and despised and live in poverty.

DUCHESS YSABELLE: And this is why you are all a-flutter. In what manner can we speak of governance without observing that we are the governed? All the pearls, and golden braid, and silken weave, cannot conceal the fact that we depend upon the good judgement and good humour of our men, and when they are lacking we suffer in consequence ... and there is no court we can turn to.

SIGNORA EMILIA: That is it Ysabelle, in its entirety! I feel this most keenly; I am not the mistress of my fate.

DUCHESS YSABELLE: And you desire the good opinion of the Duke, and feel you must speak with care.

SIGNORA EMILIA: I desire the good opinion of the Duke.

DUCHESS YSABELLE: We must both tread warily ... I am not without personal feeling in this matter. Let me attempt to lead, and you may play the accompaniment.

SIGNORA EMILIA: Thank you ... and a thought ... the women of Rome turned to Juno for protection. What does Jupiter offer women,

apart from rape in a multitude of strange guises? I do not know. If
we are to have Jupiter, let us also have Juno.

DUCHESS YSABELLE: An inspired and wicked thought! Let us insist
upon Juno.

LIBER SPHÆRÆ

SPHÆRA JOVIS

Muses, I begin with Jove; with Jove all things are full.
He protects the earth, my songs are his concern ...
Virgil, Eclogues

DUCHESS YSABELLE: Please be seated Father. Today I have placed us in the banqueting hall, and so this table and its seating lacks the intimacy of our previous gatherings.

FATHER GIOVANNI: Yes, very spacious, very grand. And what a feast of delicacies!

SIGNORA EMILIA: Ysabelle! So many dainty dishes to tempt us! I must give thanks to the cooks.

DUKE LORENZO: Ah, I see ... are you summoning the spirits of Jupiter, who love great banquets and display? Are we to be pagans?

DUCHESS YSABELLE: We are many cattle short of being pagans, Husband—this is merely a small celebration and spirits may attend if they choose. The Greeks sacrificed their cattle in hundreds ... what did they call it Emilia, a century of cattle, one hundred cattle?

183

SIGNORA EMILIA: Homer talks of *hecatombs*, a sacrifice of one hundred cattle. They counted their sacrifices in hecatombs.

DUCHESS YSABELLE: You see Husband, we are some way short of even *one* hecatomb. Why, there are no cows to be seen, none whatsoever. Do you concur that we are not pagans, Father?

FATHER GIOVANNI: There are no sacred fires here. It was the smoke and smell of burning flesh rising to heaven that honoured the pagan gods ... and even the God of Israel in the days when they burned their sacrifices in the Temple in Jerusalem. I believe these pastries and sweetmeats and this excellent vintage will merely summon smiles and good humour.

DUCHESS YSABELLE: And you will bless our repast Father, to dispel any doubts that we might be pagans?

FATHER GIOVANNI: Of course:

> Benedic nos Domine et haec Tua dona quae de Tua largitate
> sumus sumpturi. Per Christum Dominum nostrum. Mensae
> caelestis participes faciat nos, Rex aeternae gloriae. Amen.

We may now be jovial without peril to our souls.

DUCHESS YSABELLE: Thank you Father, let us eat and drink and ... as you say Father ... be jovial, and let us begin our discussion. Husband, I need not ask what you have brought. It might evoke fear if it was not so distressed by time and neglect.

DUKE LORENZO: Indeed, this eagle was once the monarch of the air and now it flies in terror of moths. I asked the Master of the hunt to question the huntsmen about eagle feathers—they pick them up and sell them, they can look brave in a cap, as you know—and he discovered this eagle that a huntsman had attempted to preserve by filling it with the sawdust from a cedar tree, and wool, and sundry other matters. Behold, it has glass drops for eyes. Very ingenious, very commendable, if somewhat lacking in refinement.

DUCHESS YSABELLE: If Jovian spirits attend at our feast they will be dismayed to see this magnificent creature brought so low. But it is an eagle for all that, and you have a purpose and a message no doubt.

Duke Lorenzo: The eagle is the bird of Jupiter. It signifies power, dominion, and victory. The Romans mounted a bronze eagle upon a staff, and in its claws it held the lightning bolts of Jupiter (for the eagle would fetch and return the bolts after Jove had cast them). The eagle was the standard of a legion, carried into battle, and it was a mark of utmost shame to lose it to the foe. And as you know the eagle is still the mark of the Holy Roman Emperor.

Duchess Ysabelle: Except the German eagle has two heads ... an even more eccentric specimen.

Duke Lorenzo: Indeed, it has two heads, one threatening force of arms, the other reciting liturgy and doctrine.

It seems to me that the essence of Jupiter is power. Mars is the power of arms and force, and as we have observed, at its root or source this power is essentially lawless and unprincipled. Jupiter has a greater power still but this power serves the needs of justice and it upholds the law. Without law there is no society, and without justice there is no law. Without power, there is no justice.

Duchess Ysabelle: These are heady propositions husband, and we will debate them in due course. Emilia, what token of Jupiter have you brought?

Signora Emilia: I have Homer. There is a passage in the *Iliad* where Achilles talks to his mother Thetis about the injustice of King Agamemnon, and so Thetis ascends to Zeus and asks a favour, which Zeus grants. Zeus summons all the gods of Olympus and announces his decree, which is that none may assist either Greek or Trojan in the coming battles. The passage is long, but I find it most revealing, and I will read it if you please?

Duke Lorenzo: I would be delighted to hear it Signora.

Signora Emilia:

> Now as the Dawn flung out her golden robe across the earth,
> Zeus who loves the lightning summoned all the gods to
> assembly on the topmost peak of ridged Olympus.
>
> He harangued the immortals hanging on his words:

"Hear me, all you gods and all goddesses too, as I proclaim what the heart inside me urges.

Let no lovely goddess — and no god either — try to fight against my strict decree.

All submit to it now, so all the more quickly I can bring this violent business to an end.

And any god I catch, breaking ranks with us, eager to go and help the Trojans or Achaeans — back he comes to Olympus, whipped by the lightning, eternally disgraced.

Or I will snatch and hurl him down to the murk of Tartarus half the world away, the deepest gulf that yawns beneath the ground, there where the iron gates and brazen threshold loom, as far below the House of Death as the sky rides over earth — then he will know how far my power tops all other gods.

Come, try me, immortals, so all of you can learn.

Hang a great golden cable down from the heavens, lay hold of it, all you gods, all goddesses too: you can never drag me down from sky to earth, not Zeus, the highest, mightiest king of kings, not even if you worked yourselves to death.

But whenever I'd set my mind to drag you up, in deadly earnest, I'd hoist you all with ease, you and the earth, you and the sea, all together, then loop that golden cable round a horn of Olympus, bind it fast and leave the whole world dangling in mid-air — that is how far I tower over the gods, I tower over men."

There are three parts to this. Firstly, there is the announcement of his decree; then there is a threat of terrible punishment; and lastly there is a boast of irresistible power.

FATHER GIOVANNI: He enacts an inviolable decree as a personal favour—how very Italian.

DUKE LORENZO: And that is the nature of power, having the freedom to act as one pleases.

FATHER GIOVANNI: I see that, my Lord ... forgive me Signora, pray continue.

SIGNORA EMILIA: Thank you Father. My reading from Homer was inspired by my thoughts on dominion, by which I signify that province of choices where a person is free to act. Zeus has absolute dominion. He can do whatsoever he pleases. He boasts that none has the power to oppose him, and that any who offend him will be struck down or sent to Hell. His decree is law. And we see that where there is absolute power there is no justice, for none may object and be heard.

DUKE LORENZO: Indeed, there is no justice in your example, merely the tyranny of the greater upon the lesser. My thanks Signora, you have delineated the history of Italy, in which the strong invariably prey upon the weak. To possess justice the power of the nobility must first be circumscribed by law ... but lawyers are tedious and long-winded, and it is always more glorious to pay mercenaries and wage war. If only we had a king or emperor to mediate our squabbles ... but instead we have both, a French king and a German emperor, a superfluity of rule.

And how is a king to be restrained? The Romans grew weary of the abuse of kings and made a republic.

SIGNORA EMILIA: And did they then obtain justice, my Lord?

DUKE LORENZO: They obtained a better semblance of it, Signora. They were most particular about dominion, setting out the rights and duties of any public official and the span of time in which they could be exercised. The scope of punishments was defined, for a Roman found it shameful to be scourged, or beaten, or crucified, like a slave. Also a right of appeal in cases where legal decisions were contested. Perhaps their greatest innovation was to place public funds under the control of the Senate, which provided an excellent means to restrain an ambitious magistrate. In direst emergencies they would appoint a dictator for a limited span of time.

SIGNORA EMILIA: Thank you, my Lord.

DUCHESS YSABELLE: Zeus reminds me of my father. He did not liked to be crossed.

DUKE LORENZO: Oh, he did not like to be crossed ... I learnt when to hold my tongue. But he gave me your hand, and so I cannot speak ill of him.

DUCHESS YSABELLE: How sweet, after all these years you are still gallant. But speaking of fathers, I have not asked Father Giovanni whether he has brought some token of Jupiter.

FATHER GIOVANNI: Thank you, my Lady. I have here this familiar tome. Once again I have brought my Ptolemy, so that we might discover how the rays of Jupiter impinge upon the soul. Before I begin I will say that Jupiter is *Fortuna Major*, a beneficent and kindly power, and when well-positioned he brings many great qualities into this world. Let me begin ...

> If Jupiter alone has domination of the soul, in honourable positions he makes his subjects magnanimous, generous, god-fearing, honourable, pleasure-loving, kind, magnificent, liberal, just, high-minded, dignified, minding their own business, compassionate, fond of discussion, beneficent, affectionate, with qualities of leadership.

> If he chances to be in the opposite kind of position, he makes their souls seem similar, to be sure, but with a difference in the direction of greater humility, less conspicuousness, and poorer judgement. For example, instead of magnanimity, he endows them with prodigality; instead of reverence for the gods, with superstition, instead of modesty, with cowardice, instead of dignity, with conceit; instead of kindness, with foolish simplicity, instead of love of beauty, with love of pleasure, instead of high-mindedness, with stupidity, instead of liberality, with indifference, and the like.

He continues at some length concerning how the influence of other planets is mixed with that of Jupiter, but I think we are now sufficiently informed to devise our own *Tetrabiblos*.

DUKE LORENZO: Thank you Father. When the soul is blessed by Jupiter we have the admirable prince, respected by all; when ill-aspected, we have the despicable prince who brings about the ruination of his state and his people. If only all kings and princes were blessed by Jupiter. I am intrigued by how easily an apparent virtue descends into a vice, as when generosity becomes prodigality.

FATHER GIOVANNI: I think Ptolemy borrows this notion from Aristotle, who noted that the impulse that leads to courage is the same impulse that leads to recklessness. In this passage Ptolemy gives us qualities that, when prudently exercised, lead to virtue, and when imprudently exercised, lead to folly.

SIGNORA EMILIA: I have a thought ... if one can say that Venus is that feeling of particular loves, narrow loves, passionate attachments, the love of one-to-one, then it seems to me that Jupiter brings a more general and less narrow disposition towards benevolence, the love of one to many ... Jupiter manifests as an out-flowing of goodness, like the cornucopia. There is a noble feeling of beneficence and charity that resembles the Christian ideal.

DUCHESS YSABELLE: I see that Emilia, like the blessed Saint Francis, being poor and humble, but rich in spirit, loving all life equally.

DUKE LORENZO: But as we discussed during the first of these pleasant meetings, we live in a world of Necessity. The cornucopia of practical benevolence is finite. We must check these feelings with reason and prudence lest we beggar ourselves.

FATHER GIOVANNI: I would say so, my Lord. There are pious Christian souls who say that we should surrender our possessions to the poor and live a perfect Christian life, depending upon God for our daily bread. Indeed, our Lord councils this, to live as do the birds:

> Look at the birds of the air, for they neither sow nor reap nor
> gather into barns; yet your heavenly Father feeds them.

But I have seen many who, through ill-fortune, are forced to depend upon God for their sustenance. Their crops have withered through drought. A river has flooded and drowned their crops. Hail has stripped their vines. Brigands have emptied their stores. They would have starved but for the industry, prudence, and charity of others.

DUCHESS YSABELLE: I agree Father ... I was about to say that we need not check our feelings of love, that love is boundless and does not diminish, but now I recall how it is with children. I love them with all my heart, but each day I find I must set boundaries to my love so that they learn discipline and prudence.

DUKE LORENZO: We return to prudence again ... she must be the queen of the virtues.

LIBER SPHÆRÆ

DUCHESS YSABELLE: Our children must learn right measure in everything they do.

DUKE LORENZO: Right measure ... you speak of the Golden Mean ... draw the bowstring too little and the arrow does not fly; draw it too far and the bow breaks.

SIGNORA EMILIA: It seems to me that when we speak of prudence we speak of practical wisdom, or right measure, or—as you say my Lord—the Golden Mean. We speak of Necessity and that miserly portion of abundance granted to us by Fortune, a measure that we must administer with prudence. Jupiter is not bound by Necessity, and so the inherent tendency in Jupiter does not tend towards prudence. The kingly Jupiter tends towards abundance, magnificence, grandeur and display.

DUKE LORENZO: An excellent observation Signora ... and how Italians love display!

DUCHESS YSABELLE: If only they did not hate taxes.

DUKE LORENZO: Herein is an essay in statecraft. Kings and princes love magnificence and despise prudence. Splendour shows that they are truly anointed by God, that they are blessed by divine providence. The more excessive the displays—fountains flowing with wine, jewels worth as much as a fortress—the more the people are persuaded that their prince is divinely appointed.

DUCHESS YSABELLE: And then there are taxes.

DUKE LORENZO: And then there are taxes. I recall an example from the days of our fathers, and doubtless you will have heard some account of events. Ludovico Sforza of Milan, known as *Il Moro* because of his complexion, ruled Milan as regent on behalf of his nephew Gian Galleazzo, who was the legitimate heir. The splendour of Ludovico's court was famous across Europe. He commissioned works from the finest artists of the day, including the extraordinary Leonardo. He blessed the city with noble buildings, showered gifts upon the Church, and enjoyed courtly diversions on a scale that even Jupiter might envy. In this manner he impressed upon the citizens of Milan that divine providence had chosen him as their Duke, and not his nephew, who died mysteriously.

But they wearied of taxes. When the French came to contest the city, the townsfolk opened the gates, and Ludovico spent the remainder of his life in a French prison.

Machiavelli of Florence expounds upon this topic in his little book for the tuition of princes. He counsels against extravagent displays and generosity. He asserts that one can purchase affection but it does not endure, for as soon as spectacles and displays and public largess cease (as they must eventually) people will grumble and grow resentful, especially if gold has been borrowed and must be repaid out of taxes.

FATHER GIOVANNI: The temptation of borrowed gold is the first folly of new princes. They desire that the world acknowledge their greatness, and so they must deck themselves with magnificence.

DUKE LORENZO: As you say Father—it is easy to be lavish with borrowed gold. With a sufficient store of corn I could be be king of the pigeons ... but only a fool would confuse the appetite of a bird with affection. So what is better than affection? Machiavelli advises that it is better to be feared than to be loved ... that it is folly to purchase affection with benevolence.

FATHER GIOVANNI: It is written: 'The beginning of wisdom is the fear of the Lord'.

DUCHESS YSABELLE: Where is this written Father?

FATHER GIOVANNI: In the book of Solomon known as *Proverbs*, my Lady.

DUCHESS YSABELLE: But are we not instructed to love God with all our hearts?

FATHER GIOVANNI: In the words of Jesus: you should love the Lord your God with all your heart, and with all your soul, and with all your mind, and with all your strength. Love brings us closer to God. But it is also written that Moses asked to see the glory of the Lord, and the Lord replied 'You cannot see My face; for no man shall see Me, and live'.

191

Here is a parable of my own devising. A boy listened to stories about the sea, and of voyages to exotic lands, so that he fell in love with the sea, and with ships. He resolved to travel to the sea, and find a ship, and so he bade farewell to his parents and set off towards the coast. The road to the nearest port travelled along a high cliff above the sea, and the wind was fierce, and waves crashed against the rocks, and white spray flew high in the air. The immensity of the sea was a steel-grey froth of waves and foam, and the love in the boy's heart—love that had sustained him throughout his journey—turned to fear. In his fear the boy had touched the beginning of wisdom.

SIGNORA EMILIA: Did he become a sailor, Father?

FATHER GIOVANNI: Did the boy become wise in the ways of the sea? Perhaps he did ... some men do, just as some become wise in the ways of the Lord.

SIGNORA EMILIA: Ovid tells the story of Jupiter and Semele. Juno was enraged to see that Semele was swollen with the child of Jupiter, and so she visited her in the shape of an aged nurse. In this guise she asked: 'How do you know this fellow was Jupiter? Men are conniving rogues, they will say anything to deceive a maiden. You should ask this so-called Jupiter to reveal himself in all his glory, just as he does when he beds with Juno his wife—then you will know if he speaks truly'.

So Semele asked Jupiter to grant her a boon, and Jupiter swore on the Styx that he would grant anything that she asked. Semele asked Jupiter to reveal himself in all his glory, just as Juno had intended. I have the *Metamorphoses* here, and I will read it, for none can better Ovid in his mastery of words:

> To keep his promise he ascends, and shrouds
> His awful brow in whirlwinds and in clouds;
> Whilst all around, in terrible array,
> His thunders rattle, and his lightnings play.
> And yet, the dazzling lustre to abate,
> He set not out in all his pomp and state,
> Clad in the mildest lightning of the skies,

And armed with thunder of the smallest size:
Not those huge bolts, by which the giants slain
Lay overthrown on the Phlegrean plain.
'Twas of a lesser mould, and lighter weight;
They call it thunder of a second-rate,
For the rough Cyclops, who by Jove's command
Tempered the bolt, and turned it to his hand,
Worked up less flame and fury in its make,
And quenched it sooner in the standing lake.
Thus dreadfully adorned, with horror bright,
Th' illustrious God, descending from his height,
Came rushing on her in a storm of light.
The mortal dame, too feeble to engage
The lightning's flashes, and the thunder's rage,
Consumed amidst the glories she desired,
And in the terrible embrace expired.

Even the most feeble of Jove's thunders was more than a mortal body could withstand.

FATHER GIOVANNI: I have always felt pity for poor Semele; Juno played a low trick upon her. But I suppose this story shows us, as does your extract from the *Iliad*, how divine majesty humbles gods and men, and in this matter the Greeks and Hebrews share a common understanding. Such power is far beyond our comprehension or emulation.

Men seek the trappings of majesty with gilt, and jewels, and banners, and trumpets, but these have no more substance than the illusions of a masque or pageant. Why, the Roman emperors declared themselves to be gods and decorated their standards with eagles and the lightning bolts of Jupiter, but alas, they were only men, and died as any other men.

DUKE LORENZO: It is your task, Father, to remind us to be humble before God.

FATHER GIOVANNI: Thank you, my Lord, I feared that you might detect the odour of treason in my remarks, that I might be a closet republican ... or worse still, that I nurture a grudge, for all of the majesty of the Church has passed me by. I console myself with the works of Solomon, who had all the glory a man could desire and yet he preferred righteousness and wisdom.

It is a sign of my declining years that I have forsworn all the trappings of glory and content myself with a worthy book and a sound night's rest.

DUCHESS YSABELLE: Come Father, despite your preference for Solomon, you are not so old. And you know very well that it is your counsel we value, not jewelled rings and golden medals, and a marbled villa in Tivoli. The rewards of the Church are awarded to allies of the mighty, and rarely to the pious.

This is Italy; the first thing a new Pope does is hand out red caps to his nephews so that he might have allies in the College of Cardinals, and in the Curia. There are cardinals who have only just begun to trim their beards, and are as proficient in Latin as a fishmonger.

FATHER GIOVANNI: This is so, my Lady, and it has been the custom for so long we have lost all shame in the matter.

DUCHESS YSABELLE: Tell me Father, do you recall a case where a Pope handed out red caps to his nieces?

FATHER GIOVANNI: You jest, my Lady!

DUCHESS YSABELLE: I do not jest! I admit that my question is rhetorical, but I do not jest, for I have a end in mind. We all know that the Church does not admit women to positions where they would be in power over men. Even when a woman is a paragon of learning and virtue, such as the famous Hildegard, she will never be permitted to ordain priests or administer the primary sacraments of the Church.

FATHER GIOVANNI: This is so, my Lady.

DUCHESS YSABELLE: There is the story of a Pope Joan, who disguised herself as a man and rose in the Church to become Pope, but when her guise was revealed, she was bound to a horse and dragged through the streets, while being stoned until she was dead. Doubtless you know this story?

FATHER GIOVANNI: I do, my Lady. According to accounts, her name was stricken from the list of Popes, and now her tale is accounted a fabrication.

DUCHESS YSABELLE: True or not, it is the exception that proves the rule ... that women who enter the Church must accept the dominion of men.

FATHER GIOVANNI: That is so.

DUCHESS YSABELLE: And now I will turn to secular law. Husband, in your knowledge, has there ever been a women who was a magistrate in this city?

DUKE LORENZO: It sounds improbable. I have never heard of such a thing.

DUCHESS YSABELLE: In the entire history of Rome was a woman appointed as magistrate? A woman with the same dominion as a man?

DUKE LORENZO: Again, I have never encountered such a thing. There were women of considerable power and influence both within Rome and without, such as Zenobia, Queen of Palmyra.

DUCHESS YSABELLE: But this was happenstance. Even today we find cases where a woman acts as regent for her son and gains fame through skillful governance and martial vigour—I am thinking now of Caterina Sforza of Forli and Imola. But what of election to office? Is there a community of men who would elect a woman to have dominion over them, in the way that cardinals elect a Pope? In the way that the Great Council of Venice elects a Doge? In the way that magistrates are chosen in this city?

DUKE LORENZO: Women would be excluded as candidates ... is this germane to our discussion?

DUCHESS YSABELLE: You have said that Jupiter signifies, among other things, power and dominion, and so I will say yes, it is germane ... to myself and to the Signora Emilia. As women we have our own view on this matter.

You acknowledge that sometimes power and dominion are granted to a woman through exceptional circumstances, and for a limited duration, as in a regency, but never to my knowledge through election or promotion.

DUKE LORENZO: It would cause an outcry if a woman was nominated for a public office.

DUCHESS YSABELLE: It would cause an outcry. The dominion of a woman ends at the walls of her husband's house, and even within the house she is concerned solely with servants, and meals, and children and the like, for she has little property in her own name. Perhaps her husband is travelling or at war, and he permits her some role in administration, but it is done in his name and with his seal.

DUKE LORENZO: Do I hear a note of grievance?

DUCHESS YSABELLE: Not for myself, I count myself fortunate and give thanks to God. However, we have chosen to discuss Jupiter and so it falls upon us to understand dominion in fullness. I have an end in sight and a path I wish to travel.

DUKE LORENZO: Then let us travel with you.

DUCHESS YSABELLE: Thank you Husband. Let us examine dominion as does a surgeon. What is dominion? It is that which is ruled over. The dominion of a man is his land, his property, his wife and children, and his wealth. If he is of noble blood his dominion includes estates, men-at-arms, servants, and tenants. If he is in mercantile trade or manufacture, his dominion includes warehouses, artisans, factors, clerks, and possibly ships and sailors, an invisible empire that he rules just as the noble rules his castles and estates. More intangible still is the dominion of the banker, who rules an empire of deposits and loans and obligations. Even the most humble man, the *pater familias*, rules over his family.

FATHER GIOVANNI: I was about to say that the dominion of the priest is still more intangible, ruling over hearts and minds, then I recalled that the Pope rules over a large part of Italy.

DUKE LORENZO: But you remind us that some have a dominion over hearts and minds, a power that comes from their inner qualities: sagacity, learning, eloquence, courage, and good fortune. I recall the priest Savonarola who, through passion, conviction, and innate *charisma*, roused the Florentines, ousted the Medici, and ruled the city for some years.

DUCHESS YSABELLE: And many women also possess the inner qualities to exercise dominion over others, but have no place or pulpit from which they may be heard. And now I approach my point: is there a place in these schemes of dominion for an ambitious woman? We have discussed this ... there is not. Not through inheritance, not in public office, not through trade, not in the Church ... there are no red caps for nieces. Apart from accidental circumstances, women are excluded from dominion, and are under the dominion of their fathers or husbands.

So we must conclude that Jupiter is not a god for women. Jupiter is not a god who cares for my ambitions or successes, no more than does Mars. I could sacrifice an hundred cattle and Jupiter would turn his head and ignore me. In the days of Rome, a man of ambition desiring power over other men might offer prayers to Jupiter, but it would be useless for a woman to pray for such a thing. To whom should a woman turn?

SIGNORA EMILIA: Now you must show us what you have brought Ysabelle!

DUCHESS YSABELLE: Now is the time. I will fetch it from concealment. Behold!

DUKE LORENZO: Ah ... you seek to trump my dowdy bird with better feathers! And brighter!

DUCHESS YSABELLE: But do you know why?

DUKE LORENZO: I do not.

FATHER GIOVANNI: The peacock is the bird of Juno, who is wife of Jupiter, and ever watchful of his philandering and adulteries.

DUKE LORENZO: I hope you do not think that of me!

DUCHESS YSABELLE: I do not think that. Emilia and I were discussing Jupiter and concluded, as you have heard, that he is not a god for women. Emilia recalled that the women of Rome turned to Juno for their protection. The peacock is the bird of Juno. Perhaps you will tell the tale, Emilia?

SIGNORA EMILIA: Before I begin I will say that Jupiter seeks to fill the world with his offspring, and violates nymphs and maidens in many guises: as a bull, as a golden shower of rain, as a swan, and so on. Juno, who is both his sister and his wife, seeks to restrain his wandering lust, and punishes his paramours according to her whim. This couple are often at odds.

I will tell the tale of Io. Ovid embroiders the tale of Io with an abundance of beautiful details. There is a tale within a tale, the story of Syrinx, and how Pan first made the pipes that shepherds use to pass the time during the heat of the day ... but I will be brief.

Zeus, seated upon his throne, spied the river nymph Io, and descended from Olympus to have his way with her. Juno, ever-watchful and suspicious, descended fast after him, and so Zeus transformed Io into a cow. Juno was not deceived by this. She took Io and she tasked Argus the Hundred-Eyed to watch over her. Argus was ever watchful because only two eyes would sleep and the rest would remain awake day and night.

Jupiter, not to be outwitted, asked his son Mercury to slay Argus. Mercury pretended to be a shepherd and lulled all the eyes of Argus to sleep using his magic wand and his shepherd pipes. Then he struck off his head. As a token of faithful service Juno placed the eyes of Argus upon the tail of the peacock, and this is why the peacock's tail is a sign of the goddess Juno.

DUKE LORENZO: Now I see. And of what use is Juno to women?

SIGNORA EMILIA: She is the queen of Heaven and protector of women. She has dominion over women, and marriages, and children, just those things that concern us, for we have little else to fuss over. She keeps watch upon erring husbands, and visits upon them a multitude of strange and whimsical misfortunes.

FATHER GIOVANNI: You would place Juno within the Sphere of Jupiter— even though there is no planet of that name?

C.A.L. 2021

SIGNORA EMILIA: Perhaps the bright star we call Jupiter is doubled, but too close to be discerned.

FATHER GIOVANNI: And remaining in a close conjunction?

SIGNORA EMILIA: They are husband and wife.

FATHER GIOVANNI: Even though one of the pair is the famously erring Jupiter?

SIGNORA EMILIA: He may err in bed, but he is constant in the sky ... apart from when he moves backwards against the stars.

DUKE LORENZO: I am curious ... if Juno could represent the case of women to Jupiter, what might she ask for?

SIGNORA EMILIA: That we can own property in our own names, and administer our affairs without the permission of a husband. That we can nominate heirs that might include both sons and daughters. I understand the argument, that this would split the wealth of families, that the wealth and power of families would be fragmented, and in Italy a family needs whatever power it can accrue. But if a man is judged according to his property, then so is a woman, and without property we will always be beholden to the demands of others.

That we need not cohabit with a man, and that we have the right to divorce. The Church will object, but in bygone days Roman women were permitted to divorce. I do not understand why a woman should endure the embrace of a man who is distasteful to her.

That we might find employment in worthy occupations, entering into guilds, or studying law and philosophy, just as you did, my Lord. And lastly ... that we should be eligible for public office and sit as magistrates and the like.

DUKE LORENZO: These are remarkable demands! I see that Juno has a practical turn of mind.

SIGNORA EMILIA: She does, my Lord, for she has a famously erring husband and must look to her own advantage ... but they are not remarkable. With the exception of divorce, which the Church forbids, the men of this court would consider these requests as their

birthright. As for eligibility, women should be judged as men are
... not according to any merit or competence , but according the
influence and status of their family.

DUCHESS YSABELLE: I see this rose has thorns. Let me intervene. I
sought this discussion, but now I will end it, for it began like a
small stream and quickly became a tumult. It seems to me that
women must demonstrate their virtues and bide their time until a
better age will see their worth. Let us return to your propositions,
Husband, something about law, justice and power.

DUKE LORENZO: Ah, indeed, let me collect my thoughts. In the case
of the sack of Rome, we have heard many reports of what happens
when men are permitted to act without restraint or fear of punishment: theft, torture, the violation of women, murder. No society
is possible under these conditions ... indeed, much of Rome fled,
for civic life had become impossible.

All societies have laws against such things, but a company of
lawyers armed with writs and restraints would not have calmed
Rome. There must be an apparatus for the administration of justice,
and it must have sufficient power to create fear among the lawless—
I speak of the Bargello and his men, the prisons and jailers, and the
hangman.

But we cannot permit citizens to be taken and punished simply
because of spite, bad report, or gossip, and so justice rests in the
hands of our magistrates, who are appointed or elected as the case
may be. Ultimately our citizens look to me to oversee all parts of
this: that laws are reviewed, that lawyers are respected, that magistrates enforce our laws and are fair in their judgements, and that
the Bargello and his men instil fear among the lawless—but do not
break too many doors or heads without good cause.

As you will know, I hear appeals concerning verdicts on a
Wednesday morning. I meet with the Bargello routinely. I have a
formal meeting with the magistrates each month. It is in this
manner that I uphold the rule of law. My good wife, in the manner
of Juno, surveys the city for any injustice done to women and
brings these to my attention. How do you accomplish this?

DUCHESS YSABELLE: I am well-known in the churches and hospices of the city. Women talk to priests, and priests arrange for them to meet with me.

FATHER GIOVANNI: Your work in the city is well-known, my Lady, and inspires great loyalty among the womenfolk.

DUCHESS YSABELLE: Thank you, Father. It was not my intention to sound boastful or to seek praise. I am conscious that the Wheel of Lady Fortune is ever turning, and any one of us might need the aid and charity of others. Who was that Roman who wrote a book about the transitory nature of power and success, how the Wheel of Fortune can bring any man low? He wrote it in prison?

FATHER GIOVANNI: Perhaps you mean Boethius, my Lady, *The Consolations of Philosophy*. He was an adviser to King Theodoric the Great, but his enemies caused him to be thrown into prison and executed.

DUKE LORENZO: An unjust end to a noble Roman. There is no accounting for the whims of fortune ... why, look at Cesare Borgia. At one point it seemed as though he was fated to rule half of Italy. Then his father Pope Alexander died unexpectedly. Cesare was taken by a fever as his enemies marshalled against him ... then he was betrayed by a friend in Naples, and transported to a prison in Spain.

And that is but the half of it. It is said that he caught the French disease in Naples, so that he wore a leather mask to conceal the ruin of his features. And he died a violent death, ambushed and stripped naked of everything but his mask. Never was a man so embraced by good fortune and then cast out into the night.

DUCHESS YSABELLE: And that is why we should be humble and charitable, lest Fortune find us obnoxious. Father, it is said that power corrupts. It is your task to guard us from the wiles of the evil one. In what manner does power corrupt?

FATHER GIOVANNI: Power resembles a reading glass, my Lady, for it magnifies all the sins, and some in particular. Who does not, at some time, desire to oppress their neighbours? Seize their jewels? Own their vineyards, and drink their vintages?

DUKE LORENZO: So true Father ... the first impulse of power in Italy is to slander one's enemies, drive them into exile, and seize their properties.

FATHER GIOVANNI: What better way to pay off one's debts? We have become a covetous people, and for this reason it is written: you shall not covet your neighbour's house, you shall not covet your neighbour's wife, or his male or female servant, his ox or donkey, or anything that belongs to your neighbour.

But why do we covet? Because our lives are precarious, and so we envy those with power and wealth. We imagine that they sleep better than we do. But they do not, for they have felt envy themselves, and so they imagine treachery in every shadow, insincerity in every smile, and inwardly recoil from every kiss as if it were from Judas.

SIGNORA EMILIA: Dante has the ninth and final circle of Hell given over to traitors.

DUKE LORENZO: And rightly so! I recall that Satan chews upon Judas Iscariot?

SIGNORA EMILIA: He does, my Lord. And Brutus and Cassius.

DUCHESS YSABELLE: So we have envy and covetousness, and perhaps murder and theft. In what other ways do those with power give offence to the Lord?

FATHER GIOVANNI: Lust and gluttony, my Lady. When I was in Rome I passed distinguished houses that catered to the immoderate lusts of the wealthier members of the clergy. These houses are now looted and despoiled, but no doubt they will return to their business as wealth returns to the city.

As for gluttony, I view this sin not merely as overeating. Some are possessed of a temperament that will not be restrained by prudence or sufficiency, tending always to excess. Our cardinals compete to create the finest palaces and villas, and the only criterion by which they are judged is excess. It is in these monuments to power and extraordinary wealth that they parade their vanities and hold banquets unseen since the most unprincipled eras of Roman history.

I will mention one other aspect of this power that causes me offence. These prelates are charged to provide guidance to the people, and as they lead dissolute lives, they must necessarily become the most consummate hypocrites. They preach, but they do not practice. In this matter I accept any criticisms the Lutherans care to make.

DUCHESS YSABELLE: Truly Father, you would say such a thing? Giving credence to the Lutherans?

FATHER GIOVANNI: I would, my Lady. Impious hypocrites offend me more than pious Lutherans.

DUCHESS YSABELLE: You think the Church has become wicked?

FATHER GIOVANNI: I believe the church is cursed with too many nephews. The wastrel sons of noble families are appointed bishops and cardinals. They are more inclined to the pleasures of the flesh— which they have abundant wealth to enjoy—than to upholding and spreading the word of God.

DUKE LORENZO: You speak truly, Father. The princes of the Church are princes first. They govern cities and states as princes, they plot and scheme as princes, they build their palaces as princes, and they entertain as princes. They dress as priests, and we kiss their rings, but we know they are princes and that in their hearts they remain sons of the Farnese, or the Colonna, the Orsini, the d'Este, the Medici, or the della Rovere. If there is some spark of piety or holiness in the man, then we give praise to God. Alas, we cannot repair the Church unless we repair Italy and rectify human nature.

DUCHESS YSABELLE: This talk of power and sin is unsettling.

DUKE LORENZO: It is. I feel as if I have slept in a strange bed and must now examine myself for fleas and lice.

DUCHESS YSABELLE: We should eat and be merry ... Father, what is our next assignation among the Spheres.

FATHER GIOVANNI: It is Saturn my Lady—remote, austere and cold.

DUCHESS YSABELLE: In that case we should be merry while we can. And what locale is best suited for examining the Sphere of Saturn?

SIGNORA EMILIA: A prison!

DUCHESS YSABELLE: You jest, Emilia!

FATHER GIOVANNI: A prison would be the perfect place to console oneself with philosophy. But perhaps we can find a locale less dark and damp ... my bones will no longer suffer the damp. It should be remote from the cares and intrusions of this world.

SIGNORA EMILIA: A high place, where we can look down upon all the kingdoms of the world.

FATHER GIOVANNI: And in your fancy are we to be tempted by Satan?

SIGNORA EMILIA: We are now wise to the temptations of power, so we shall tell Satan to run along, for we have become philosophers.

FATHER GIOVANNI: And shall we live on locusts, and wild honey, and dress in the skins of animals?

DUCHESS YSABELLE: We shall do no such thing!

SIGNORA EMILIA: Then a tower, so that all the world lies below us, and stars are seen at all the quarters of the globe. And we should have philosophical instruments ... do not ask me what they are, but we should have them. And innumerable books on the curiosities of natural philosophy ... Albertus Magnus ... and geometry, all in Greek and in the writing of the Arabs. And a stuffed crocodile. And a skull. And an hourglass.

DUCHESS YSABELLE: You have given the matter some thought, Emilia.

DUKE LORENZO: I understand the sense of this ... a remote spot, like a hermit's cell, where one can turn one's back upon this world ... forty days and forty nights, as Christ did in the wilderness of Judea. But I am ever practical ... how might one realise this without an excess of inconvenience? We have the castle at San Martino; it is but an hour by carriage, and it has a tower over a wild chasm. Perhaps we could adapt it to philosophy?

Duchess Ysabelle: Will the castellan have the means to host our party... maids, and servants, and cooks, and escorts, and so on and so on? And Father, are you agreeable to such an inconvenience?

Father Giovanni: I have often imagined myself in such a tower as the Signora Emilia describes. With an astrolabe, and an armillary sphere, and a quadrant, and innumerable books—as you say, in Greek, by the great geometers. It is a foolish fancy. I would be agreeable to meeting at San Martino, and I would enjoy viewing the chasm from such an elevation. I do not know about a stuffed crocodile ... but I am open to the thought.

Duke Lorenzo: I will write to the castellan, and see what I can arrange.

Sphæra Saturni

DUCHESS YSABELLE: Father, there you are ... my pardons ... I am quite out of breath ... once I would have taken the stairs two-at-a-time. I hope your chamber is acceptable.

FATHER GIOVANNI: Thank you, my Lady, very adequate, my needs are simple. When I travel I sleep where I can—in the vestry of a church, in a friary, in a monastery. A simple pallet is all that I require.

I was enjoying the cool air as it rises out of the chasm. There is a noise of rushing water.

DUCHESS YSABELLE: The Duke tells me a river falls into the chasm and disappears into a cave. It is a wild spot; I am sure the pagans would have had a sibyl telling oracles or some such foolishness ... but I am not clambering down rocks and stones to find out. Perhaps Emilia will go down there, she has a passion for such places.

FATHER GIOVANNI: I believe she might—there is now a fashion for witnessing the past. Artists sketch in the ruins of temples and sell engravings to travellers. Poets seek out the tumbled vanities of the past and reflect on vanished kingdoms.

DUCHESS YSABELLE: Here is Emilia ... Emilia, you may wish to seek out the depths of the chasm ... there may be a cave of some antiquity. Perhaps one of the men-at-arms knows the path?

SIGNORA EMILIA: Then tomorrow I will seek out the castellan and perhaps he will suggest a guide. Look, the moon is yellowed and gibbous ... but does it wax or wane?

FATHER GIOVANNI: It waxes, Signora. When the Moon sets after the Sun, it is waxing. That bright star in the twilight is Venus, called Hesperus or Vesper. In the light of dawn she is called Phosphorus, or Lucifer.

DUCHESS YSABELLE: Lucifer?

FATHER GIOVANNI: A relic of ancient times, my Lady, for the name means only that it is a bright star presaging the light of dawn ... just as John the Baptist heralded the coming of our Lord.

DUCHESS YSABELLE: Then I am relieved. I do not wish to have a devil peering through my window when the birds begin to sing. Where is my husband? He has been absent for hours.

FATHER GIOVANNI: I have not seen him either, my Lady ... some business with the castellan I expect. While we wait I had hoped to show you Saturn. I also wished to show you these items. The Signora Emilia desired that we be philosophical ... ah, here is the Duke ... good evening, my Lord.

DUKE LORENZO: Ah, welcome all, and please forgive my lateness.

DUCHESS YSABELLE: The castellan?

DUKE LORENZO: Indeed. As it is autumn we must review the store of food; it is intended to be sufficient for a siege ... and also to supply the city in a time of great need. Each year we purchase new provisions and sell the oldest part of the store. The older food could be distributed to the poor via the parishes, or it could be sold at a discount in the poorer districts, but I have discovered to my cost that the world is filled with rogues. In practice it ends up in the market and drives down the price of this year's harvest ... and so the farmers burn my effigy, and throw stones at my carriage.

We had a notion to transport it to a neighbouring city so as to let them deal with it ... or find a quartermaster who will take it to feed some army in the field ... but the trouble with mercenaries is that one never knows whom they will be fighting next. Or we could sell it to the Venetians.

Forgive me Father, let us hear about philosophy.

FATHER GIOVANNI: Thank you, my Lord, and I regret that your leisure should be sullied by such matters. We were viewing the evening sky, and I was about to find the planet of Saturn, but first I would like to display these two items—the Signora Emilia had observed that the Sphere of Saturn is the sphere of philosophy and so we should view some tangible philosophy. The first item appears unremarkable. It is this collection of tables; they are named *Alfonsine Tables*, and are compiled in Spain but widely copied and reprinted, complete with numerous errors.

They are compiled using the methods of Ptolemy in his *Almagest*, and show where we may expect to find the Sun, Moon and planets in the sky. If one has mastered the arts of horoscopy, then one can then say whether fair or foul influences rain down upon us from the stars.

SIGNORA EMILIA: This is the secret book of astrologers?

FATHER GIOVANNI: In a manner of speaking ... but it is also an arithmetical wonder. It requires an extraordinary diligence to devise these tables from an understanding of epicycles.

SIGNORA EMILIA: How extraordinary! May I hold it, Father?

FATHER GIOVANNI: Indeed.

SIGNORA EMILIA: So many numbers ... I have never seen so many numbers.

FATHER GIOVANNI: These are places upon the Sphere of the sky.

SIGNORA EMILIA: Marked out with philosophical rulers and such like?

FATHER GIOVANNI: You have it Signora. I have one here.

209

DUKE LORENZO: Ah, an astrolabe! I sailed from Pisa to Genoa and the master of the vessel had an astrolabe.

FATHER GIOVANNI: It was not an easy thing to find, and I am sworn to guard it as if it were the relic of a saint. There are some Venetians in the lower town who trade in silk, and I found a Venetian who had been a ship's master and is now weary of the sea and its trials.

DUCHESS YSABELLE: And what is it, pray tell?

FATHER GIOVANNI: It is what the Signora called a *philosophical ruler*, for it measures out places in the sky just as one might mark out a piece of cloth for a dress. There is more: it is a model of the sky as it moves in time, a thing of wondrous ingenuity and construction. They were first devised in the far East, but they are now made in Flanders and Milan and other places where they excel in craftsmanship. It is held up to the sky and then one sights a star like this, and I observe its altitude and do something with this plate that is called a *rete* ... I cannot demonstrate it, it is beyond me. Let me explain the sky, for the sky comes first, and the model comes afterwards.

DUCHESS YSABELLE: You can explain the sky?

FATHER GIOVANNI: After a fashion, my Lady. Permit me to demonstrate. The Sun has just set, and the brightest region of twilight is there in the west, so if I stand with my arms in a cross, and my right hand points to the setting Sun, then I am facing south, which is where we find the Sun at noon.

Now, if we all look to the south, there is a notional arc in the sky, which is the path the Sun follows during the day as it moves from east to west, and even at night we can still imagine it. And this arc is higher in summer, when the Sun is higher at noon, and lower in winter, when it hides behind the mountains.

SIGNORA EMILIA: In winter some valleys scarcely see the Sun, and snow lies until April or May.

FATHER GIOVANNI: Indeed. The path that the Sun follows among the stars is called the Ecliptic, and upon it we find the signs of the Zodiac. The planets also move in the same plane.

Duchess Ysabelle: And why does the path of the Sun move up and down as the seasons change?

Father Giovanni: Because the sky is tilted. One might imagine that the stars would rotate about the zenith, but this is not the case. Each night the stars rotate about a point in Ursa Minor, over there ... but there is another slow rotation, a yearly rotation so that the plane of the Sun moves around us. In summer the plane of the Sun is high, and in winter the plane of the sun is low. This is why the astrolabe is such a wonder, for it contains all this in brass and fine markings.

Duchess Ysabelle: And why does the plane of the Sun go up and down—it seems like an unnecessary complication.

Father Giovanni: Perhaps the Lord desired that we should have four seasons. It is a mystery.

Duke Lorenzo: Perhaps it is like being on the deck of a ship in a swell; at first the sea is above you, and then it is below you, and so on.

Father Giovanni: Except, my Lord, the ancients insist that the earth does not move.

Duke Lorenzo: In that case, it is indeed a mystery.

Duchess Ysabelle: Father, it seems unfair that you should be burdened with a mystery that perplexed the ancients ... please go on.

Father Giovanni: Thank you, my Lady. Now upon this Ecliptic— the arc of the sky where we find the Sun—we also find the signs of the Zodiac. As it is now harvest time and the Sun has just set, we see the autumn and winter constellations before us in the sky: Virgo in the west, setting with the Sun, and then towards the east, Libra, Scorpio, and Sagittarius, with Capricorn rising.

Duke Lorenzo: That bright star with a yellow hue and a fan of three stars to the right ... that is Antares in Scorpio. Many mistake it for Mars.

Father Giovanni: Indeed, my Lord, it has a similar colour.

Duchess Ysabelle: Do you know, all these years of my life and I have never once paid attention to the movements of the sky.

Signora Emilia: But tonight the wonders of creation are displayed before us, for we are in possession of a Tower of Philosophy.

Duke Lorenzo: Are you satisfied with the tower Signora? We are so much closer to the stars.

Signora Emilia: It is admirable, my Lord, just as I had hoped. And Father Giovanni has brought us an instrument of philosophy that mirrors the sky and demonstrates a similitude between what is above and what is below. And a book of movements filled with numbers that shows that the creation is both rational and comprehensible.

Duke Lorenzo: I had hoped that this remote place would find us far above the concerns of everyday life, but it seems they have followed me here in battalions, and I must think only of corn and olive oil.

Signora Emilia: I am sorry, my Lord. Perhaps your cares and troubles will find the narrow winding stairs of this tower too arduous, and remain in a huddle at the bottom.

Duke Lorenzo: I do hope so ... Father, I have interrupted your speech, please, be kind enough to show us Saturn.

Father Giovanni: Thank you, my Lord. Saturn is in Sagittarius, so we should find him easily in the south, but somewhat towards the east. There, that star with a light brown tint, as you say, similar to Antares.

Duchess Ysabelle: He does not twinkle like the other stars ... he has a steady, baleful light. And yet he seems so unremarkable. I suppose we should not judge him solely by his size—there are fatal poisons that require but a few grains.

Father Giovanni: Saturn is known as the Greater Misfortune, *Infortuna Major*, or the Greater Malefic. Mars is the Lesser Misfortune, just as Jupiter is *Fortuna Major* and Venus is *Fortuna Minor*.

Duchess Ysabelle: So we should seek out Jupiter and enjoy his influence.

FATHER GIOVANNI: Alas, he is below the horizon, but Venus is still visible in the west.

DUCHESS YSABELLE: And the great mass of stars are beyond Saturn? And although they move about us each day, they move as one piece, while these wandering planets may do as they please?

FATHER GIOVANNI: Indeed, my Lady, the stars are unvarying in their positions, as if painted on a dome that moves. Each planet has its own movement that is best explained with circles and epicycles and other notions that Ptolemy uses. So the planets cannot do as they please; they must move in perfect circles as ordained by God, and it is their motions or dance relative to each other that influences our hearts and minds, and alters the destiny of kings and nations.

DUCHESS YSABELLE: But if their motions are strictly ordained by circles, then how are we free.

FATHER GIOVANNI: I take the view that the stars make for us a changing landscape of clement and inclement fortune, just as some roads are smooth in parts and rutted in other parts. Is this not what astrologers do ... advise on fortunate occasions?

DUCHESS YSABELLE: I see ... thank you Father. Emilia, have you viewed the sky to your satisfaction? You have viewed the Greater Misfortune and soaked in his rays? The Duke is here, we can go below, there is some wine to refresh us.

DUCHESS YSABELLE: Let us go down then, I will return later when it is no longer twilight and the sky is darker.

DUCHESS YSABELLE: Husband, the servants have been working to make this room acceptable. We found profuse droppings of bats and pigeons, and it has taken a many buckets of water carried up from the courtyard to remove the dirt from the floor. Some men-at-arms brought this table and these chairs up the stairs. The servants must imagine that I am moonstruck, and as for the castellan ... but, as you say, we should never explain or justify.

DUKE LORENZO: Just so! If we choose to spend an evening in an old guardroom at the top of a tower ... then we shall. The tapestries do make the space more homely. I see that I will have to convey my gratitude to your host of Myrmidons.

SIGNORA EMILIA: You speak of Myrmidons, my Lord. I will speak of Spartans, who shunned comfort. I find this place entirely congenial to the mood, for the Sphere of Saturn is without luxury or plenty or pleasure.

FATHER GIOVANNI: This is true Signora, austerity is a mark of the Sphere. Indeed, it is a relief to me that we shall not spend this night on beds of nails as holy men are said to do in the Indies.

DUCHESS YSABELLE: Then are the chairs too comfortable for this occasion? Shall we throw these cushions into the chasm? And is the wine too palatable? Should we prefer vinegar?

FATHER GIOVANNI: A more acid vintage might be preferable. Sackcloth and ashes, all the mortifications of Lent.

DUCHESS YSABELLE: Now you jest, Father. Is Saturn truly so terrible? Shall we find out? Shall we begin? Let us begin! Emilia, I see you have your customary volumes. Ovid again? Hesiod?

SIGNORA EMILIA: You know me so well, Ysabelle. Yes, Ovid and Hesiod. I will begin by admitting my perplexity. I have found Saturn to be confusing and contradictory.

According to Ovid, the Romans recalled a golden age of abundance and harmony, when men were so moderate and reasoned in their passions that laws were not necessary. There were no slaves, for the land gave forth its bounty without labour. The ruler of this happy time was Saturn. Then the god of the Roman state became Jupiter, and Saturn was remembered as a happy memory celebrated each year in the Saturnalia, in which all of Rome was given over to license and wine and gambling, and slaves and masters changed places. This is the first tale: that long ago Saturn was a wise king who ruled over a happy world.

The Greeks tell a different story. The god the Romans called Saturn the Greeks named Cronos, and he was a dark god of the ancient world. In the beginning there was the sky, called Ouranos, and the earth, called Gaia. Ouranos and Gaia had many strange offspring that the Greeks called Titans. Ouranos oppressed Gaia, and so Gaia gave her son Cronus a sickle, and with it he castrated his father.

DUCHESS YSABELLE: That is certainly terrible.

SIGNORA EMILIA: There is worse. Cronos became the ruler of the Titans, but he feared that one of his own children would kill him, and so he ate his children. Only the youngest was spared, for the mother gave Cronos a stone wrapped in swaddling clothes and he ate the stone instead.

    The youngest child, whom the Romans called Jupiter, was hidden away in Crete until he was grown, and he caused his father to vomit forth all the children he had eaten—Ceres, Juno, Neptune, Pluto, and Vesta. Then Jupiter made war upon his father and the Titans. The Cyclops forged thunderbolts for Zeus, and with these he defeated the Titans, banishing them to the utmost dark that the Greeks named Tartarus, so that it was Jupiter, his siblings, and the children of Jupiter, who ruled this world.

DUCHESS YSABELLE: So Saturn castrated his father and ate his children? He is truly a most terrible god!

SIGNORA EMILIA: I think perhaps these might be allegories, Ysabelle. The Greeks, being excessively and unnecessarily clever, were fond of such things. They liked to confuse the name of the god Cronos with the word for time, which is *chronos*, so that Cronos became the god of eternal time ... and time eats all of his children. Is that not a splendid allegory?

FATHER GIOVANNI: There may be some truth to that, Signora, that these tales were never to be confused with history. I have wondered about the Titans, the gods before Olympus. Perhaps they are indeed allegories, for no man or woman ever worshipped them. They lived in a time before men, and are perhaps the inventions of priests and storytellers.

DUCHESS YSABELLE: And what was the fate of Saturn?

SIGNORA EMILIA: He was banished from the company of gods and no longer rules in this world. He lives alone in the utmost dark, having no role in the daily lives of men. He still bears the sickle or scythe; the Greeks recall that he castrated his father, and the Romans recall that once he was a god of farmers.

DUCHESS YSABELLE: And this Tartarus ... where is it?

SIGNORA EMILIA: Hesiod says that if an anvil fell out of heaven it would take nine days to strike the earth, and if it carried on falling it would take nine further days to reach Tartarus. And Homer places Tartarus somewhere in the forgotten bowels of Hades.

DUCHESS YSABELLE: So the Titans resemble the wicked angels that rebelled against God and were cast down into the abyss?

FATHER GIOVANNI: There are similarities.

DUCHESS YSABELLE: And Saturn is among their number?

SIGNORA EMILIA: He is, but as we have seen this evening, he also resides in the sky ... but of all the planets his Sphere is furthest from this Sphere of Nature. Perhaps he returns to the abyss when the night is over?

DUCHESS YSABELLE: How confusing ... you are correct Saturn is most confusing. Wicked and confusing. Thank you Emilia. Father, I am intrigued by that wooden box you have brought.

FATHER GIOVANNI: I have two things to show you, but I will first reveal the contents of the box. Behold!

DUKE LORENZO: A sheet of lead with a hole pierced through it. And perhaps some writing.

FATHER GIOVANNI: There is writing ... it is Latin, scratched I believe during the heyday of Rome.

DUKE LORENZO: May I inspect it? It is crudely written. It would seem to be a curse.

FATHER GIOVANNI: Gravediggers working in the old graveyard near the Duomo found it and called upon a priest to remove it. The priest brought it to me. It is indeed a curse: a woman betrayed by a lover calls upon some spirit to wither his manly portion. It was rolled-up and pierced through with an iron nail, but the nail has

rusted away leaving some brown marks here. A Roman would have called it a *tabella defixionis*, a curse tablet.

DUCHESS YSABELLE: A curse? It looks alarming and unwholesome!

FATHER GIOVANNI: I left it in a bowl of holy water for a week, saying over it the words that priests say to cast out unclean spirits: *Adjure te, spiritus nequissime, per Deum omnipotentem* ... and so on. I assure you, my Lady, the spirit is long gone.

DUCHESS YSABELLE: And the connection with Saturn?

FATHER GIOVANNI: Lead is the metal of Saturn. When cut it shows a bright silver, but it quickly tarnishes to a dull grey and in time it turns almost to black, as you can see. Why Saturn? This is black magic without a doubt, and Saturn, cast out into Tartarus, bears some kinship with Satan. At least to the Romans it must have seemed that way ... that Saturn ruled the darkest of spirits.

DUCHESS YSABELLE: Father, you are sure this curse brings no ill-fortune among us?

FATHER GIOVANNI: Holy water is most efficacious in such cases. The salt and water are blessed and charged with the intent that they should drive away all the powers of the evil one and his spirits, in the names of Jesus Christ, the Holy Spirit, and Almighty God. I have some with me, for I sprinkled some in this room when I first arrived.

SIGNORA EMILIA: Might a spirit have lingered about this tablet? King Solomon placed spirits in bottles and pots ... the Arabs have many tales of spirits in bottles that seek vengeance when released.

FATHER GIOVANNI: The nail, which would have bound it, rotted to dust many centuries ago. Fear not, the spirit is back in Hell. Let me return this tablet to its box and I will read from Ptolemy as I am wont to do.

DUCHESS YSABELLE: Yes, please do Father.

FATHER GIOVANNI: Then these are the words of the wise Greek concerning children of Saturn:

> If Saturn alone is ruler of the soul and dominates Mercury and the Moon, if well-placed with respect to the cosmos and the

angles, he makes his subjects lovers of the body, strong-minded, profound, austere, of a single purpose, laborious, imperious, vindictive, lovers of property, avaricious, violent, amassing treasure, and jealous; but if his position is the opposite and without dignity, he makes them sordid, petty, mean-spirited, indifferent, mean-minded, malignant, cowardly, diffident, evil-speakers, solitary, tearful, shameless, superstitious, fond of toil, unfeeling, treacherous in friendship, gloomy, taking no care of the body.

DUKE LORENZO: That is not a pretty picture Father.

FATHER GIOVANNI: There is worse, much worse. I have this from Alcabitius, who wrote in Syria, but I have his *Introduction to the Art of Judgement in the Stars* in Latin, for it has become popular among those who study such things:

> He is bad, masculine, in daytime cold, dry, melancholy, presides over fathers ... over old age and dotage and over elder brothers and ancestors, and over honesty in speech and in love, and absence of impulses, and over experience of things, keeping of a secret and its concealment, much eating and silence, deliberate dealings, over understanding and the faculty of distinguishing; he presides over lasting, permanent things, like land, husbandry, farming, tilling the land, and over respectable professions which have to do with water like the commanding of ships and their management, and the administration of work, and shrewdness and fatigue, pride, kings' servants, the pious among the peoples, the weak, slaves, the worried, the low born, the heavy, the dead, magicians, demons, devils and people of ill-fame—all this when his condition is good.

> But when he is evil he presides over hatred, obstinacy, care, grief, lamenting, weeping, evil opinion, suspicion between men ; and he is timid, easily confused, obdurate, fearful, given to anger, wishes no one well; further, he presides over miserly gains, over old and impossible things, far travels, long absence, great poverty, avarice towards himself and others, employment of deceit, want, astonishment, preference for solitude, wishes that kill by cruelty, prison, difficulties, guile, inheritances, causes of death. He also presides over vulgar trades like those of tanners, blood-letters, bath attendants, sailors, grave-diggers, the sale of ironware and objects of lead and bones, as well as working in leather. All this when he is unfortunate. To him belong hearing, comprehension, the viscous, sticky, blackish thick humours, and

of the parts of the body, the right ear, the back, the knees ... the bladder, the spleen, the bones, and of diseases, gout, elephantiasis, dropsy, hypochondria, and all chronic illnesses which come from cold and dryness.

DUKE LORENZO: 'All the chronic illnesses which come from coldness and dryness'. And death itself—I saw a corpse once in the Alps, it had not decayed.

DUCHESS YSABELLE: A corpse? A man or a woman?

DUKE LORENZO: A man, perhaps a goatherd, or a hunter. His leg was broken, he must have fallen. I mention it because the mountain path was bitter cold, and my lips were so dry and cracked they bled, and at the mention of cold and dry, the memory returned.

DUCHESS YSABELLE: What were you doing in the Alps?

DUKE LORENZO: A drunken jape, an exercise in youthful folly. After a night of wine and song we walked out into the light of dawn, climbed the tower of some church or other, and saw the Alps ... from Padua one can see the Alps ... one can even see the Campanile of San Marco in Venice on a clear day. At that moment we thought to journey into Germany ... why, we would pay our respects to the Holy Roman Emperor.

Italy being formed as it is, we thought we knew mountains, dismissed all advice, had no care for distance or difficulty. We went north into the Alps. The trees ended, we mistook one stony path for another, and ended up in the snows even though it was July. There was no wood for fire, no running water to drink. When we saw the frozen corpse by the path, the last of our courage departed, and we turned back. For me this is Saturn: a frozen corpse, cold and dry, the shape of life with all warmth and moisture stolen from it.

DUCHESS YSABELLE: God be praised, you returned from the icy wastes and you are still among us.

FATHER GIOVANNI: My lord, your misadventure in the mountains has the quality of a parable ... indeed, there is such a parable, the Three Living and the Three Dead. You have doubtless heard it. Three princes are hunting in the forest and they encounter three dead. The dead speak: 'we are your forefathers ... honour us, for life is fleeting and before long you will join us'.

DUKE LORENZO: Well observed Father, although my tale should be titled 'Five Fools and One Corpse'. Of the five on that cold, stony path, three are indeed dead ... Antonio in a brawl in Pisa, Feliciano from plague, and Lucca struck his head on a low branch while hunting ... God rest their souls, they were good companions but not blessed by good fortune. Here is my parable: no matter what road we choose, we will tread the same stony path with death at its end.

Yes my good Wife, I am aware that our discourse has wandered, and I am at fault. Regarding the excellent Ptolemy and Alcabitius, it seems to me that Saturn is the god of those who are exiled from life and society ... because they are old, because they are destitute and must beg from others, because they are despised for their occupation, because they are moonstruck ... or perhaps because their disposition tends towards arrogance and gloom, preferring their own opinions to any others, so that they are quarrelsome companions.

FATHER GIOVANNI: Yes, like Saturn they are driven towards the periphery where all is cold and dark, and there is no ease or comfort. Each parish has those who have been ill-served by Fortune and live apart. Many have been betrayed by Time. Alas, it is the fate of the aged that they become exiles from good society as infirmities of flesh and mind take hold.

SIGNORA EMILIA: That is so Father. What do we most admire in a person? Strength, grace, beauty, wit, eloquence, quickness, suppleness of mind and body. The aged lose the qualities we most admire in the young. They would sing ... with a voice that wavers and does not hold the tune. They would dance ... but have no grace. They would recite a poem ... but fumble the verses. They sit and nod in conversation but have no comment for they cannot hear but one word in three. If they flirt, they are most cruelly mocked. If perchance they should offer to entertain with a memory of bygone days, they forget the listener has already heard the tale, and more than once. If they offer counsel or opinion it is condescendingly ignored, for the young prefer the counsel of their peers, with whom they share their ventures.

DUKE LORENZO: Cruel but true Signora ... it is often said that Time is a thief that steals what we most value. The day comes when we are not fit for society and are best suited to the company of dogs and small children.

DUCHESS YSABELLE: I can think of few desirable qualities that come with age. Perhaps wisdom, although I have grown to doubt that.

FATHER GIOVANNI: It is wise to care for one's soul, my Lady.

DUCHESS YSABELLE: That is true ... old age is a time when one can care for one's soul. The young are more concerned with vanity than piety. Husband, I see books before you but you have not yet told us what you have brought.

DUKE LORENZO: I fear you will mock me for my choice. It is once again Ficino, his *De Vita Libri Tres*, and relevant to our topic.

FATHER GIOVANNI: This is so, my Lady. It is a work well-chosen.

DUCHESS YSABELLE: Then we should listen to Ficino. What does he say on this occasion?

DUKE LORENZO: I will begin with an introduction, for the origin of this matter lies with the Greeks, who were first to understand the four humours of the body and how their admixture brings us health or sickness. There is yellow bile, which is warm and dry, having the quality of fire; blood, which is warm and moist, and having the quality of air; phlegm which is cold and moist, having the quality of water, and black bile which is cold and dry, having the quality of earth. From these we derive four temperaments or dispositions, these being choleric, sanguine, phlegmatic, and melancholic.

    Some say that just as there are four elements and four humours and four seasons in a year, so there are four seasons in life: the child is spring, which is warm and moist; the youth is summer, which is warm and dry; the mature man is autumn, which is cold and dry; and that of the old man is winter, which is cold and moist. Others say winter is cold and dry.

DUCHESS YSABELLE: Italy has winters of every complexion: warm, cold, dry and moist.

SIGNORA EMILIA: Ysabelle, I believe these seasons are not of Italy, but of philosophy.

FATHER GIOVANNI: Oh indeed Signora, philosophical seasons! The Lyceum—the temple of Apollo Lyceus where Aristotle met his students—had very particular winters, dependably cold and dry.

DUCHESS YSABELLE: I see. Philosophical seasons. Father, Emilia, I am close to laughter. As for the final season of life I find that the aged are cold. They sit too long and the fire in their bodies does not kindle. It could be noon in August and my mother would call for a fire. She complained of dryness ... in the lips, in the mouth, in the eyes, and she rubbed lotions into the skin of her hands. But my recollections do not constitute philosophy ...

DUKE LORENZO: I am with you in this matter, dear Wife, that old age is cold and dry. And now for the heart of the matter. Aristotle believed that solitary study and contemplation has a desiccating influence upon the body so that black bile predominates, and the soul is overwhelmed by melancholy. In some it causes despondency and despair and self-loathing; in others, genius. He argues that just as wine can have several effects upon the drinker, so black bile can lower the spirits to the utmost despair, or it can raise them to the realm of the pure intellect, in which the forms of the divine become apparent.

DUCHESS YSABELLE: And what are these forms of the divine?

DUKE LORENZO: The truths beyond appearance. Root causes. Eternal forms.

SIGNORA EMILIA: Geometry.

DUKE LORENZO: Indeed, geometry. And the forms of the Good and the Beautiful.

FATHER GIOVANNI: Regarding black bile, the Greeks recognised an elevated and excited state of mind that we still call *frenesia*, or *furor*,

223

in which it seemed that a god takes possession of the soul and divine power speaks through it. So we speak of inspiration, as when a divine spirit breathes into the soul, and brings forth prophecy, music, poetry, and the highest forms of philosophy. This is *melancholia fumosa*, as we might say, 'hot melancholy'.

Those gifted with such frenzy grow weary of this world. When the soul flies so high that the vanities of this world become apparent, then the everyday works of man appear tedious and worthless, and so there is black or cold melancholy.

There is another malady of the soul that afflicts those who devote themselves to solitude and study. We call it *acedia*; there is restlessness, an inability to study or pray, there is boredom, anxiety, insomnia, and guilt. It resembles unrequited love. The soul seeks what it does not attain and cannot find relief or peace. It is common among monks.

SIGNORA EMILIA: *Acedia* ... so it has a name. Some days I cannot settle to any purpose. I fret. I wander about and discover dirt the servants have missed and organise a cleansing. There is haste, and flurry, and universal industry until the mood passes and I can settle again.

DUCHESS YSABELLE: And all of this is the fault of black bile? And how does it relate to our subject, which is Saturn?

DUKE LORENZO: Ah, Saturn rules the spleen, which is the seat of black bile. The rays of Saturn arouse the spleen to release its black bile, which makes a person ill-tempered, grasping, suspicious, anxious, avaricious, slow, of fixed purpose, and a nay-sayer, with never a good word for any proposal. A holder of grudges, and a purveyor of short measures.

Or, and here is the peculiarity of this humour—just as you say Father—it may raise the soul so that one becomes a philosopher who touches upon the divine, for Saturn is the final Sphere before the stars, and from that remote outlook one might view the mysteries of the creation.

And now I am ready to come to Ficino, who was a martyr to melancholy throughout his life. This occasions no surprise, for he was a scholar of singular attainment and spent his days recovering Plato and his followers from ancient folios written by indifferent scribes.

DUCHESS YSABELLE: And so his soul shrivelled like a raisin?

DUKE LORENZO: His soul was deprived and divided. Here is how he describes it, in his own words:

> The cause is, first, that the more difficult the work, the greater concentration of mind it requires; and second, that the more they apply their mind to incorporeal truth, the more they are compelled to disjoin it from the body. Hence their body is often rendered as if it were half-alive and often melancholic. My author Plato signified this in the *Timaeus*; he said that the soul contemplating divine things assiduously and intently, grows up so much on food of this kind and becomes so powerful, that it overreaches its body above what the corporeal nature can endure; and sometimes in its too vehement agitation, it either in a way flies out of it or sometimes seems as if to disintegrate.

SIGNORA EMILIA: Perhaps the body, and by this I mean the animal soul that inhabits the body, resents being diminished and denied nutrition; like a plant that is left without water, it cannot grow as it should and so it sags and wilts.

FATHER GIOVANNI: Undoubtedly Signora; each portion of the soul requires its own nourishment, and if the contemplative soul takes all, it is to the detriment of others.

DUKE LORENZO: And so Ficino recommends that to avoid melancholy, one should fortify the spirit or quintessence, for it is this spirit that joins soul to body; in this way body and soul rejoice in amicable and harmonious communion. I will quote from him again ... here ... I have marked the passage:

> This quintessence can be ingested by us more and more if a person knows how best to separate it, mixed in as it is with other elements, or at least how to use those things often which are filled with it, especially in its purer form. Such things are: choice wine, sugar, balsam, gold, precious stones, myrobalans (which is the cherry plum), and things which smell most sweet and which shine, and especially things which have in a subtle substance a quality hot, moist, and clear; such, besides wine, is the whitest

sugar, especially if you add to it gold and the odour of cinnamon and roses. Then too, just as foods we eat in the right way, although not themselves alive, are converted through our spirit to the form of our life, so also our bodies rightly accommodated to the body and spirit of the world (that is through cosmic things and through our spirit) drink in as much as possible from the life of the world.

My understanding of this is that spirit in the greater world and spirit in the body are of similar nature, and by enjoying those substances rich in spirit we refresh and stimulate the spirit within the body ... in a manner that resembles drinking to relieve a thirst.

DUCHESS YSABELLE: If one takes a raisin and places it in water for a day it swells and once again resembles a grape. Ficino would have us counter bitterness and blackness with sweetness and brightness. I think a woman could have taught him how to unshrivel his soul in a trice. A hot bath, a fresh linen chemise, a few roses, and sweet perfume.

SIGNORA EMILIA: A lute played below one's window. A song of adventure and romance.

DUKE LORENZO: You have it in a nutshell; one should counter the malice of Saturn with the joys of Venus, Jupiter and the Sun. And he recommends the power of music to charm the soul.

SIGNORA EMILIA: He does?

DUKE LORENZO: It was his belief that song, having the quality of speech and air, is close in nature to the quintessence, and so it has a singular virtue to resuscitate the spirit. He was accomplished with the lute, and it is said that he sang the hymns of Orpheus which he found in some scroll or other, so that some accused him of being a pagan. But he was a priest of the Church, and claimed these matters concerned natural virtues, and had nothing of the Devil in them. You are correct in your observation that a woman could have taught him these things, but he was ill-formed and perhaps he lacked instruction.

DUCHESS YSABELLE: In what way ill-formed?

Sphæra Saturni

DUKE LORENZO: I understand that he was small and bent and lacked some fluency in his speech. And irascible.

FATHER GIOVANNI: I have heard this also, my Lord, from some who knew him.

DUCHESS YSABELLE: Poor man, I am not amazed that he was afflicted by melancholy.

SIGNORA EMILIA: These hymns of Orpheus, are these the songs that Orpheus sang to charm men and savage beasts, and with which he was able to gain entry to Hades itself to retrieve his love?

DUKE LORENZO: So I would imagine, Signora. I do not know where Ficino found them.

FATHER GIOVANNI: Perhaps I can assist, my Lord. Many years ago, in the time of Cosimo de' Medici, a Giovanni Aurispa travelled to Constantinople and spent years learning their tongue so that he could discover and purchase ancient works. Indeed, he purchased so many works that there were complaints to the Byzantine Emperor that he was looting the city of the works of the Church Fathers, so he bought mostly heathen works to appease his accusers. These works he brought to Florence on account of the passion of Cosimo de' Medici for antiquities. Then he taught and lectured in Florence for some years, and I expect that his students purchased copies of his manuscripts for their own use.

There was also Plethon, a Greek who had a passion for Plato. He came to Italy with a great many Byzantines for the Council of Florence in the time of Cosimo de' Medici, and was an advocate for the ancient scholars of Greece, but whether he brought the hymns I do not know.

SIGNORA EMILIA: I would sing these hymns so that I might charm beasts.

DUKE LORENZO: Perhaps we can discover a manuscript. With what beasts would you commence your serenade?

SIGNORA EMILIA: I thought I would begin with my dogs, my Lord, as they are generally attentive. I doubt that even Orpheus could charm cats with song alone.

FATHER GIOVANNI: It is said that Orpheus charmed savage Cerberus with his lyre ... are we wandering, my Lady ... ?

DUCHESS YSABELLE: Indeed Father, but there is some charm to it. However, I have not yet disclosed what I have brought.

DUKE LORENZO: Then you must tell us.

DUCHESS YSABELLE: I have brought an hourglass ... but I left it in my chamber below and so I must claim to have brought Time itself. We will observe a moment of silence and I will tap on the table for some heartbeats . . . . there, our lives are ten heartbeats less than they were, and we are that much closer to our deaths.

    I do not wish to be sombre, but our days in this life are short, and we are bound into an earthy vessel that will return to the dust. Everything in this world tarnishes and grows dim and dull like lead ... apart from gold.

    When we are young and growing, and filled with dreams of a boundless future, we do not imagine that the flowing tide will turn back, and that the world will close in upon us until it is a relief to die.

    Is this Saturn?—it seems to me that it is. The Moon and Mercury and Venus are young and look up to the Sun, but Saturn is old and slow and has nowhere to go, for he is exiled in darkness, and there is only further darkness beyond.

    Do you fear to grow old, Husband?

DUKE LORENZO: When I was a youth I thought that I could be the equal of any man: in the field of battle, in tourney, in the hunt, at court, in disputation. We were all mad to show our qualities. The day came when I knew that I had done what I could. There were better men, and there would always be better men, younger men, all as mad with ambition as I had been. Youth and renown lasted for only a moment.

    I am not reconciled with growing old. Fine food and a comfortable chair are no recompense for a fierce horse, and the roar of the crowd as one charges forward, lance *en couchant*.

Duchess Ysabelle: But at least my heart is not so alarmed as it once was, and wielding a lance is the least of your many talents. Father, do you fear to grow old?

Father Giovanni: God did not intend me for a warrior, but for a scholar. When I was young I could read a chapter and recall details for weeks, or even years. My memory brought forth passages from the Bible untaught and unsought; the art of memory was artless.

Then I found myself resorting to notes written on scraps of this and that, and I would discover the notes and have no clue what I had been reading when I made them. Then I would lose the notes and be as innocent of learning as a child. Now I depend upon some reading from my youth, and convince myself of the vanity of learning, for as Solomon says: 'of making many books there is no end; and much study is a weariness of the flesh'. Yes my Lady, I do fear growing old, for my purpose is to serve others, and not to be a burden to them.

Duchess Ysabelle: Very true Father, our children will have trials of their own. Although the Bible commands them to honour their father and mother, I would prefer that they do not honour me in my dotage for too long. Emilia, do you fear to grow old?

Signora Emilia: I do. I fear for my girls. I fear all the pain I must watch them endure. We spoke of this some months ago ... that pain seems ... unreasonable, beyond necessity. My girls will marry and leave with their husbands, and depart from my life, and my heart will ache for them. They will be urged to bear children; perhaps one will die in childbirth as so many do. I will struggle to be Christian ... my Lord, Father, Ysabelle, I speak honestly if unwisely ... Saturn is the curse placed upon us by God, that we grow old and sicken and die. We are in Tartarus with the wicked old man and his sickle, cast away in darkness, and shackled to these frail bodies of pain and decay.

Duchess Ysabelle: For all the joy of being a mother, one must fortify one's soul against the loss of a child. No doubt my sons will want to gallop at full tilt at other men, and they will see no harm in it. I will suffer a thousand agonies and say Hail Mary until St. Peter closes the gates of Heaven out of weariness.

SIGNORA EMILIA: Do you fear growing old, Ysabelle?

DUCHESS YSABELLE: I do. I fear that I will be alone in the world. I meet with many elderly women; their husbands have died, their children have no patience, and their only companions are priests and the blessed sisters.

You must not die, Husband; we must comfort each other.

DUKE LORENZO: Then I will not die, but I may become bored and irritable.

DUCHESS YSABELLE: Then I will find a young scholar who will read to you. And poets and minstrels will come to our court to entertain us. I will summon travellers to tell us how Germany fares, and France, and what new inventions there are, and how the Great Turk threatens Venice, and so you will not be bored.

DUKE LORENZO: Then I will only be irritable. My father perfected the art. He became a true child of Saturn as he aged.

DUCHESS YSABELLE: He did indeed! I thought that perhaps that Mars was the worst of the Spheres, but it seems that the ancients were correct, that Saturn is indeed the greater misfortune, and Mars the lesser. I hear you Emilia, that Saturn is the curse placed upon us.

DUKE LORENZO: A curse indeed. When we are young our thoughts are filled with love and war, and an increase in all things. As we age our thoughts reflect upon decrease, weakness, pain, and loneliness. The bars of our prison become apparent.

It seems to me that we have come full-circle. When first we met together we began with the Sphere of the Elements. We observed that the body is subject to the vicissitudes of Nature, and Necessity forces unwelcome truths upon us. Now we discover the author of this Necessity, the grim warder who sits in the far darkness and shows us his hourglass and sickle.

FATHER GIOVANNI: The ancients spoke of *carcer*, a prison, and *vinculum*, a shackle or bond, for they understood that the soul is bound to the body, and imprisoned in Time, where everything that begins must end. And yes, my Lord, we have come full-circle. When the ancients desired to show their understanding of Time, they showed a serpent biting its tail.

DUCHESS YSABELLE: And this is allegory once again ... like eating children?

FATHER GIOVANNI: I would say that this is allegory, my Lady.

DUCHESS YSABELLE: But if it is mere allegory we may choose any creature that bites its tail. Cats and dogs both pursue their tails. Why a serpent? Is the serpent perhaps a sign of wickedness, of deceit?

FATHER GIOVANNI: You wonder if this serpent tempted our first parents and brought them into suffering and mortality?

DUCHESS YSABELLE: I had that thought. And the blessed John speaks of a serpent-dragon with horns and crowns, the deceiver of the whole world. Is not Satan the father of lies, and the deceiver of the world?

FATHER GIOVANNI: You suspect some kinship between Satan and Saturn? I will not dispute this notion, other than to observe that Satan comes from the writings of the Jews, and Saturn from the writings of the Greeks and the Romans. It is true however that Saturn is an ally to serpents and dragons, for they pull his chariot across the sky.

SIGNORA EMILIA: And he is master of the Titans, who took many strange forms and are bound in Tartarus like the fallen angels. And I have another thought: Apollo slew the great serpent Python, just as Michael contends with Satan.

DUCHESS YSABELLE: It seems that we have no good thing to say about Saturn. He is a friend to wicked serpents, and he sends us melancholy and black bile, so that our souls shrivel like raisins.

FATHER GIOVANNI: I think perhaps I can vouch for Saturn ... not a recommendation, but an observation. It is this: in any matter where people come together with a common purpose, there is a rule that binds them.

LIBER SPHÆRÆ

DUKE LORENZO: As in the rule of St. Benedict, or St. Francis, a rule so that men or women may live together in harmony and with a common purpose?

DUCHESS YSABELLE: Or marriage, where man and woman are joined together by consent.

FATHER GIOVANNI: That is my meaning: that there is an allegiance to persons, or to a cause, such as one finds in public office, in a company of soldiers, in the Church, and, as you say, my Lady, in marriage. Once allegiance is sworn there are duties and obligations and one is no longer free to act as one chooses.

SIGNORA EMILIA: And an allegiance that brings joy to some may be a burden to others.

FATHER GIOVANNI: You divine my intention, Signora. Saturn binds all things into a common purpose. It is through his rule that we are subject to Time and Necessity. Some—perhaps they are children of Venus—will live joyfully in this world and they will praise God for its beauty. Others will feel oppressed, and their souls will be shrivelled like raisins. They will curse the cause of their affliction.

Some time ago I spoke of the game of chess, and how the players bind themselves according to the rules of the game.

DUCHESS YSABELLE: I recall. You had conversation with the Jews of Ferrara, who believe that all things are God, and I wondered how God could be a stone. This was your reply ... that if God played chess he would abide by the rules and be as any other player.

FATHER GIOVANNI: That was it! We are all bound together in this game that the Lord has made for us. The ancients, not being wise in scripture, thought that Saturn, the most ancient of the great gods, was the architect of all that is finite and outside of eternity.

DUKE LORENZO: We resemble mariners cast away upon an island. We must live according to the sustenance we find, and we cannot help but wonder what greater lands lie across the sea.

DUCHESS YSABELLE: I would curse any who abandoned me to such a fate.

SPHÆRA SATURNI

FATHER GIOVANNI: My lady, recall the story of Job. Satan petitioned God to test Job's faith, and afflicted him with terrible sufferings, but Job never wavered in his love of God.

DUCHESS YSABELLE: I would not curse God, Father, only Saturn.

SIGNORA EMILIA: I will observe that the race of women bears some blame for our predicament, for all the souls in this world enter it through our bodies.

DUCHESS YSABELLE: I would never have thought of that, Emilia. I would never have thought of it ... but I see that it is true ... that we are accomplices.

SIGNORA EMILIA: We cast away and abandon our children into this forbidding world. Like the people of Israel in Egypt, they are strangers in a foreign land.

DUCHESS YSABELLE: Do not say that Emilia, I will not sleep ...

SIGNORA EMILIA: It is the black bile speaking Ysabelle; pay it no mind.

FATHER GIOVANNI: It is indeed the voice of Saturn speaking. We have risen through all the Spheres that are human; our minds are raised to the Sphere of causes, and causes are like the wheels and gears of a mill.

DUCHESS YSABELLE: Our souls are turning into raisins?

DUKE LORENZO: Soon you will be reading Euclid and entertaining us with triangles.

DUCHESS YSABELLE: I will become indifferent to comfort, tidiness, and good food. I shall wear old, shabby dresses and neglect my hair. I will be as irascible as Ficino. Soon you will wish to have your wife returned to you.

DUKE LORENZO: Father, Signora, I think it is time to quit this sphere.

FATHER GIOVANNI: And I concur, but would make one more observation. It is through reason that we understand causes, and it is through reason that we comprehend those circumstances that lead to suffering. We should recall the beasts of the field, who have no understanding of time or causes.

They possess habit, and so they can live from day to day, but they live in the present. They do not reflect upon experience, and so lack hindsight or foresight. They will die, but do not know it. They are for the most part indifferent to the suffering of others. They have no concept of good or evil, or sin. They suffer as we do, but they are innocent of the causes of suffering.

We possess divine reason and our minds are raised up to comprehend time and causes. We anticipate the sufferings of old age, and so we blame Saturn for the ills that we perceive. But it is the gift of higher reason that is at fault, the same reason that understands how causes carry us from a beginning to an end, so that we understand the pattern of life in time. If we were to extinguish our faculty of understanding, then we would be as ignorant as cattle, and we might as well stand in a field and eat grass.

DUKE LORENZO: Many drink to oblivion Father. They have seen enough, and would forget.

DUCHESS YSABELLE: Well observed, Husband; it is a common impulse, for we are not all made to be philosophers. Father, your point is also well made and brings great clarity to our situation. The world is fallen and we possess the understanding that it is fallen. We wish that it were raised ... but, as the *Bible* declares, the day of the Lord will come when it comes, and no man will know that day.

Have we more to say as to Saturn? Have we concluded our meetings? My head says that we have, but my heart is not in agreement.

FATHER GIOVANNI: There is only the Sphere of the stars to detain us, and it raises more questions than I have answers.

SIGNORA EMILIA: I am done with Saturn, but I would like to see the stars again.

DUKE LORENZO: And I. The night is clear, and the view from above is beyond compare.

DUCHESS YSABELLE: Then let us ascend to the roof.

STELLATUM

For I have swift and speedy wings
With which to mount the lofty skies,
And when thy mind has put them on
The Earth below it will despise.
Boethius

SIGNORA EMILIA: This sky is quite glorious.

DUKE LORENZO: I have spent many a night by a camp fire looking up at the stars.

DUCHESS YSABELLE: Then Husband, you can be our guide.

DUKE LORENZO: I will be a poor guide. I know only a few stars by name. When I am at camp I seek out Ursa Major ... there ... you must know it ... some call it the Wain or the Plough ... and it points me to Ursa Minor, the Little Bear, and there we find the Pole around which the sky turns. That is North. When scouting far from road or habitation I would set a stone or branch in the direction of the Pole so that by daylight I could mark bearings to landmarks, and I would make a note in my journal.

Duchess Ysabelle: Then this is North, where I am pointing?

Duke Lorenzo: It is. The north wind blows down from the Alps from that quarter ... do you know his name, Father, the name of the wind?

Father Giovanni: I believe it is Boreas, my Lord, but the Romans called it Aquilo.

Duke Lorenzo: Ah, yes, Boreas, Aquilo, thank you Father. A freezing wind that chills to the bone. Over there is Cassiopeia, the stars resemble the letter 'W'.

Duchess Ysabelle: I see it ... I recall the name ... remind me, who was Cassiopeia?

Duke Lorenzo: I forget ... another of Jupiter's paramours I would imagine.

Signora Emilia: I know the story, my Lord. Cassiopeia was the wife of King Cepheus of Aethiopia. The king boasted of his wife's beauty and offended the nymphs of the sea, so Neptune sent a great monster to ravage their kingdom. An oracle advised that their daughter Andromeda must be sacrificed to the monster. She was chained to a rock by the sea ... from where she was rescued by the hero Perseus, who slew the monster. Some say he uncovered the head of Medusa the Gorgon, and turned the monster to stone.

Duke Lorenzo: You are a wellspring of ancient legend, Signora; now I recall the names.

Signora Emilia: I have a fondness for heroes, my Lord: Bellerophon, Theseus, Perseus, Hercules, Jason. They fought monsters.

Father Giovanni: And they are in the stars above us: Cassiopeia, Cepheus, Andromeda, Perseus and the winged horse Pegasus. Even the monster, whom some say is Cetus, the Whale, but I take it to be Draco, the serpent-dragon that coils around the Pole, for he is contiguous with the group.

Duchess Ysabelle: Can you point out this Draco, Father?

Father Giovanni: The stars of Draco are unremarkable. They lie between Cepheus, Ursa Minor, and Ursa Major. In books that

chart the sky, the constellation is drawn as if it were a serpent or dragon coiling about the axis of the world. Some say this monster is Ophion, others that is is Typhon, a terrifying monstrosity put down by Jupiter with his thunderbolts ... much as Satan was put down by Michael. I think these stars are but a memorial of his defeat, for by tradition he is confined below this world, and suffers and groans among the fires of Mount Aetna.

DUCHESS YSABELLE: We share this world with monsters who seek to overwhelm us and bring about chaos and death. If one forgets for a moment that the Greeks were heathens and did not possess the word of God, one might confuse this Typhon with the enemy of our Lord. I begin to wonder if it matters what we call these ancient serpents.

FATHER GIOVANNI: I have had this thought this many times, my Lady.

SIGNORA EMILIA: And I. Whether we read Hesiod, or John of Patmos, there is a serpent-dragon lurking in fire and darkness that seeks to claim this world.

DUCHESS YSABELLE: A cheerless thought, but we are here to view the night sky and so I will put these thoughts aside. How far to the starry dome? Emilia, did you say something about an anvil falling from Heaven, and it took ... what ... seven days?

SIGNORA EMILIA: Nine days. The anvil of Hesiod took nine days to fall from Heaven to this world, and another nine to land in Hades. I think Hesiod was a storyteller first, and not so much a philosopher.

DUCHESS YSABELLE: Indeed. I can think of no reason why angels might require an anvil in Heaven.

SIGNORA EMILIA: Perhaps they were beating swords into ploughshares?

FATHER GIOVANNI: Very amusing Signora, very droll. My lady, if I might answer your question concerning distances, distances can be measured through an application of geometry, by using a base and two angles. If one angle is a right-angle, then only a base and one angle are required. By using this method the Greeks of old measured the size of this world, the distance to the Moon, and the distance to the Sun.

DUKE LORENZO: We have fallen away from so much understanding, Father. The Greeks were like gods in these matters.

FATHER GIOVANNI: This is true, we are like children in our understanding of the Spheres.

DUCHESS YSABELLE: So how far is the Sun, Father?

FATHER GIOVANNI: A long way; a very long way.

DUCHESS YSABELLE: I think Hesiod gave us a better answer with his anvil!

FATHER GIOVANNI: Forgive me, my Lady, I forget the answer … the Greeks measured in stadia, and a stadion is about 160 paces, so about eight stadia to a Roman mile. I recall many, many thousands of stadia. If you had the winged horse Pegasus, he would grow weary of flying.

DUCHESS YSABELLE: And the starry dome? How far to the starry dome?

FATHER GIOVANNI: Far beyond the Sun. We have no base of a sufficient length to present us with angles. The dome is far beyond the Sun, far beyond Saturn. Those who have passed through the Spheres say that this vast world appears to be but a pinprick.

DUCHESS YSABELLE: And who has been to Heaven and back?

FATHER GIOVANNI: Why, in *Corinthians* the blessed Paul tells us that he ascended to the Third Heaven, which I take to be the place where the ascended Christ rules in glory. He tells us nothing of distance or stars. Among the pagans, Cicero describes to us the dream of Scipio Aemilianus, who ascended through the Spheres. He tells us that each Sphere revolves at its own pace and together they harmonise to make music, as in the strings of a lute.

DUCHESS YSABELLE: So it is the soul that makes the journey, and we have no need for winged horses to transport us above this world.

SIGNORA EMILIA: But it would be an excellent adventure, to fly past the Sun, past Mars and Jupiter. I would not like to fall like Icarus—I would ensure that my steed was proof against the heat of the Sun, and its wings were properly secured. And one must take care to fly wide of Cain, who lives in the Moon, and may wish to seize a mount and return to this world.

DUKE LORENZO: You must avoid the baleful glare of Mars, and the lightnings of Jupiter.

SIGNORA EMILIA: And I expect Saturn would be cold, bitter cold. I would take my best cloak and fur-lined gloves.

FATHER GIOVANNI: You would need a guide to conduct you.

SIGNORA EMILIA: As Dante was guided by the blessed Beatrice?

FATHER GIOVANNI: Indeed, a guide like Beatrice, lest you are turned back at the starry firmament. It is written that the Celestial Jerusalem has twelve gates, and they are warded by angels.

SIGNORA EMILIA: I have no ambition to enter the Heavenly City, for that would be the act of a proud, vain, and foolhardy temperament. For me it would be enough to see the stars for what they are. Are they ascended souls, or bright angels, or fiery spirits ... as when a burning log explodes, and scatters sparks into the sky? Or perhaps they are flames, like a lantern seen from many miles across a valley on a dark night. See, that distant light over there, it seems little larger than a star.

DUCHESS YSABELLE: I suspect that if the good Father had a sound opinion on the stars he would have told us. Is that so, Father?

FATHER GIOVANNI: That is so, my Lady; I am familiar with everything the Signora suggests. Souls, angels, spirits, sparks ... who can say what the stars are or why they shine as they do? The ancients tell us that parts of the sky have influence and meaning—the stars of Leo increase the dignity and influence of the Sun, the stars of Capricorn add their power to Saturn. Poor Venus is afflicted in Virgo—but I have no notion as to how this was discovered. Here again, the Greeks surpass us in their understanding.

Stellatum

DUCHESS YSABELLE: Do the Greeks tell us why the sky turns about the Pole?

FATHER GIOVANNI: They do. According to Aristotle, everything that moves is moved by some other thing, and that second thing is caused to move by some third thing, and so on, so that we have a chain of causes with no end to it. This resembles the problem of the chicken and the egg.

To resolve this puzzle of causes and satisfy the demands of reason, Aristotle proposed a first cause of movement, a Prime Mover that initiates all movement, but does not move itself ... like the first hen, made whole and entire by God on the fourth day of creation, and source of the first egg.

DUCHESS YSABELLE: A first hen ... I suppose there must have been. But I do not understand this first Mover. If this Mover does not move, how can it be the cause of movement?

FATHER GIOVANNI: Imagine a comely maiden. She does not move. Nothing is required of her, and yet gallants come from afar to sing her praises and win a smile. So it is with the Cosmos; it is moved by love of its Creator.

SIGNORA EMILIA: But the gallants move towards the maiden, they do not circle her.

FATHER GIOVANNI: But they might move in circles when they have approached as close as they dared, moving around her according to the purity of their love.

SIGNORA EMILIA: Why, that is how Dante has it in the *Paradiso*!

FATHER GIOVANNI: Indeed he does; the blessed spirits and angels move in circles. The Cosmos is shaped as a sphere, for a sphere is the most perfect shape, and it moves in a circle, for a circle is the most perfect way in which it can move.

DUKE LORENZO: That is an elegant analogy, Father—the comely maiden I mean, and her suitors.

FATHER GIOVANNI: I deserve little praise, my Lord; this matter of the movement of the Spheres goes back to antiquity.

Duchess Ysabelle: So the Prime Mover does not move, but all things are moved by it, as if by love.

Father Giovanni: Not 'as if', my Lady ... they are moved by love. My lord, you expounded on Ficino, and Socrates in the *Symposium*, how all things pursue beauty, for beauty is the exterior form of goodness, and the source of goodness is God. All things are moved by their desire to return to God. It is love that turns the stars, it is love that makes the world go around.

Duchess Ysabelle: And this Prime Mover is God.

Father Giovanni: In the mind of Aristotle, yes.

Duchess Ysabelle: How extraordinary ... so all this movement of Spheres and stars comes from love?

Father Giovanni: Indeed.

Duke Lorenzo: Father, might I object that it appears that the heavens circle around us, and not God as one might expect?

Father Giovanni: My lord might recollect some person who imagined the world revolved about them?

Duke Lorenzo: Oh very good Father, very good. Yes, I have met many such. They jostle to be at the centre of every happenstance.

Father Giovanni: The fallen imagine all things circle around them; the blessed see that God is the centre, and all things circle about God.

Duke Lorenzo: So this movement around us is merely an appearance ...

Duchess Ysabelle: A falling star! I saw a star fall from the heavens!

Signora Emilia: Where! Show me ...

Duchess Ysabelle: Over there ... a flash, less than a heartbeat. Do angels still fall away from God, Father?

Father Giovanni: Perhaps it was a messenger, sent down into this world, just as Jove sends Mercury on his errands.

Signora Emilia: Or an angel disenchanted with Heaven?

Stellatum

FATHER GIOVANNI: Or enchanted by this world ... by the sight of a comely maiden. There is a story—I think you know it—told by the Church Fathers, who had it from the Jews, that there were (or are) angels set to watch over this world. Some were tempted by the beauty of the daughters of men and fell to earth, so that they might couple with them. They taught these women the arts of magic and divination, and the secrets of the stars and planets. The offspring of these women and the fallen angels were wicked, and God cleansed the world with a great flood.

SIGNORA EMILIA: Another star falls! Over there! Surely it must be dreary in Heaven.

DUKE LORENZO: Did you wish upon it, Signora?

SIGNORA EMILIA: Alas, I did not. The fall was too brief for a wish ... I had none prepared. A flying horse—next time I will wish for a flying horse and ride through the air like Bellerophon. I have a thought; if God cleansed the world of wickedness, how is it that we are still so wicked? This argues that angels are still falling to earth and teaching secret arts.

FATHER GIOVANNI: Or that there are those in the Church (and it is chiefly clerics) who call upon spirits to instruct them in the arcane arts. The angels who fell with Satan remain devoted to wickedness, and seek to bind our souls to their cause with pacts.

DUCHESS YSABELLE: Have you encountered such wickedness, Father?

FATHER GIOVANNI: I have witnessed some small signs of it. It is not uncommon to discover a manuscript. A man is laid out on his deathbed, and he asks for a priest to take away a book he has copied, lest his kin are dismayed. The priest has no idea what to do with it, and so it is passed from hand to hand until it reaches me. I drown such books in holy water until they are quite ruined, and then bury them in the ground, where they moulder away into dirt.

I would say that there is more curiosity in this world than deviltry—it is one thing to copy a work, it is another to follow its instructions.

DUCHESS YSABELLE: But some men call upon fallen angels to instruct them in wickedness?

FATHER GIOVANNI: If they do, then they call upon the princes of Hell, who dispose of vast legions of devils. There is a book named after Solomon and it contains their names and seals. It is written that Solomon built his temple in Jerusalem with the aid of these devils.

DUCHESS YSABELLE: He must have been young and foolish to conjure such servants ... but he grew wise and wrote books of wisdom.

FATHER GIOVANNI: These are my favourite books, my Lady.

DUCHESS YSABELLE: And are there women who call upon devils from ancient books?

FATHER GIOVANNI: They would need some knowledge of Latin.

DUCHESS YSABELLE: I suppose they would. Our sex is excused from wickedness, Emilia!

SIGNORA EMILIA: On account of ignorance ... a thought that brings me no joy ... but I am certain our sex can be just as wicked with potions and poisons and philtres, like Circe and her daughter Medea. And unless I have misheard, Father Giovanni has just told us that the fallen angels first instructed women in the wicked arts?

FATHER GIOVANNI: I did Signora.

SIGNORA EMILIA: Which proves our sex can be wicked without Latin ... and we have priority in this matter of wickedness.

DUCHESS YSABELLE: And so God must cleanse the world again, but not with a universal flood ... according to John, evil will be routed with a multitude of tribulations.

FATHER GIOVANNI: That is so. It is written in the book of Isaiah that the sky will be rolled up like a scroll, and all the stars will fall. John repeats this also ... rolled up like a scroll.

SIGNORA EMILIA: Then I had best make haste to enjoy the stars before they are all swept away. We are fortunate to have this time with them.

DUKE LORENZO: We are, Signora, most fortunate.

STELLATUM

DUCHESS YSABELLE: When the sky is rolled up the glories of Heaven will be revealed.

SIGNORA EMILIA: But will they be the glories of Dante or the tribulations of John? Must I hide myself away from great terrors? The Book of the Seven Seals, the Four Horsemen, the trumpets, the seven angels bearing bowls filled with the wrath of God? Will we be marked for redemption, or will we be taken by devils into the pit of eternal fire?

FATHER GIOVANNI: The gospels concur with John, that there will be many tribulations. But my heart is drawn to the vision of Dante. *Omnia vincit amor*, as Virgil expresses it ... but I do not mean (as he did) an infatuation. I mean the love of God that binds all things into One. The love that moves the Sun and stars.

DUKE LORENZO: Bravo, Father! The love that moves the Sun and stars ... it is many years since I read the *Paradiso*, and there was much I did not understand.

SIGNORA EMILIA: It is a work that bears many readings, my Lord.

DUKE LORENZO: I am certain it does. I would read it again ... I have it somewhere in an excellent edition. Now that we have ascended through the Spheres I feel my mind is more receptive to his *Cantos*.

DUCHESS YSABELLE: I would read it too. Aha, I know, I will combine three virtues: those of learning, education and industry. I will find a page who deserves some education and have him read it to me ... while I sew. Alessandro's boy ... Riccardo, he will do. And Emilia, I will tax your understanding of Dante, be sure of that!

SIGNORA EMILIA: Then I must read it once more too ... perhaps we can share some sewing.

DUKE LORENZO: And what of me? Must I read alone and have no conversation?

DUCHESS YSABELLE: You do not sew, Husband.

DUKE LORENZO: When required I can repair harness with an awl and linen thread.

Duchess Ysabelle: You would remove the contents of the stables into my chamber? As if we did not have grooms for that task!

Duke Lorenzo: Then I could offer some service in the matter of reading.

Father Giovanni: Perhaps I might join you, my Lord?

Duchess Ysabelle: Oh Father, how discourteous of me, I did not think to prevail upon your time, for I know you would not refuse even if it caused you inconvenience. Husband, of course, now that we have completed the Spheres, we will set aside some evenings to study the *Paradiso* and reach a common understanding.

Duke Lorenzo: Excellent. I will enjoy that. Now that we have marvelled at the glories of the starry dome and seen that it is not yet rolled up, and that the End is not yet nigh, we can return into the world.

Signora Emilia: Your troubles remain huddled at the foot of the stairs, my Lord, awaiting your return.

Duke Lorenzo: This is so Signora, and I see the advantage in having a tower for Philosophy—the cares of the world seem distant. Perhaps there might be some wine remaining?

Duchess Ysabelle: I believe that there is ... but Nature requires that I descend.

Duke Lorenzo: Alas! Never was the opposition between our celestial and earthly natures more clearly illustrated.

EPILOGUE

SIGNORA EMILIA: Ysabelle, what a delight! I saw the glint of arms in the distance and thought that perhaps we were prey to brigands ... but then I saw your brave colours.

DUCHESS YSABELLE: I thought I would surprise you and escort you the last few miles to the city gates. It will increase your fame by some small amount.

SIGNORA EMILIA: I will be the talk of the city to arrive so, in the midst of such a host. Join us please ... Lucetta, Maria, make a space so that your godmother can climb in and join us.

DUCHESS YSABELLE: There ... this is cosy. Lucetta, Maria, how is your grandfather?

LUCETTA: He is well, my Lady.

MARIA: He took me upon his horse and I saw a boar.

DUCHESS YSABELLE: And were you frightened? Was it fierce?

MARIA: It was as huge as a horse!

LUCETTA: It was never so large!

MARIA: It was as large as your pony!

SIGNORA EMILIA: It was a good size, and you each have a tusk to prove it.

MARIA: May I show it? Please?

SIGNORA EMILIA: It is in the baggage. You may show it to your Aunt Ysabelle when we have unpacked.

DUCHESS YSABELLE: And did your mother join the hunt?

SIGNORA EMILIA: I did! I feathered that boar with arrows before it ran onto a spear.

DUCHESS YSABELLE: And you Lucetta, did you join the hunt?

LUCETTA: I rode a pony but I did not see the boar charge, for grandfather said I must stay back behind the men-at-arms. They made a great noise to frighten the boar.

DUCHESS YSABELLE: A good thing too; it takes the skill of a warrior to handle a horse when a boar breaks cover. Your mother can ride and use a bow like the horsemen of the East ... I have seen her.

SIGNORA EMILIA: My father taught me. He has no passion for books or learning, but he is skillful in all the arts of hunting.

DUCHESS YSABELLE: And is he well?

SIGNORA EMILIA: He grows old. To ride as he once did it is necessary to fall off many horses, and he has paid his dues in that respect, and now he is not so nimble. He is still a better horseman than most, but he grumbles and gripes. He was delighted to see his granddaughters ... is that not so? He gave you both a fine bow and arrows, and now you must practice.

MARIA: Where may we practice, Mama?

SIGNORA EMILIA: We will find a place, be sure of that. Ysabelle, I have so much to tell you.

DUCHESS YSABELLE: Join me when you have settled the children and you are refreshed.

EPILOGUE

[SOME TIME LATER]

SIGNORA EMILIA: All is unpacked and restored to some order. Are you well Ysabelle?

DUCHESS YSABELLE: I am well. I wrote to you to say that the Duke had some sickness and could not eat for a week; now he is regaining his strength. The boys are well but they have become unruly with Master Lombardi, and so I seek a new tutor.

SIGNORA EMILIA: I am relieved to hear the Duke is recovering. Concerning Master Lombardi, would he be a better match for Maria and Lucetta?

DUCHESS YSABELLE: He has a gentle manner, they might enjoy his instruction.

SIGNORA EMILIA: Do you continue with the *Paradiso*? What *Canto* have you reached?

DUCHESS YSABELLE: We have paused. We were dismayed by your absence.

SIGNORA EMILIA: I was dismayed to be so far removed. I return with good tidings however. I spoke at great length with my father concerning marriage, and my desire to be chaste and have no more children.

DUCHESS YSABELLE: And was he comfortable with this?

SIGNORA EMILIA: More than I thought possible. I told him that I had come close to death following the birth of Maria, that a priest was summoned, that I received the Last Rites. He said the oddest thing.

He told me that many years ago he had met the Duchess Lucrezia of the Borgia family in Ferrara, when she was married to Duke Alfonso d'Este. He spoke so wistfully ... I could tell that an arrow from Cupid's bow had pierced his heart, that she was his secret and unrequited love—his Laura, his Beatrice!

DUCHESS YSABELLE: Ah, the Borgia daughter ... I am not surprised that Cupid's arrow found its mark. I saw her once when I was still unmarried—at a christening I think—very striking and graceful,

249

she charmed all who knew her, for her father was the Pope of course, and her mother a known beauty. I have heard gossip that during her father's absences she would sit on the Throne of St. Peter and administer the Vatican, having cardinals at her beck and call.

SIGNORA EMILIA: I have heard the same stories—perhaps it was you who told them. My father told me that this Lucrezia had innumerable children, some of great ability and renown, but she did not live to see their accomplishments, for she died after childbirth.

DUCHESS YSABELLE: Ahhh ... now I understand. I recall the circumstances, very sad; she had many children, but God called her away. It seems your father has a heart. He cares for you.

SIGNORA EMILIA: For so many years I did not think so. You have met him; he is a robust and hearty man, not given to sentiment, and he has never possessed much delicacy of feeling. But it seems that he has finally understood that the making of heirs is a business of pain and blood, and women go to war against Fortune and Nature. I should not carp ... for he has agreed that I will not marry again, and that I should retain my dowry and make a life for myself and Lucetta and Maria.

DUCHESS YSABELLE: And your dowry?

SIGNORA EMILIA: The matter is settled; all of a sudden the lawyers concluded their quibbling.

DUCHESS YSABELLE: The Duke took an interest. He declared that he would review all cases involving widows, for it is our Christian duty to ensure that the weak are treated fairly. Do not thank him, for he conceals his affections behind a mask of duty.

SIGNORA EMILIA: You will thank him?

DUCHESS YSABELLE: I will. And now you are free. As you once told me, widows are the only free women in Italy. What will you do?

SIGNORA EMILIA: I have obtained from Venice a collection of letters that were made by a Laura Cereta of Brescia, in the time of Pope Sixtus. She lost her husband as I have done, and did not marry, but remained chaste and entered into public debate. She has much to say about the lives of women and how they may be amended. She has a great indignation that we are so confined and ill-used in marriage, and denied the means to show our qualities, which is through learning and the administration of public affairs.

DUCHESS YSABELLE: You would be a scholar?

SIGNORA EMILIA: I had thought to make a school for girls, to teach them Latin and rhetoric for public discourse. The primary aim of the Trivium is to prepare a young man for life in the community of men, where every matter of consequence is decided. How can our sex be counted as having any value if we are not so prepared?

DUCHESS YSABELLE: You will be condemned for preparing women to debate every matter with their husbands, when they should submit to his wiser discourse.

SIGNORA EMILIA: You speak truly. It would take a fierce spirit to endure such censure. Perhaps if I am subtle and disguise my intentions ... there are convents that teach girls to read and write, and they are approved.

DUCHESS YSABELLE: They have a narrow purpose: they hope that clever girls will join their community and so teach those who have no learning and cannot read scripture. They do not instruct the girls in wilfulness. What is the value of rhetoric if it is not to argue to some purpose? You would teach women to be wilful. Eve was wilful ...

SIGNORA EMILIA: Now that you say it, I see that it is true. The difficulty is not Latin, or even rhetoric, it is the matter of wilfulness.

DUCHESS YSABELLE: The Church approves obedience: that priests are obedient, that men are obedient to priests, and that women are still more obedient than priests or men.

SIGNORA EMILIA: I see that you give me good council. Laura Cereta says something of the sort: that men will praise a pretty woman in possession of learning as if she was a performing dog, but if she ventures an opinion of which they do not approve, they will charge that she is a Jezebel and cast her out of a window.

DUCHESS YSABELLE: That is my fear, and I bear you too much affection to see you used in this way.

SIGNORA EMILIA: So long as one wears the aspect of Venus, then all is well, for men are charmed ... but wear the aspect of Mercury, or Mars, or ... Heaven forbid ... Jupiter, and they are outraged that a woman has departed from her place in Heaven.

What I discovered in our journey through the Spheres is that regardless of our form, whether we are outwardly shaped by Mars or Venus, our inner aspect is determined by the stars, and, like the First Man of the *Pimander*, the soul has no sex. The soul may incline towards any of the Spheres according to the influence of the sky at birth, and that our first obedience is to our own nature, as God has formed us. If we possess the freedom to rise through the Spheres, then we cannot be confined in this earthly world by custom and narrow opinion.

When I spoke with you some months ago, I said I feared I was unruly ... and it is so, I find that I am unruly. Diana is unruly and runs around forests, hunting this and that; I am unruly and rush from book to book. I am not to be confined or silenced or brought to heel.

DUCHESS YSABELLE: I see that. There is some part of Mercury in you, and some part of the Moon. I find my greatest sympathy lies with Venus and Jupiter.

SIGNORA EMILIA: I see Juno.

DUCHESS YSABELLE: I did not see that ... truly, I did not see that.

SIGNORA EMILIA: You care for women. You have more kindness than I possess. You are also fierce in matters of justice.

DUCHESS YSABELLE: You honour me ... I thank you. It seems to me that we have become quite familiar with these Spheres ... do you think that we have become pagans, Emilia?

SIGNORA EMILIA: Pagans? Perhaps ... in a small way ... but no more than Dante.

DUCHESS YSABELLE: That is true. Dante is not condemned for being a pagan.

253

SIGNORA EMILIA: I see that there are powers within the soul ... that the soul is a *microcosmos*, a little world that reflects the greater, just as Father Giovanni said. It cannot be wrong to have a greater light of understanding ... to open the shutters and let the Sun in ... to see our souls more clearly, to see how we are strong and how we are weak, to see where we have virtue and where we have vice.

DUCHESS YSABELLE: I agree. Tomorrow I will go to the chapel of Santa Chiara and pray for guidance ... and talk to Father Giovanni ... it seems to me that it cannot be a sin to be a little wiser than we once were.

Printed in Great Britain
by Amazon

80809330R00154